STRICTLY FORBIDDEN

PLAYBOYS OF NEW YORK BOOK 2

JA LOW

JA LOW BOOKS

Copyright © 2020 by JA Low

All rights reserved. No part of this eBook may be reproduced or transmitted in any form, including electronic or mechanical, without written permission from the publisher, except in the case of brief quotations embodied in critical articles or reviews.

This is a work of fiction. Names, characters, businesses, places, events, and incidents are either the products of the author's imagination or used in a fictitious manner. Any resemblance to actual persons, living or dead, or actual events is purely coincidental. JA low is in no way affiliated with any brands, songs, musicians, or artists mentioned in this book.

This eBook is licensed for your personal enjoyment only. This eBook may not be re-sold or given away to other people. If you would like to share this eBook with another person, please purchase an additional copy for each person you share it with. If you are reading this eBook and did not purchase it, or it was not purchased for your use only, then you should return it to the seller and purchase your own copy.

Thank you for respecting the author's work.

Cover Design by Outlined with love

Editor by Swish Design & Editing

1

LENNA

"Have any plans for tonight?" Logan Stone, my boss asks.

"It's my anniversary, actually," I reply, which makes him frown.

Nothing can dampen my spirits tonight as I think Justin is going to ask me to move in with him.

We've been together for two years, and it's the natural progression of our relationship. We live together, and then a year or two later he proposes, rather romantically, of course. Our engagement announcement will then end up in the *New York Times* for everyone to see.

A year after that, we will get married in an elegant affair, probably at the famous Waldorf Astoria.

We will honeymoon in the Caribbean or maybe Europe, and then two years after our wedding, we will be met by the pitter-patter of little feet. We will have a boy first, that will make his mother happy, and then we will have a daughter two years after that.

If you haven't guessed, I'm a planner. Not obsessive or anything, just in my head. You can't verbalize your five or ten-year plan to men because that freaks them out, but you can subtly work them toward your timeline.

That's what I'm doing with Justin.

"Have anything special planned?" Logan asks through gritted teeth.

Logan and Justin don't get on *at all*. They went to college together, and something about Logan stealing his girl from Justin, or vice versa, I'm not sure which, because I don't really want to get stuck in the middle of my boss and my boyfriend as I know it won't end well for me.

"Not really. I think dinner somewhere," I reply.

Justin told me he was organizing everything when I asked him what we were doing, so I'm assuming that means we are doing something.

"That's nice," Logan answers curtly.

"What's nice?" Noah, his twin, enters our conversation.

"Lenna and Justin are going out for dinner tonight. It's their anniversary." Logan almost chokes on the word *anniversary*.

"Oh." Noah smiles. The romantic in him seeps through. "I hope he's going to take you somewhere nice because you deserve it."

"It's a surprise," I add.

"Ohhh." Noah grins. "Do you think he's going to pop the question?"

Logan chokes on a bottle of water beside me.

"You all right, there?" Noah asks his brother, who simply nods in reply.

"No. I don't think so…" Maybe Justin's timeline is a little more advanced than mine if he is. It's not like we haven't talked about our future, but I am kind of happy with just living together first.

"Well, he would be an idiot if he didn't. You're a catch, Lenna. Don't forget that." Noah wraps his arm around my shoulders and pulls me into him in a semi-like hug.

I've known Noah and Logan for the past five years. They hired me to head up the human resources department for their company, being with them from the conception of their business to where they are now has been utterly amazing. I've been able to grow my team over the years, something I would never have been able to do in another company.

"Don't we have a meeting?" Logan asks with a scowl on his face, changing the subject.

"Yes. Yes. Let me grab the paperwork and meet you in the conference room in five," I tell him.

Logan nods and walks away.

"Ignore him. He's just jealous," Noah tells me.

I wish.

Shit, that thought shouldn't have crossed my mind, especially not when I'm happily in love with someone else. I'm no better than the other women in the office who crush all over the Stone brothers.

Of course, you'd have to be blind not to realize how gorgeous they are.

The way they fill out a suit is lady porn at its finest, but they do have a reputation around town. They aren't called the *'Playboy Twins of New York'* for no reason.

Noah's gorgeous, but for some reason, he doesn't do it for me like Logan does. Maybe it's his grumpy disposition or his workaholic nature that gets me going. Not like it matters because I'm in a happy, loving relationship, and my stupid little crush on my boss is inconsequential.

"Jealous?" I question Noah.

"Yeah. Jealous that he's not getting laid." Noah bursts out laughing, and a tiny portion of me deflates. As if Logan Stone would be interested in me. Ugh, I'm such an idiot.

"Noah," I groan his name in warning.

"I know. I know. Don't write me up for saying that," Noah quickly adds when he realizes I'm *not* laughing at his joke.

"You can't say those things in the office," I remind him of our strict sexual harassment rules.

"I know." He rolls his eyes at me. "But you're family, Leens. So, that should come under different rules. I would never joke like that to anyone else."

I know he wouldn't. I'm just annoyed that my stupid heart got all aflutter over the thought that Logan might be jealous over Justin.

"Come on, we're having a meeting," I remind him.

"Fine," he huffs.

Heading back into my office, I grab the paperwork off my desk as my phone lights up with a message.

Justin: Going to be running late. Dinner at 9pm is that ok?

Really? He's working late on our anniversary.

Me: You can't push it back. It's our anniversary or did you forget?

The little bubbles startup then disappear. He's probably trying to work out his best response. Justin is charming and is used to getting what he wants, and I know that I'll give in to him, which is so annoying.

Justin: Babe. I'm sorry. If it wasn't an important client, I wouldn't be pushing our dinner back.

Of course, I understand he has super important clients he needs to look after. Ugh. I'm just—there's nothing I can say that doesn't make me look bad in this situation.

Me: I know, babe. Just disappointed.

Justin: I promise to make it up to you.

Me: You better.

I've been sitting at the restaurant for twenty minutes waiting for Justin to arrive. He's not answering any of my calls or text messages. *Where the hell is he?* I'm now onto my second glass of wine, I've devoured both of our bread rolls, and the staff keeps looking at me with pity thinking I've been stood up.

"I'm so sorry, babe." Justin finally rushes into the restaurant, looking freshly showered with some wilted-looking daisies. Bending down, he kisses my cheek and hands me the flowers. Honestly, they look like something he's picked up at some convenience store in the bargain bin on his way here. I place them on the table, my blood boiling, but I say nothing.

"I'm not that hungry, I ate with the client." He rubs his flat stomach.

Honestly, at this point, I consider stabbing him with my bread knife. He throws his cell onto the table and calls over the waiter to order a drink, totally oblivious to my mood. Eventually, he faces me and smiles. "Happy anniversary, babe." Reaching out and taking my hands in his across the table, he looks at me with those smoldering eyes that usually melt my icy heart, but this time they don't because I am too damn angry.

"You're late." I pull my hands from his.

"Oh, come on, Leens. I'm not *that* late." He rolls his eyes in jest, chuckling at my tone. His dismissive reaction makes my blood boil even further.

"You're thirty minutes late," I state, not backing down. I always back down when it comes to Justin, not being the one to rock the boat in our relationship.

"Am I?" By the way his head draws back, I can tell he's shocked that he's even late. "I did stop to get you some flowers."

Oh, for fuck's sake, as if that makes everything all right.

I can't help myself as I look down at the sad excuse for a bouquet and blurt out, "They are half-dead."

"Don't be so ungrateful." His curt tone shocks me.

How dare he.

How dare he have a go at me when this is all *his* fault.

Silence falls across the table as an intense stare-off begins between us.

"I'm going to the bathroom. Hopefully, that will give you enough time to calm down, so we can have a lovely dinner like I had planned." He scraps his chair loudly against the cement floor and strides off to the bathroom. In his haste, he leaves his cell behind, and it lights up with a message. I don't normally read his messages unless he wants me to, but the couple of words I saw flick up on the screen gave me pause to pick up his phone. I type in his passcode so I can read the message.

Dani: Thanks for tonight, I had fun. I can't wait to catch up again when I'm in town. Miss you. xoxo

My hands begin to shake as I read the message over and over again. *What the hell?* Clicking on the message, I scroll further down and come across an array of dick and titty pics between the two of them with dirty talk, back and forth—also, messages about their hookups.

I'm going to be sick.

Quickly, I place his cell down again as I see Justin returning from the bathroom.

"Have you calmed down yet?"

I am literally going to murder the selfish prick. How fucking dare, he.

"Sure have," I say through gritted teeth.

"Good." He smiles. "Because there's something I've been dying to ask you, and I don't want your mood to ruin it." My eyes fall to where the bread knife is located, and my brain contemplates how I can possibly stab him and get away with it. I've watched enough of those cop dramas to know there's a possibility.

"How was your meeting?" I change the subject completely.

"Oh, it was good." Not even a damn flicker of discomfort talking about him fucking another woman before meeting his girlfriend for dinner on their anniversary.

"Did you get everything you needed out of the meeting?"

"Sure did." He smiles. "One of the best meetings I've had in a while. Got so much accomplished. They are going to be coming back next month to continue talks."

What a fucker.

He's talking about the woman coming back in a month so he can fuck her again.

I. Am. Raging. So much so, I can hear my breathing is louder than normal being forced out through my nose.

"So, Dani's a good client, then?"

Justin stills, his face begins to pale at my question.

"Yes," he answers cautiously.

"She's the best you've ever had?"

"Client... she's the best client I've ever had," he corrects me.

"And do many clients send you pictures of their tits?"

Justin places his wine glass onto the table, but it misses and smashes against the concrete floor. The restaurant stills, and everyone goes silent.

"She messaged you, thanking you for a wonderful night."

The waitress rushes over to help clean up the mess. Her eyes widening when she hears my question.

"It's not what you think, Lenna," he tries to reassure me.

"Oh, it's exactly what I think. You've been fucking around with this 'client' for months now." I use air quotes. "You've fucked her before coming out to our anniversary dinner."

The waitress gasps at my comment and looks between us. I am sure she has no idea whether to flee or keep listening.

"Babe." Justin tries to reach for me, but I move out of his reach.

"I think you should leave. *Now.*" The waitress turns to Justin as she folds her arms over her chest and stares him down.

She's obviously not intimidated.

"Fuck off," he tells the waitress. "This has nothing to do with you."

She takes a step forward. "Actually, it does. This is my restaurant, and what I say goes." He stares up at her. "And I think *you* should *leave*."

"Lenna." Justin looks back at me.

I agree with the waitress. "I think you should go, too. We're done,"

He pushes his chair back loudly. "You're all a bunch of bitches," he screams at us both. "Dani's a far better fuck than you, anyway," he spits at me in retaliation. "Can't believe I wasted two years on you," he yells out as he leaves before a male bartender pushes him out the door.

Tears fall down my cheeks at his cruel words.

"Ivan, tequila," the blonde waitress calls to the bartender. "What a dick." She sits opposite me. "I'm sorry he said those things to you, you didn't deserve that."

"Thank you." I hiccup through my tears, embarrassment turning my face bright red as the rest of customers continue to stare at me with a mixture of pity and annoyance.

"Don't waste your tears on that man, he simply doesn't deserve them." She reaches out and cups my hand with hers. "He's done you a favor. It may not seem like it tonight or even tomorrow, but there will come a time when you will be so thankful he fucked up, and you didn't get stuck with him and his cheating pin dick." She gives me a warm smile as a shot of tequila lands in front of me. "Drink up." The blonde throws hers back as do I.

"I needed that." The alcohol burn soothes my pain somewhat.

"You probably need another five, but at least it's a start."

"Probably, but I better get going..." Standing up from the table, I ask, "How much do I owe you?"

"On the house, sweetheart." The blonde waves her hand around at me.

"No, I can't."

"I insist. I also insist that you stay and help me finish the tequila." She gives me a wink.

"I..." I begin to argue, but something stops me. Honestly, I don't want to go home. I don't want to deal with what just happened. I want to drown my sorrows in tequila, so I say, "I'd love to."

She squeals with delight and rushes around, pulling me into a tight hug. "Girl, we are going to wash that man right out of your hair."

I like this girl.

"What's your name?" she eventually asks, moving me toward the bar.

"Lenna, and yours?"

"My name's Stella."

2

LENNA

My head's pounding as I roll over in my bed and turn off the blaring alarm. So, this is what dying feels like. Squinting, I try to work out what the time is on my bedside clock, but it's too blurry. My stomach gurgles, and I jump out of bed and hightail it to the bathroom where I empty the remnants of last night. I stay there for what seems like an eternity before I slowly crawl back to my bed and grab my cell phone. This is going to be the first time in my whole career that I've decided to take a day off. I can't face the office this morning, especially not with the hangover from hell.

I type out a text message to Noah as he will be more understanding than Logan.

Me: Sorry to do this. But I'll be working from home today. Not feeling very well, might have food poisoning.

Noah: Nice story. I'll play along with it. Have fun in bed with Justin.

Damn! I don't want him to think I'm staying in bed with that idiot.

Me: Justin and I broke up last night. I need a mental health day, is that okay?

Noah: Shit. I'm going to fucking kill him.

This makes me smile. Noah is like a brother to me, and I've always wanted a brother to protect me.

Me: Get in line.

Noah: Take as long as you need off. We've got you.

Hours later, I'm feeling slightly more human. I've got a pint of ice cream, and I'm wearing my ugliest yet comfiest pajamas while catching up on episodes of *Hart of Dixie*. The buzzer to my apartment sounds, and my stomach sinks. Please don't be Justin, it's still too soon to hear from him. Slowly, I make my way over to the video screen to see who it is. My body stills, my stomach turns. There standing at my door is none other than Logan Stone.

My boss.

What the hell is he doing here?

"Logan?" I question through the speaker.

"Can I come up?" He looks directly at the camera, and I instantly melt.

"Sure." Pressing the buzzer, I catch a glimpse of myself in the mirror, and I look like crap. My hair's a mess, my face is pale, and I don't have much time to fix myself. Quickly, I run into my room and throw off my holey outfit and grab a pair of black leggings and an old university T-shirt as I hear a knock at the door. Quickly, I drag my fingers through my hair then pull it up into a messy bun. Calmly, or as calm as I can be, I walk to the door, then count to three while schooling my thoughts, opening the door with a smile.

"Noah told me what happened." He looks guilty over this bit of information, then pulls out from behind his back a large bouquet of flowers. This time they aren't close to dead and don't look like they're from a twenty-four-hour store discount bin. They are a gorgeous bunch of blush pink peonies. "I just..." He stands there, awkwardly. "I'm sorry," is all he manages to say, then shoves the flowers into my chest.

"Want to come in?"

Logan hesitates before taking a step inside my apartment.

"I brought Italian, too."

It's from the place down the street from work that we all love. How did he know I was craving their mozzarella sticks? Once Logan's inside, instantly, everything seems rather small with his large imposing body. Closing the door behind him, the delicious smell fills my apartment. He makes himself at home—he's been here plenty of times over the years but never for a social visit. Grabbing a vase from the shelf, I fill it with water and put the flowers in and place them on my dining table.

"Here," he says, handing me a plate of gooey goodness. "Thought you might need to soak up the alcohol."

"How did you—"

"EJ told me." A frown falls across my face. "He owns the restaurant you were in last night, Stella's his assistant."

I blink a couple of times, taking in the information he's just laid out for me. Of all the places, it was at one of Logan's friend's restaurants. I'm not sure if I'm mortified or relieved.

"I'm sorry, Lenna. You didn't deserve that." His kind words come out on a whisper. "Come, sit, before the food goes cold."

Not knowing how to take Logan's sympathy, or is it pity? We both take a seat on my couch and silently begin to eat our Italian meal.

"What are you watching?" he asks.

"Um... just a show."

"Which one?" he asks as he continues to dig into his food.

"*Hart of Dixie*," I confess.

"Cool. Haven't watched that one. Why don't you hit play?" he gestures to the television. *Who the hell is this man?* But I do as I'm told and try and shake off the anxiety that's plaguing me knowing Logan Stone is in my apartment, and the barrier of being in a relationship that used to be between us is no longer there.

3
LOGAN

"**Y**ou made it." Anderson slaps me on the back.

"Of course, I wouldn't miss your party."

Anderson's parties are legendary—no expense spared, over the top, the best alcohol, the best drugs, every damn everything right at your fingertips.

"Where's Noah?"

Anderson shrugs his shoulders. "Probably in a bedroom with some chick."

Nodding my head in understanding, I say goodbye to my friend and head into the throbbing masses of people that are in various states of dancing or making out. Some popular international DJ is pumping some house beats through the stereo system.

"Hey, Logan." Jade slides up to me. "You wanna pick up where we left off?" she whispers seductively into my ear.

I'm only human.

When a cheerleader asks you to continue fucking her, who am I to say no? Grabbing her hand, I push my way back through the crowd and toward the staircase, which leads up to the bedrooms. Pushing her up against the wall as my mouth meets hers in a hungry kiss, I give her a taste of what's about to happen. She giggles as our *lips part, looking up at me through those blue doe eyes that appear all innocent, but in actual fact, she is dirty as fuck. Grabbing her hand again, we race up the stairs, pausing at the top to claw at each other.*

"Your phone is either vibrating in your pocket, or you're just happy to see me." Jade chuckles, stopping our frantic kiss.

It takes me a couple of seconds to clear my hormonal cloud and realize that she's right, my cell is, in fact, ringing. Looking down at the screen, I see it's Dad. Jesus, this man has bad timing. "I'll meet you inside. It's my dad. I'll be quick."

Jade nods and seductively walks into the bedroom.

Letting out a heavy sigh, I click to answer. "Hey, Dad."

"I can't go on, buddy," *he cries down the line. He's been saying this for months since his gold digger whore of a wife ran off with his business nemesis after bleeding him dry and forcing him into near bankruptcy.*

"Dad, Noah and I will see you next week."

"I've fucked everything up. I have nothing," *he slurs his words. He's always been a social drinker, but it's been getting worse since the whore left him.*

"I know it's a bit rough at the moment, but I promise it will get better." *I've been talking my dad off the ledge for weeks, and it's as draining as his nightly phone calls.*

"They kicked me out of the country club tonight." *He lets out a frustrated sigh.*

"Dad, they canceled your membership, remember?"

"I gave them so much money. Those fuckers owe me."

Pinching the bridge of my nose in frustration, I say, "Dad, go to bed. We can talk about it properly in the morning."

"He took everything from me. Everything." *He begins to ramble about his archenemy.*

"No, he did you a favor taking that whore away from you. He can deal with her now."

"Don't talk about your stepmother like that."

"Are you fucking serious right now, Dad?" I see all shades of red. "You fucked around on Mom while she lay dying of cancer. Then you married some gold-digging whore, and now you're heartbroken because she ran off with someone richer."

"I loved your mother," he spits out.

"No, you didn't. You let some floozy with big tits distract you from the shitty cards you were dealt with. You chose to follow your fucking dick instead of your vows."

"You've never been in love, so you don't understand," he cries.

"Fuck you! I loved Mom. I know what love is, you self-centered asshole." The line goes silent for a couple of moments. He's worked me up, and everything I've been bottling spews out, "You need to grow the fuck up. Noah and I are sick and tired of having to babysit you. What about us? We've had to struggle with Mom's death while you moved on with Shelley as if Mom never meant a damn thing. We sat and grieved while you shut us out. We had to deal with the whispers around town as you flaunted your younger woman in the face of all Mom's friends.

"We stood by you even though we hated you because you were the only family we had left, but you didn't care. You never checked in to see if we were okay? You sure as hell didn't consult with us when you got married. So, I'm done, Dad. I'm done being your support. Go cry to someone else because I don't care anymore. There's no one else to blame for the situation you are in than yourself. This is your karma for cheating on Mom, and you know what? You fucking deserve it. I have to go, Dad."

"I'm sorry," he squeaks out, but I hang up on him before he can say anything else.

WAKING WITH A START, my chest is bathed in a light sheen of sweat. Closing my eyes, I count to ten, trying to calm my racing heart. My last words to my father haunt me most nights. For years, I've played the what-if game and nothing changes, the outcome is still the same.

I killed my father.

I pushed him too far with my tough love, and he killed himself that night. I was more interested in getting my dick sucked than listening to a man who was truly struggling. There aren't many times I've wanted to turn back time, but that conversation is one of them.

It takes me a couple of beats to orientate myself and realize that I'm not in my own home and most definitely not in my bed. Looking down at the brunette quietly snoring against me, I'm definitely not in my own home.

Shit! We must have fallen asleep while watching television. I honestly didn't mean to stay this long. I thought I'd drop off some food from Lenna's favorite place, give her a bunch of her favorite flowers, and then be on my way.

EJ filled me in about the drama that happened in his restaurant last night, and it wasn't until Noah told me that Lenna wouldn't be in because she and Justin had broken up that I put two and two together. I asked EJ to double-check, and it was Lenna.

Noah was going to pop over and check in on her, but honestly, I didn't like the idea of my brother comforting her. She's in a vulnerable state, and if I'm honest, I don't trust the bastard. Even though we have strict rules about fraternization with our staff thanks to the emotional legacy my father left us, I know him.

Noah would have come over with wine, flowers, and her favorite meal. He would have tried to comfort her, and the next thing they'd be in bed together. And if I'm honest, I don't think I could cope if those two sleep together.

It was hard enough watching her date that fucking douchebag, Justin, but my own twin. No. No way in the world.

I know I shouldn't be here as I look down at a sleepy Lenna.

I've overstepped a line, one that I have wanted to step over from the moment we hired her, but one that should never be crossed.

Ever so gently, I try to extract myself from her couch. Bit by bit, I slide out from underneath her, the tiniest of moans falling from her lips as she gets herself comfortable again on the couch. Taking her in one last time, committing her to memory, I exit her apartment as quietly as I can.

Looking down at my cell, it flashes 2:38 a.m. across my screen. Rubbing my weary face, I open my Uber app and order a car home where I'm supposed to be.

After a short car ride home, I walk back into my apartment and head into my bathroom to freshen up. I look like a mess as I stare at my reflection in the mirror. The nightmare of *that* night floods back through my conscience, the similarities between Dad and myself become glaringly obvious—the shape of my jaw, the arch of my left eyebrow, which raises in the exact way his used to. The main difference between us is that I've learned from his mistakes—never mix business and pleasure.

That was *his* downfall.

You came close tonight.

Temptation.

Lenna is an utter temptation for me, especially feeling her curves against my body and her warm breath against my skin. She was so close. Too close. This is the reason why Noah and I wrote the non-fraternization rules into our company's employment contract because situations like tonight are going to lead me down a path like my father.

I can't.

No, I won't be like him.

"How is she?" Noah asks as he makes his way into my office.

"She seems okay." Looking up from my computer, he has his head tilted, and the strong eye contact shows his concern.

"Okay? Just... okay?" I can tell instantly he's not convinced.

"Yeah, I mean, she didn't talk about it."

"She didn't talk about it?" Noah repeats my words back to me.

"Yeah."

"What the hell did you do all night?" Those familiar eyes bore into my own.

"We ate take-out and watched TV," I reply, feeling like I'm under a microscope.

"And that's all?" he pushes, not seeming convinced.

"Yeah, that's all," I say defensively.

His eyes squint. "Nothing else happened?"

Raising my voice a few octaves. "Noah!"

"Lenna just broke up with her boyfriend of two years. I would hardly be jumping her."

Noah's eyes widen in surprise. "I'm an idiot. How did I not see this earlier?" He slaps his thigh, a large smile settling across his face. "You have a *thing* for Lenna."

"I most certainly do *not*," I add quickly.

"Yes, you do," he pushes.

"Because you went straight to hooking up with her when all I meant was what did Justin do."

My stomach sinks with the realization that I've just outed myself.

"No. It's not like that at all. I assumed it would be something you would do. You know... comforting a woman in her time of need. Taking advantage of a vulnerable woman. That's more your M.O. than mine."

Noah just chuckles. "Yeah, yeah, deflection at its finest."

"I'm not deflecting." Goddammit, my brother is really pissing me off.

"Yes, you are. Don't forget, we are the same." Noah taps his head.

"Like hell, we are." Anger starts bubbling to the surface. "You're still hung up on some woman you met on holiday. I would never do that."

"That's because I have a heart, and yours is made of stone." Noah cracks up laughing. "Stone. Get it?"

Rolling my eyes. I think, *Seriously, how are we related.*

"I have a heart. I just choose to share it more wisely than you do."

Noah's always the romantic, the one who sees the world behind his rose-colored glasses.

"I have more of a chance hooking up with 'island girl' than you ever will with Lenna," he teases.

"True, because I will never ever hook up with her."

"Never say never, brother." Noah chuckles as he leaves my office.

4

LENNA

"Come in." His deep timbered voice bellows right through me. "Stay standing, please."

I do as I'm told as Logan stands from his desk and walks toward me with those blue eyes assessing me as he moves. Goosebumps prickle my skin as he walks behind me.

"Did you do as I asked?" His warm breath caresses the back of my neck.

"Y-Yes." My voice shakes with anticipation.

"I don't believe you." His words are sharp and penetrating. "Maybe I should see for myself." Logan moves closer, pressing himself against my back, I can feel his hard plains against my soft curves. A hand lands on my hip, strong fingers dig into my flesh. The sound of the metal teeth of my zipper echoes through the room, then my skirt falls to the floor.

"Spread your legs, Lenna," he commands, and I do as I'm told. Fingers skate across my belly and over my heated skin, the tips of his fingers drag ever so lightly across my lips. The sensation of his fingers against my soft skin arouses me. "You're so wet for me," he purrs against my ear. "I'm pleased."

Biting my lip in anticipation as his fingers travel further south *before parting my lips and disappearing into me, my legs go limp at his first touch, and I lean back against him.*

"You're so ready for me, Lenna." As another finger disappears with the other filling me up, he says, "You like my fingers, don't you?" he asks as his teeth sink into my shoulder, and I lose the ability to speak. Instead, I mumble something incoherent in response.

"You like the way my fingers find the perfect spots, don't you?"

Yes. Yes, I do. More. I need more.

"I could do this all day, making you wet with my fingers."

Don't stop, please don't stop.

The bundle of nerves that he seems to be able to reach with his long fingers is bringing me closer and closer to climax. I feel my orgasm building with each deep thrust inside of me, with each flick of his thumb against my clit. The man has magic fingers. I don't think I'm ever going to look at them the same, knowing what magic they bring with them.

"That's it, isn't it." He chuckles in my ear. "You're close, so fucking close." My pussy contracts around his fingers at his words. "Give it to me, Lenna. Show me just how much you love my fingers."

I'm close, so close.

BEEP BEEP BEEP BEEP

What the...

The blaring alarm pulls me from my dream instantly.

Nooo... I was so close.

Flopping back down against my sheets with frustration, I rub the sleep from my eyes.

Dammit!

These sex dreams I've been having about Logan for the past couple of months are driving me crazy. Every single time I'm about to fall over the edge, my damn alarm clock cockblocks me, and I wake up extremely frustrated.

Ugh.

***

"L... E... N... N... A," Noah whines popping his head into my office. I know that tone, he wants me to do him a favor.

"Whatever it is, the answer is no." I shut him down before he gets the chance to ask me whatever it is he's about to ask.

"But you don't know what I want. You might like it."

"Highly doubt it," I reply while raising a brow at him.

"Fine!" he huffs as he takes a seat. "Can you be Logan's date for this fundraiser tonight?"

No.

Nope.

Nada.

I shake my head over exaggeratedly.

"Please," he whines again, throwing those puppy-dog eyes at me that all the women go crazy for. They don't work on me, he's the wrong twin.

It's funny how Noah and Logan are identical twins, yet they're so different. Noah is, of course, just as handsome as his brother, but for some reason, my stupid heart doesn't flutter when I'm around him. This stupid crush I have on Logan is becoming worse, and I'm finding it harder and harder to push it down, deep, deep down inside of me.

Since breaking up with Justin, all my pent-up hormones have bubbled to the surface and keep coming out in sex dreams about my boss, which is most inconvenient.

Logan's been keeping his distance for the past couple of months since he fell asleep on my couch after my breakup with Justin. I know he's torturing himself over it, feeling like he crossed a line that night.

As far as I'm concerned, he didn't cross it far enough.
Stop it.
Stupid hormones.
But I also hate that our friendship is suffering now because of it. I miss the great banter between us, the times when he would grab me my favorite cup of coffee from the store below the office, or even our random lunches at our favorite Italian place. He's subtly put a divide between us, and as much as it stings, I understand why.

Over the years, as the three of us have grown closer to each other, the more I have been let into their personal lives, and especially about their father, but that part has mainly been through Noah. Logan is tight-lipped as always when it comes to that subject.

"Please, Lenna," Noah pleads with me again.

"Give me a good enough reason as to why you can't go, and I'll consider it." Sitting back, I cross my arms.

"Easy." He grins. "Loco Linda."

Linda was an ex-employee who had an unhealthy obsession with Noah.

"How do you know she's going?" Once we let Linda go, she kind of disappeared off the face of the earth, and we hoped it would stay that way.

"Because she's dating Graham Davies."

My eyes widen. "He's like... old enough to be her grandfather."

Noah nods his head.

Graham's a real estate agent, one of the best in New York.

"Anderson saw them at some party, and he asked." Well, that isn't surprising considering Anderson literally has no filter. "Apparently, she's on her meds, and he's looking after her, but still..."

"Fine."

Noah's mouth drops open, and he gives me an incredulous

stare that I've given in so easily. But I know what he went through with Linda, and the last thing he would want to do is see her again. I better get a great bonus this year for doing this.

"Thank you sooo much." He smiles. "I've organized for some dresses to be dropped off and a hair and makeup consultant to come to the office."

"You knew I'd say yes."

Noah gives me a wicked grin. "Yeah."

Damn, I must have 'sucker' written across my forehead.

"You owe me." He chuckles when I point at him.

"I sure do. You're a champ, Leens."

"You have to tell Logan." His face drops. "Fine," he groans out while standing from his seat.

"And don't forget we have an interview in an hour in the conference room."

Logan Stone in a tuxedo—that has always been my kryptonite.

Tonight is going to suck.

5

LOGAN

Noah walks into the conference room and sits beside me. "Lenna is going to be your date tonight for the fundraiser."

"Like hell she is."

No. I'm not doing it. I've been keeping my distance from her because, honestly, I can't look her in the eye, not after what I have done to her in my mind most nights. I swear I've worn callouses on my hand with how much I can't stop thinking about her, and about that night, when we fell asleep together. It's driving me crazy. So us two being alone together is a bad idea.

"You have to."

"The great thing about being an adult is I don't have to do shit I don't want to do," I explain my reasoning to Noah.

"Loco Linda is going to be there," he adds.

Right. Okay. He's got me there. That woman made my brother's life hell. Actually, she scared all of us, but I can't be alone with Lenna.

"There will be hundreds of people there. She won't even see you. Man the fuck up and go."

Noah stills, he turns and looks at me. There's anger bubbling right under the surface. I can see it by the way he's holding his chin high at my comment.

"You're in a mood today."

"No, I just hate when you flake on me," I state as I try and distract myself with a bit of paper.

"You look like shit, too." I don't need Noah poking around in my head at the moment. "Did you go out?"

"No, I did not go out," I reply curtly.

Noah continues to stare at me, the intensity becoming hard to tolerate.

"Then why do you look like that?" He raises his brow at me.

Let it go, Noah.

He's so annoying sometimes.

"Sorry that I am letting the whole twin 'thing' down with my looks." Using air quotes, I try to distract him with a joke.

"We all know I'm the better looking of the two of us, anyway." He chuckles, easily distracted by my deflection. "Are you okay, though?"

"I'm fine," I snap at him when really I'm not. Between the nightmares about my father and the sex dreams about Lenna, I'm on an emotional rollercoaster at the moment, and I want to get off, but my mind has other plans.

The door to the conference room opens and in walks the woman I've been trying to avoid.

"I told him," Noah happily explains to Lenna.

She looks over at me.

Damn! It's not like I can say no to her being my date to this event because we've done it many times before.

"He doesn't look happy about it?"

"Logan's in a *mood*."

Those molten chocolate eyes look over at me, questioningly.

"I think he just needs to get laid," Noah whispers behind his hand for the empty room to hear.

"Noah!" I shout, reprimanding my brother, which makes him laugh.

"Chill... it's only Lenna."

Yeah, right! I wish it was that simple.

"You can't say those things."

"Fine!" Noah rolls his eyes at me.

What! Are we five again?

"Can we please get back to this interview." Trying to bring back some semblance of professionalism from my brother, Lenna straightens and launches into her spiel. "We've chosen the best candidate for the Director of Social and Content Marketing. She comes highly recommended with the right skillset and experience for the job. I think she will be a great asset to our team. Plus, I like her."

This grabs my attention because Lenna doesn't usually take an instant liking to anyone who comes in for an interview, let alone rave about that person. That's why she's the best at what she does. This person must be exceptional.

"She sounds great. Bring her in, Lenna," Noah replies.

She nods, stands, and opens our conference room door. "Let me introduce you to Chloe Jones."

Noah and I both stand to greet our newest employee.

Oh, shit! The realization hits Noah as she walks into the room. It's the woman my brother hasn't been able to stop thinking about for the past couple of months.

We tried to do an undercover boss at one of our resorts, but that didn't work out because people soon realized who we were, and once the resort got wind we were there, everything changed.

We met this group of girls who were on their friend's

honeymoon. Apparently, she left her fiancé at the altar because he knocked up one of her bridesmaids—way too much drama for me. Anyway, my brother was besotted by the so-called bride, but it kind of all unraveled quickly when he put his big foot in his mouth. I mean the woman had a lot of baggage, so it was probably for the best.

Until now.

Panic crosses her face upon recognizing us as well.

"Chloe, let me introduce you to the owners of The Stone Group... Logan and Noah Stone," Lenna introduces us.

Chloe holds out her hand to shake as if she hasn't met us before. I'll give her props for her professionalism.

"It's great meeting you both. I've heard so much about the company, and I'm looking forward to working with you."

Wondering if Noah's going to lose it, I look over at my brother.

"It's a pleasure, Chloe." Standing, I give her a wide smile as I shake her hand.

Noah follows me.

Lenna then leads Chloe out of the conference room.

"What the fuck," my brother curses, finally breaking his façade.

"Small world." I chuckle, my mood turning around at my brother's distress. "At least she was professional."

Noah nods, still looking a little stunned by what's just happened. "Look, I like her... she seems great at her job. But if you can't handle being around her, we don't have to hire her."

"What?" Noah gives me a look. "No, she's perfect." I can see he's struggling with seeing her again by the way he is shifting from one foot to the other. "But maybe we should catch up before she joins the team to chat, and get everything that happened between us out in the open."

"You can't sleep with her," I warn him because I know that's exactly what he's thinking about.

"What! No, of course, not. I didn't on our trip, and I won't now."

I'm not convinced by my brother's protests. This could go one of two ways, fingers crossed it goes the way I want.

"Just fix it up. I like her, and her ideas are spot on."

A while later Lenna pops her head into my office. She's wearing a white blouse that is semi-sheer, and I can see the lace camisole she's wearing underneath, and the thought of lace against her creamy skin drives me fucking crazy. Don't even get me started on her pencil skirt and the way the material hugs her curves so tightly, it does something to me. There's nothing about her outfit that should have this effect on me, but for some reason, it does. My eyes fall to her shapely calves. Never in my life did I ever think calves would do it for me, but—

Oh my God, I am literally losing my mind. It's up and disappeared like some hormonal teen that can't control his urges.

My fingers dig into my thigh, trying to calm whatever is going on with me. Those stupid sex dreams about Lenna have done something to me, and *all* I can think about is the things I've done to her on my damn desk.

Her screams.

Her moans.

They are haunting me.

"She's great, isn't she." Sitting down in front of me, her berry-scented perfume swirls all around me, and I can't get enough.

"Yeah." My answer is less than enthusiastic.

"Are you okay, Logan?" Concern laces her question.

How the hell do I tell her I'm moody because I can't stop thinking about fucking her?

"Are you mad about me coming tonight?"

"What! No. Of course, not," I try to reassure her.

"You seem a little off today?"

"Yeah, I... just..." Looking up into her chocolate eyes, which are swirling with confusion, I melt instantly.

"Just not getting enough sleep, that's all."

"I know there's a lot going on at the moment, especially with The Hampton's resort, but we have it all under control. Plus, we've just hired our new Director of Social Media Content, so we've got things covered."

Ever the optimist.

"True."

"Is there anything else worrying you?" I see the concern on her face as her eyebrows are drawn together and those chocolate eyes stare at me.

Over the years, Lenna has become close to Noah and me. Like Noah said before, she's family. She's been with us since the beginning, helped us build the company to where we are today, and she's been there through thick and thin with her unwavering support. Lenna knows about what happened with our dad and why we have the strict rules around the office.

"Are you still having nightmares?"

I feel ashamed that as a fully-grown adult, I'm having nightmares, and it's hard to admit, so I just say one single word, "Yes."

Lenna reaches out and touches my hand, giving it a tiny squeeze. "Do you think you should see someone about them? They are becoming more frequent, Logan."

How do I tell her, she's the reason why? Some stupid Pandora's box of feelings has been opened, and now it's totally fucking with me again.

"I'm fine. I think it's just stress, and it's manifesting into those dreams."

She doesn't look convinced by my reasoning. "Maybe try some meditation before bed," she tells me.

I nod in agreement, but the only form of meditation that I have been having is my hand around my cock while thinking about her bent over my desk.

6

LOGAN

"Hope you get laid tonight." Noah comes into my office and stands at the bathroom door as I finish getting ready, and I ignore his comment.

"Can't believe you're bailing on me." I side-eye him from the mirror.

"I have PTSD from Loco Linda." He chuckles.

"How did it go with Chloe?" Changing the subject, I turn and join him back in my office.

"Good. Really good, actually." There's hope on his face as he says it, and I know this isn't good.

"You know the rules, Noah," I warn him.

"Oh, for fuck's sakes, Logan. I know the fucking rules. You don't have to keep reminding me." My eyes widen at his tone. "Chloe and I are cool. I'm not interested in her. Now just drop it." The tone of his voice says otherwise, but I guess I have to trust him. He hasn't fucked up yet with anyone from the office, so I can't see Chloe being any different.

"You ready?" Lenna arrives, forcing us to stop bickering.

Looking up to where she's standing, my heart literally stops, and I forget to breathe. She's dressed in a simple black evening dress, her brunette hair is pulled up into an elegant bun, and her makeup is natural which shows off her molten chocolate eyes.

"Looks like Cinderella is ready for the ball," Noah jokes, pulling me from the spell she has put on me.

Grabbing my wallet and cell from my desk, I kick him in the shin as I pass, but all I hear is his laughing behind me.

"Everything okay?" Lenna asks.

"My brother's just being his usual dick self," I grumble while striding down the office corridors. We walk in silence through the emptied office, down the elevator, and through the foyer toward the waiting limousine. Lenna hurries along behind me, rushing to keep up. I hold open the door for her to slide in before joining her in the back seat where we sit in silence as I brood.

"Logan," Lenna says my name pulling me from my thoughts.

Turning, I look over at her.

"You can drop me off around the corner, I don't have to go with you tonight."

What? No.

"We can tell Noah I went with you."

"Why would I do that?"

"I feel like maybe I'm adding to your stress." She nervously plays with her hands in her lap.

What! How? Damn, she knows me too well.

"I'm sorry, Leens." Letting my head fall back against the limousine's back seat, I say, "I didn't mean to make you feel like it's you. Believe me, it's not." She doesn't look convinced, so I wipe my hand down my face in frustration. "I don't feel like myself today, and I think it's thrown me out of sorts."

Looking over at her, I reach out and place my hand on hers, which I know is a mistake, but I feel like I need to reassure her. As soon as our skin touches, the electricity between us is palpable, and I want to snatch my hand away from the burn. I can't let myself feel that spark that's between us. I know she feels it too because her teeth sink into her bottom lip on contact.

"You're the only one who makes these things bearable." These words make her smile, but it's the truth. We have fun together when I let myself relax around her. "I promise I'll improve my mood."

"Okay." She removes her hand from under mine. "Logan..." she says my name a couple beats later. "You know you can talk to me... anytime?" I hear the sincerity in her voice, and it warms my heart. "You don't always have to be an island."

"It's just easier sometimes."

She nods in understanding.

"Ready?" I ask as the limousine slows down near the red carpet.

"Born ready." She gives me a confident smile.

Stepping out of the limousine and into the bright lights of the flashes of photographers, I wait for Lenna at the vehicle's door. Holding my hand out for her, she takes it and steps from the limousine. The reporters scream our names, but I'm not in the mood to chat with them. Once Lenna's out of the limousine, I hold my arm out, and she takes it, so we can walk the red carpet together.

I HAVEN'T BEEN LEFT ALONE all night. This is why I like having Noah with me because he's the buffer between them and us. He's a hell of a lot friendlier than I am, that's for sure. I dislike the schmooze. I hate the people trying to get something out of you because you are successful. These being the same people who refused to invest in our hotels when we asked them years ago because we were too young. Funny how the tables have turned, and now they are scrambling to be a part of our business.

Thankfully, it's just a cocktail party tonight and not a sit-down dinner. I don't think I can cope plastering this smile on my face for much longer.

Looking around the ballroom, I try to see if I can find Lenna. She disappeared off to the bathroom a while ago and hasn't resurfaced. She's probably stuck chatting with someone who's trying to get in with us through the back door. Excusing myself from my current conversation, I head on toward the ladies' room, trying not to look too much like a creeper standing outside for a couple of moments to see if Lenna comes out.

Five minutes later and no such luck.

"Excuse me..." I reach out and grab one of the waitresses. "I seem to have lost my work colleague. She went to the bathroom but never came back. Would you mind double-checking for me?" The young girl nods her head. "Her name is Lenna Lund, she's brunette, and wearing a black evening dress."

The girl nods and enters into the bathroom, but moments later, she comes out again.

"Sorry, there's no one in there by that name. I called out, and no one answered."

"Thank you." Pulling out my cell, there aren't any text messages from her or even a phone call. I quickly send off a text, hopeful she will get back to me soon. I continue walking around the ballroom, scouring the crowd, but there's no sign of Lenna.

Where the hell is she? I'm starting to get a little worried, but she wouldn't just disappear like this. An uneasy feeling settles in my stomach, so I decide to walk outside. Maybe she needed some fresh air? After all, these things can get claustrophobic. I look around the dark, empty red carpet, and there is no one around anywhere.

"Can I help you get your car, sir?" one of the valets who is helping at the event asks, surprising me from the corner where they are standing.

"I'm looking for someone, and I thought they might be out here." *Maybe he's seen her.* "A beautiful brunette, dressed in a black dress, she wouldn't have happened to walk past, did she?"

The valet thinks over my strange request.

"The only brunette that's walked out here was with another man."

My stomach sinks.

Did Lenna pick up?

No, she would never leave a work function.

"But they looked like they were arguing," he adds.

Did she try and get away from some guy, and he followed her out here?

"Which direction did they go?"

He points toward the private garden off to the side.

"Thank you."

Rushing off, I hope that if it was Lenna, she's okay.

7
LENNA

I excuse myself from Logan's conversation, one too many champagnes has me heading toward the bathroom. I wait patiently until I can pop in and do my business.

"God, Logan Stone looks delicious," someone states.

"He certainly knows how to pull off a tuxedo," another muses.

"I bet he looks better out of it," another adds, and they all burst into giggles.

"Did you see his date?" There's grumbling which I can't make out then one says, "Lucky bitch. I wonder if she's sleeping with him."

"No way, she works for him. There's no way he would sleep with her."

That voice.

I know it well. *Loco Linda.*

"I bet I could tempt him," someone else adds.

"Oh, I did a number of times," Loco Linda adds, and her friends all gasp. "I had both of them."

"You lucky bitch, Linda," the girls tell her.

But it's a lie, and I know it.

Noah and Logan never slept with her. She may have wished they did, but I know for certain it never happened. Stepping out of the bathroom stalls and into their space, I say, "Hi, Linda," as I start washing my hands in the sink beside the group of young women.

She pales upon seeing me.

"It's been a while." I look directly at her through the bathroom mirror. Her friends are as slack-jawed as Linda is right now. "It's a shame you're still lying about the guys." Turning toward her this time, so she gets my full attention, I continue, "I'm sure your doctor would be interested to know you're still living in a fantasy world." Pulling out a few pieces of paper towel, I dry my hands.

"How dare you," one of the girls tries to stand up for her friend.

"Linda *never* slept with Logan or Noah."

The girls look to their friend for reassurance, but there's nothing but silence.

"Shall I tell your new friends about how we know each other?"

"No, I'm good," Linda says quickly.

"Linda?" one of the girls questions her.

"She's right, I never slept with them. I was trying to impress you." Tears begin to well in her eyes. It's incredible how good an actress she really is. "I'm sorry." She begins to break down, and they quickly rally around Linda, pulling her to them as they tell her it's going to be okay.

Turning on my heels, feeling more than accomplished, I make my way out of the bathroom. My work here is done.

Pushing through, I walk slap bang into a hard chest. I look up and see those dark eyes I know so well.

"Wow, little lady." He tries to steady me, but I jump out of his arms quickly.

"Justin?"

"Lenna," his voice turns to steel as he says my name.

"Hey, baby." A blonde sidles up to his side, and a hand snakes around him possessively. Believe me, she can have the jerk.

"I've got to go." Turning on my heels quickly, I rush through the crowded ballroom. I haven't seen Justin since that fateful night in the restaurant months ago. He tried to contact me twice, sent me flowers once, but that was the total extent of his pathetic apology.

"Lenna..." he calls after me.

No, I have nothing to say to him. Quickly, I move through the crowd, smiling and exchanging pleasantries with people I know while trying to find the damn exit. I walk out the front doors and into the cool night air. I suck in a couple of breaths in an attempt to calm my nerves down.

"Lenna..." Justin finds me outside.

Oh, for fuck's sake!

"Just leave me alone, Justin." I move away from him, and wonder if there are any cabs available?

"Please, can we talk?"

Shaking my head, I make my way down the deserted red carpet, not wanting to speak with him. "No, I have nothing to say to you." My steps quicken as he gets closer.

"Lenna..." He grabs my arm forcefully, swinging me around into him, and that's when panic finally sets in. "Lenna..." He looks down at me, but this time he says my name softly.

"Justin," the woman from earlier calls out into the darkness. "Babe, where are you?"

Justin pulls me to the right and down a deserted path into a private garden area.

"Let. Go. Of. Me." Trying to shake his hard grip away from my arm, I realize he won't budge. "Why don't you go back to your date."

"She'll wait," he states cockily.
Ugh, this guy repulses me.
"I have nothing to say to you." Looking him in the eyes, I stand my ground.
"Well, I have a lot to say to you." Folding his arms across his chest, his eyes glare with anger as he takes a step toward me.
"I don't want to hear it, Justin."
"Well, you're gonna hear me." His tone sends a cold shiver all over my body.
"Make it quick." Trying to act confident, when in actual fact, I'm shitting myself,
"You embarrassed me at the restaurant, getting me kicked out. I'm actually blacklisted there now."
Well, halleluiah. This makes *me* happy. Let's face it, he's angry because his ego took a hit, not that he broke up with the supposed love of his life. *Asshole!*
"That's not my fault."
"Yes, it is, that bitch kicked me out because of *you*. This is all *your* fault." His voice continues to rise higher and higher.
"You were the one cheating on me." To be honest, I'm not sure why I'm fighting about this. It's over, and I don't want him back or have anything to do with him.
"They didn't mean anything."
"They?" Oh, goddamn, of course, there was more than one. I'm such an idiot.
"Babe..." his voice softens, "... you were working such long hours. Anytime I would come over you were exhausted, and I didn't want to stress you out by trying to jump you as soon as I walked in the door." Oh, he was doing *me* a favor by cheating on me, I get it now. "They were simple stress relief, so I could be the best partner for you."
"Are you delusional?" Stupid! Don't engage, Lenna.
"Babe," he coos again. "I did it for us."

My eyes widen. What an absolute narcissist. He cheated because it was what was best for *us*? I just can't deal with this anymore.

"Is that it?" Folding my arms across my chest while glaring at him, anger bubbles through my veins.

"What do you mean?" He seems confused.

"Is that all you needed to tell me? Because honestly, I am done with this situation."

"You're an absolute bitch," he snarls at me. "I don't know why I even bothered trying to explain to you my reasoning. You've always been a selfish bitch."

Wow! "Okay, I'm done now." Turning, I begin to walk away from his bullshit. I don't need it, and I don't want to hear any more of his idiotic reasoning.

"You are done when *I* say you're done." He reaches out and grabs my arm, holding firmly, so much so I am sure it will bruise. It makes me scream as he swings me around back into him, his forcefulness surprising even me.

"Please, Justin, let me go. You're scaring me." I look up into his red face, the little vein on his neck popping with anger.

"I'm sorry, baby. You make me so frustrated when you don't listen to me. I didn't mean to scare you." He caresses my cheek with his palm, and it disgusts me. "I just want you to understand where I am coming from. I'm not the bad guy in this scenario."

"Okay, Justin."

"You believe me, don't you?" he asks.

"Yes." Because at this moment I'll say absolutely anything to get the hell away from him.

"I miss you," he tells me tenderly. "Do you miss me?" Hope flashes across his face, and I know I can't lie because I don't want to give him false hope, but I also don't want to anger him again.

"I..."

"Lenna." In the distance, I hear someone call my name. *Logan?*

"Who the fuck is that?" Justin growls and curses. "Are you seeing someone else?"

"Lenna, where are you?" Logan calls out again.

Turning around in the direction the voice is coming from, I'm relieved to hear a familiar voice.

"Who is he?" Justin demands.

Moments later, Logan appears from behind the bushes. He pauses when he sees Justin and me together. Worry laces his face when I see his forehead crinkle, then as he takes in Justin with his arms around me, I see him swallow hard, and his head shakes infinitesimally in disbelief and perhaps even hurt.

"I always knew you were fucking him," Justin curses. "The whole 'he's my boss' bullshit."

"We didn't start until you fucked up," Logan adds.

My eyes widen in surprise.

Did I hear him right?

"I've been looking for you all night, sweetheart." Logan strides over to me quickly, taking my face in his palms. He looks down at me, and for a split second, I feel like what's happening between us is real, and then before I can even process what's happening, he's kissing me. Those lips that I've been dreaming about for years are finally on mine.

His hands tighten around my face as his tongue does a long sweep across my own. I feel like I'm floating, or I am having an out-of-body experience. My hands reach out and rest against his hard chest. My fingers dig into the ripple of his abs as our kiss intensifies, and then as quickly as it began, it's over.

"Fucking bitch," Justin seethes beside us.

Logan wraps his arm around my shoulder, tucking me under him protectively.

"Why don't you fuck the hell off," Logan swears. "I won. You lost."

Justin's eyes narrow in on Logan, and for a moment, I think he's going to challenge him as he takes a step forward.

Logan tenses beside me.

"She ain't worth it," Justin snarls, turning on his heels and leaving us shaken in the moonlight, walking back to his waiting blonde.

"Are you okay?" Logan turns me around, checking me over as if he can see visible scars.

"I'm fine." Actually, I am feeling a little shaky, but I'm not sure if that was from my run-in with Justin or from Logan's kiss.

"He didn't hurt you, did he?"

I shake my head as silence falls between us.

Logan reaches out and scratches his neck nervously. "I'm sorry I kissed you…" I'm seconds away from saying I'm not sorry when he continues, "It was a mistake, Lenna." Those words crash down on me like a cold bucket of water.

"I know." Rubbing my bare arms as the cool night begins to seep into my bones, I'm feeling a little shaky from my run in with Justin. "Thank you. But I think I've had enough excitement for tonight. I'm going to get going." My throat's beginning to constrict, and I know I'm seconds away from bursting into tears.

"I'll come with you." Logan places his hand against the small of my back as we walk silently out of the gardens and back onto the red carpet. "Let me just call my driver, and he can take us home."

"No." Moving away from him, I turn and making my way to the cab stand. "I'd rather grab a cab."

"Lenna," Logan calls after me.

Looking up, I can see the confusion on his face, so I say, "We're all good, Logan. I'm just tired."

"You sure?"

I nod as a cab pulls up in front of me.

"Night, Logan," I call out as I open the door of the cab and slide in.

"Night, Leens—" His words are cut off as I shut the door behind me.

8

LOGAN

I fucked up with Lenna last night. Kissing her was one of the biggest mistakes I have ever made. It's changed things between us now, I know it. She couldn't get away from me fast enough last night.

Seeing her there in the darkness with Justin, made me angry. I hate the fact she was with him. Justin never deserved Lenna. He certainly doesn't deserve her now after cheating on her. Unfortunately, ego got the better of me, and I kissed her to prove Justin's point. I knew it would piss him off, and fuck did I want to hurt that fucking weasel. The problem is as soon as my lips touched hers, Justin faded away, and I was consumed by her. Her soft lips, the tiny sighs that fell from her as our kiss intensified. The touch of her hands against me, her fingers running along my abs. My dick grew instantly hard, and it took everything in my power to pull away from her at that moment —*every damn thing.*

"Heads up, dickhead," Anderson screams before launching a basketball at me. The hard ball hits me square in the chest, taking my breath away for a couple of moments. "You're a million miles away. Wake the hell up, pussy. We're about to play a game," he warns me.

Rolling my eyes, I pick up the ball and throw it back at him.

"First Noah's away with the fairies, now you. What the hell is happening with you both?"

One guess, *Noah's thinking about Chloe.*

"You know the new girl we hired is the chick from the island."

Anderson stills. "Which chick?" His eyes narrow in on me.

"The one Noah tried to hook up with but failed." Anderson shrugs. "The one who's friend you spent all night with."

Ah, now he remembers. I see the sly grin lighting up his face.

"Hang on... she works with you guys?" he asks as he bounces the basketball a couple of times in front of him.

"Yeah, Lenna found her. She's good at what she does."

"Do you think she did it on purpose?"

That thought had crossed my mind, but Chloe genuinely looked shocked when she first saw us in the conference room. "No, she seemed genuinely surprised that it was us."

"Small world, huh?" Anderson chuckles.

"You can say that again. Just hope it doesn't complicate things." I let him know my reservations.

"You seriously think Noah would do that?" Anderson passes the ball to me.

"I'm not sure." I pass the ball back to him.

"I don't think he would. I mean, Noah has so much tail on speed dial he doesn't need to go chasing one from the office."

He throws the ball back to me. "Yeah, but there's something about this one that got to him."

Passing the ball back, I reply, "Probably the challenge. She's the first woman to ever say no to him." Anderson throws the ball back at me. "I trust him, I think." Passing the ball back, I bite my bottom lip because I am unsure.

"Guess we'll soon find out when she starts." Anderson chuckles, which unnerves me. "How did last night go with Loco Linda?" He changes the conversation's direction, and I am happy about that.

"Never saw her." I pass the ball back.

"How's my girl, Lenna?" Anderson winks at me. He loves winding me up by flirting with Lenna in front of me. Thankfully, she isn't interested. I mean, I don't think she is, anyway. "I heard she was your date last night." Of course, Noah would have told him about that.

"Her ex was there."

Anderson stops bouncing the ball. "Anything happen?" Concern lines etch across his face.

"He cornered her in the garden and was yelling at her."

"Fucker." Anderson squeezes the basketball so tightly I think it's going to burst.

"But..." *Should I tell him?* I mean, Anderson is the biggest gossip known to mankind, but I kind of need someone's advice on how to handle what I've done. And by someone, I mean, not Noah.

"But what?" Anderson eyes me suspiciously.

"Justin is a fuckhead, and I—"

"You what?" Anderson's voice rises with alarm.

"I kissed her." I scrunch up my face into a frown because I already know what he's going to say.

"You fucking what?" he yells.

"It was trying to teach Justin a lesson. He was abusing her and saying he always knew we were sleeping together. I just said yeah, we are, and I don't know why."

"I know why." He smirks. "'Cause you have a thing for her."

"I do not." Pegging the ball back at him, I frown.

"You do, too." He pegs it back harder at me. "From. Day. One. It's obvious, I mean it is to everyone on the outside." He grins.

"We are just friends," I argue.

"Friends that kiss." He laughs.

"It was a one-time thing, and it will never happen again," I add.

"Never?" Anderson raises a brow.

"Yes. Never."

"Damn. You have way more discipline than me. Once I've had a taste, I don't think I could stop till I have eaten her all up." He chuckles at his dirty innuendo joke.

"She's an employee. We have strict rules."

"Then fucking don't tell anyone." Anderson shrugs.

"I just told you," I argue.

"Not sure what you're talking about." He grins. "You told me shit. Come on, let me whip your ass." Anderson throws the basketball back at me with full strength behind it.

9

LENNA

Things have been tense between Logan and me since that kiss months ago. He's put a massive wall up between us, making sure I know my place. Which is, I'm his employee and nothing more. I know there can never be anything between us, and I understand his reasoning. He's suffering so much pain from his father's death, but instead of seeking help to work through it, he's bottled it up, and its manifested into these strict non-fraternization rules. Honestly, I miss our friendship and the easy banter we had around the office. There's nothing but invisible tension swirling between us, and it sucks.

I'm so thankful Chloe joined the team. Having someone to laugh and hang out with makes the tension between Logan and me more bearable. It's also nice not having a colleague who's more interested in trying to hook up with their boss than doing their job.

Over the past couple of months, Chloe has invited me to hang out with her amazing girlfriends, something I've never really had in my life before. They are a fantastic bunch of women from all walks of life—Emma, the former supermodel now fashion entrepreneur, and Ariana, an award-winning architect. Then there's Stella, who in the craziest twist of fate, she was the woman who helped me the night I broke up with Justin, and EJ, the owner of the restaurant, that's Chloe's brother. Maybe there's a reason they were brought into my life.

Yeah, because you are lonely. That's true.

I've always been on my own, and I guess I have covered up my loneliness by being a workaholic. So, it's nice to finally have a tribe.

We are on our way to Vegas this weekend for Chloe's brother's restaurant opening. Never before have I been on a girls' trip, so not really sure what to expect, but we are currently on a private plane heading to Vegas. Honestly, I don't know how I am ever going to be able to go back to commercial flying because this jet is so luxurious. There's no sweaty man sitting beside you, no cardboard box airplane food, and no waiting in lines. *This is the life.*

Eventually, the jet lands, much to my annoyance as I never wanted to get off. The desert heat hits you as soon as you walk outside the jet, or it could be the copious amounts of champagne we drank on board that's made my feet wobble.

"Vegas, baby," Emma screams into the desert air.

"I've never been to Vegas before." Stepping from the jet into the glorious sun, I shield my eyes from its harsh rays with my hand.

"You shouldn't have said that," Chloe whispers to me.

Why? Now I'm worried.

"We're going to have so much fun." Emma smirks.

"Vegas is Emma's town, and she loves showing it off," Chloe warns me.

"I'll look after you, Leelee. Don't you worry," Emma tells me as we jump into the waiting limousine, but it's the look she gives me that has me concerned. The driver takes off, and it's not long before we arrive at the hotel.

"I'll meet you guys a little later," Chloe tells Emma and me as she heads into the hotel with Stella to catch up with her brother, EJ, before the opening of his restaurant.

After freshening up in my room, I cross the corridor to Emma's room. The door is slightly ajar, so I walk in and say, "Hello."

"Oh, hey, boo." Emma slinks into view. "You ready for me to pop your cherry?" she seductively coos.

"Not really," I answer hesitantly, which just makes her laugh.

"I promise you're going to have *so much fun*."

Hours Later

"I LOVE VEGAS," I scream from the sunroof of a stretch Hummer that we have somehow acquired. Dressed looking like what can only describe as a hooker, but Emma assures me it's very Vegas, my hair and makeup are perfect—well, not so perfect now that I'm screaming out of the sunroof, although we aren't going fast because we are stuck in traffic. Emma's been plying me with these slushy cocktails that everyone walks around the strip drinking.

Those things mess you up!

But they taste amazing.

Emma joins me through the sunroof and starts catcalling guys as they walk past.

"Show us your dick," she screams at some poor guy. He turns red and disappears into the crowd.

"You can't say that," I yell at her.

"Of course, I can. They've been yelling all kinds of bullshit at me all my life. They should be able to handle it back."

Pondering her logic, I suck some more fruity slushy up through the oversized plastic straw.

"Hey, hot stuff," Emma yells at some other guys who stop, turn, and look her over appreciatively.

"You look like fun," one of them calls out to her.

"I am," she flirts.

"Need any helpers?" one of the young guys asks.

"Little boy, you couldn't handle all this." Emma wiggles and runs her hands down her body seductively from the sunroof.

"Oh, I'm man enough for you, sweetheart," he retorts, grabbing himself on the crotch.

"Really?" Emma gives him a once over and smirks.

"I'd rather her." She points her manicured red nail at me, and the guys elbow each other, chuckling and revving each other up.

"Show us," one of them calls out.

Emma giggles. "In your dreams, little boy."

"Not my dreams, love, my fucking spank bank for use later."

The Hummer takes off with a jolt, and the conversation is cut off much to the guys' disappointment.

"How are you so..." trying to find the right words, "... confident with men?"

Emma pulls us back down, and we land with a thud against the leather seats of the vehicle. "I didn't have the best life growing up. I learned to survive." She looks off in the distance, her cheery disposition vanishing almost instantly.

Now I feel bad.

"I'm sorry, I didn't mean to..."

She shakes her head, her hair not moving from its perfect position, not even a strand—there must be a full can of spray holding it together.

"It's all good, Leelee." She gives me the most glorious smile that her eyes sparkle. "I'll tell ya one day all about it. But we're in Vegas now, and there are no bad times to be had in Vegas."

"You're so cool." The words slip from my mouth before my brain realizes what I have said out loud.

"You're pretty cool, too." Emma smiles as she sucks on her alcoholic slushy.

"Not in my everyday life, I'm not." Twisting the giant plastic sippy cup in my hands, I try to void what I want to say. "I'm too…" my brain is fuzzy, "… what's the word? Too… uptight."

"No, you're professional," Emma adds.

"Yeah, exactly. That's all he ever sees." My eyes widen as I realize I said it aloud again when really, I was trying to internalize it. *Stupid truth serum.* I take another sip.

"Leelee." Emma perks up. "Do tell."

"Nothing." Quickly sucking on my straw, hoping it will stop me from spilling anything else from my loose lips as I swallow as many mouthfuls as I can.

"Oh, no, you don't." Emma arches a well-manicured brow at me. "There's a story there, and I need to know what it is."

I've kept what happened between Logan and me a secret from everyone, but I know I need to talk about it. "If I tell you something, will you promise not to say anything?" She crosses her heart with her finger. "I mean it… I could lose my job over this."

"I promise, Leelee. What's said in Vegas, stays in Vegas. Remember?"

"Well, I… kind of kissed my boss."

Emma fist pumps the air. "Hell, yeah, that's my girl."

I appreciate her enthusiasm, but she hasn't heard the rest of it yet. "Yeah, but we have super-strict non-fraternization rules." Emma nods her head in understanding. "And the company is *not* going to fire the owner, are they?"

Emma frowns at my comment. "Oh, Leelee, they aren't going to fire you," she tries to reassure me.

"I know because he's pretending as if it never happened." I let out a long sigh.

"But, you kind of want it to happen again?" Emma smirks.

"Of course." Surprising myself with my honesty, I groan loudly.

"But because of the rules, it can't, or... he won't let it happen again?"

"Both," I reply.

"Was it good dick?"

"What? No..." Emma frowns. "I mean, I wouldn't know. We only kissed."

"Oh..." She taps her red nail against her chin. "Then how do you know if he's any good in bed? He could be a dud for all you know."

"I doubt that."

"Not all confident men know what they're doing," she tells me.

"Yeah, but the way he kissed me..." I bring my fingers to my lips, "... I just know he would be amazing in bed."

"Ohhh..." Emma fans herself. "I can feel the heat steaming off you as we speak just thinking about him."

I giggle. "Yeah. But I can't have him."

Emma nods in agreement. "It's hard to forget good dick. Once you've had it, nothing else compares, and it leaves you in a frustrated mess where even your stupid vibrator can't sustain you anymore."

Mmm, I don't think she's talking about me anymore.

Shaking her head, bringing herself back to the now. "Fuck, good dick."

"Isn't that what we want?" I'm a little confused.

"No. I don't mean fuck good dick as in..." she thrusts her hips and hands as she humps the air, "... I mean fuck good dick." As she flips the air off with her middle finger. "We're in Vegas. We are two hot chicks."

Well, one ex-supermodel and one girl who does a mean set of paperwork.

"We don't need *those dicks*. We can find other dicks out there. We might have to fuck a couple of bad dicks, but once we find the next good dick, it will replace all the images of the previous good dick." She raises her slushy drink in the air, and we cheer. "To finding new good dick."

This is going to end horribly. I just know it.

10

LOGAN

The hotel is packed with paparazzi and screaming fans, all waiting for the celebrities to walk the red carpet into EJ's restaurant opening. What an amazing turn out for him, it couldn't have happened to a better man.

"Is there another entry?" Noah moans.

"I don't think so. Suck it up, princess," Anderson jokes.

We head on over to security and get our names checked off, then walk the red carpet, smiling graciously before moving inside.

The restaurant looks amazing. It's as if we've stepped into a luxurious New York-style loft. The place is pumping with people having a good time. EJ must be so proud because he is literally killing it tonight.

We head on through the crowd and spy EJ with a beautiful blonde who's dressed in red on his arm. He's a bigger player than Anderson, and that's saying a lot.

"There's EJ," I tell the guys, and we move closer to him.

"EJ," Anderson calls out, gaining his attention.

"You made it," EJ greets us.

"Man, this is fucking awesome," I tell him.

"Congrats, man," Noah adds.

"Thanks, guys. And thanks so much for coming." He beams, he's totally in his element. "Come… let me introduce you to some important people." He moves over to where a group of girls are standing with their backs to us. "Boys, let me introduce you to my sister, Chloe." The beautiful blonde turns, and that's when I realize it's Chloe. Our Chloe Jones from the office. *What in the hell?* She looks just as surprised to see us as we are to see her. Then the penny drops, and I look over at my brother.

Oh, shit.

He's hooked up with EJ's sister. Oh, Lord, no. EJ is going to kill him if he finds out. Hopefully, this will make Noah forget whatever feelings he might have had for her.

"EJ, why are my bosses here?" Chloe asks her brother, who looks totally confused by her question.

"Chloe works for us," I add, trying to help him out.

"You work for them?" EJ points at us before bursting into laughter. "What a small fucking world."

"You never listen to me," Chloe moans to her brother.

Well, that's kind of obvious. Otherwise, he would have known about all this.

"I do…" But his words don't sound convincing.

"I had no idea you guys knew my brother," Chloe states.

"Everyone knows EJ," Noah tells her.

"Gotta go." EJ waves his hand in the air, and next thing he's off to do something.

My head turns, and I notice a stunning brunette wearing a black skin-tight dress, but her entire back is exposed. It's hot. The hem of her dress falls at the base of her pert little ass. My fingers itch to sink into her plump flesh. I watch in slow motion as she turns around, and familiar chocolate eyes stare back at me. The same pair that haunt my dreams night after night.

"Lenna?" I'm shocked, especially seeing her in Vegas, but more so seeing her dressed like that. My eyes trail over her, lingering a little longer than I should on the deep 'V' of her dress, then over the swell of her breasts. I bite my lip, trying to hold back a moan I know I want to let out because never in my wildest dreams would I ever expect Lenna to be dressed this way. Okay, that's a lie. In my dreams, she's dressed like this, and things end up going a different way to how I know they will go tonight.

"Oh... hey, boss." Her tone indicates she couldn't care less that I'm here, and that seeing me in Vegas has no effect on her. She moves toward us but on wobbly feet. I've never seen Lenna this drunk. She giggles with a woman who has black hair beside her, and who is holding her up.

"First time in Vegas," Chloe adds as if that explains why my HR Director currently looks like she's part of a *Girls Gone Wild* tour.

"I popped her cherry," the raven-haired beauty says beside her, with a seductive tone. *Did they hook up?* Oh man, the images that are playing in my mind about what that could mean is *not* good.

"I looove Vegas," Lenna declares, way too loudly. "What happens in Vegas stays in Vegas. Shh..." She places a finger over her red lips.

"What exactly has been happening?" I ask as concern begins to take over.

"Oh, pretty boy... wouldn't you like to know?" Lenna stumbles and presses a finger against my chest. She's never been so forward or flirtatious with me before. "Ohh... you're hard." She giggles.

Fuck, she has no idea how hard I am about to get if she touches me like that again.

"Okay, maybe that's enough drinks for tonight." Chloe

places her arm around Lenna, moving her away from me. I can see she's concerned over her colleague and how she's acting in front of her bosses. "Come, let's grab a water," she declares as she tries to lead Lenna away from the group.

"I'll take her." The words are out before I realize what I have said, so I quickly add, "I'm getting a drink anyway." I need one after seeing Lenna dressed like pure and utter sin.

Chloe hesitates.

"It's your brother's night, enjoy," I tell Chloe as I place an arm around Lenna to hold her steady.

"You better not fire her over this," the raven-haired beauty yells at Noah.

"Of course not," Noah states.

There's no way in the world I'm letting Lenna go anywhere else tonight looking like this.

We make our way through the crowd. She's tucked up against me and is not wearing a bra? *Oh, Lord, help me.*

"One water and bourbon. Neat, please," I order from the bartender. He nods and efficiently grabs my order.

"I'm okay," Lenna groans out from beside me. "I don't need a babysitter."

I could argue differently, but I don't. Instead, I take her all in because she's refusing to look at me. Her normally straight brunette hair has been turned into soft waves that fall against her creamy skin. Reaching out, I move the hair that has fallen in front of her face back over her shoulder. The slightest hitch of breath is heard, and it hits me deep in my soul. She's affected by me the same as I am with her.

"I like your hair," I say as I lean against the bar.

"Thanks, it was all Emma's idea." She shrugs.

"Who's Emma?"

"The supermodel standing with us tonight." Lenna looks up at me. "How did you not notice her?" *Is she talking about the raven-haired girl?* I mean, she's attractive, but I am too busy looking at Lenna to care about anyone else.

"I didn't notice."

The bartender taps me on the shoulder as he places the drinks in front of me.

"Here." Handing her the large glass of water, she throws it back quickly, and I smirk.

"Are you seriously telling me you didn't notice the supermodel standing beside me?"

"Honestly," I state. "I was too busy looking at you."

Lenna's dark lashes blink a couple of times in surprise. "I'm so fucking stupid," she mumbles to herself. Then before I know it, she's turned on her heel and disappears into the crowd.

For fuck's sake! I quickly throw back my shot of bourbon and head after her. I didn't think she could be that quick, especially as she's been so wobbly on her feet, but she's gone. Looking around frantically, I know I shouldn't have said anything. If something happens to her, I won't be able to live with myself.

Movement out the front door catches my attention, and I head toward it. Pushing open the doors, I'm thrust back onto the red carpet where the paparazzi are still hanging around. Flashes go off, blinding me momentarily as I catch Lenna exiting to the left and heading through the foyer. Ignoring the people calling out for me, I follow after her.

"Lenna." Grabbing her arm, she swings around unsteadily, and I catch her in my arms. There are tears welling in her eyes.

"Please, Logan, I've had enough for tonight. I want to go to my room." There's hurt written clearly across her face, and her body is tense as she holds onto her stomach.

"Let me walk you to your room, please."

She hesitates for a couple of beats, her body relaxing as she gives in. I link her arm with mine, and we walk through the foyer in silence. I press the brass button of the elevator, then we step into the steel box. Lenna pulls herself away from me as we stand quietly watching the flashing lights as we ascend higher and higher.

"You can't say those things to me, Logan," Lenna tells me. She's wrapped her arms around herself protectively.

"I know." Looking down, I stare at the tiles of the elevator floor.

"Did I do something wrong, Logan?"

Her question catches me off guard, so I look over at her, and she appears so small and vulnerable right at this moment.

"Of course not."

The elevator stops and the doors open. Lenna rushes past me, but her heel catches on the door's lip, and she takes a tumble across the carpeted floor.

"Hey, are you okay?" Upon reaching her, tears have well and truly fallen down her cheeks.

"Just leave me alone, Logan." She looks up at me with defeated eyes.

"I don't think I can," I reply, helping her up off the floor, her chest pressed against mine. One of my hands is resting on her hip while the other is linked with hers. Those molten chocolate eyes look up at me, they are slightly red from her salty tears, but still as gorgeous as ever. My heart is pounding in my chest as the world begins to vanish around us. Just the sound of our labored breaths fills the hotel corridor.

I'm not sure who makes the first move, but the next thing I know, my lips are against hers. Fingers are in my hair while my hand is gripping a cheek of flesh. Then my back hits a wall, and it takes my breath away. A warm body is pressed against me. Lush breasts rub against my chest.

"Key," I pant into Lenna's ear because I'm seconds away from fucking her against this wall.

She pulls herself away from me, her lips looking swollen from my frantic lips. Her cheeks are pink and rosy with need.

Her nipples are taut and pressed against the thin fabric of her dress. She shakes the small clutch in her hand and turns on her heel as her hips swish seductively down the corridor. She stops outside of her hotel room, tilts her head to the side, and looks up at me.

"You coming in?" She raises a brow in a dare.

LOGAN

Of course, I follow her. One taste and I've gone insane. Every fiber in my body is pushing me toward those doors, my brain has no control over my body or my dick. They each have minds of their own.

Stepping across the threshold, I know I'm going against everything, e*verything* I have been screaming and shouting at Noah about. But in this moment, I know I'm going to fail to adhere to my strict rules. The thought of not continuing what Lenna and I have started in the corridor...

I. Just. Can't.

Stepping into the hotel room, Lenna's heels are thrown to one side. Then the barely-there black dress is cast aside like sexy little breadcrumbs for me to follow. She's standing at the edge of the bed in nothing but a G-string. Her pert ass is on display like the perfect juiciest peach you have ever seen, one that is so ripe you want to sink your teeth right into it as soon as you have it in your hands. She turns her head to the side, and vulnerable eyes stare back at me.

"You are the most beautiful woman I have ever seen."

Slowly, she turns around and exposes herself to me. Fuck! My dick comes alive instantly.

Her tits. Damn! They are as perfect as her ass. Dusty pink pert nipples beckon to me.

"I want you, Logan." Her honesty catches me off guard.

"But..."

No, please don't stop now. I've never wanted anyone more than I do right now.

"But what?" I take a step toward her hesitantly as her chocolate eyes look me over.

"I don't want to cause you any more pain, Logan."

Her words stop me, even at this moment, through the hormonal haze she's putting me before her own needs. "I have wanted you for so long," she confesses. "But If you say the word, I will get dressed and never speak of this moment ever again."

"Lenna..." Her name falls from my lips with concern as I shuck off my suit jacket.

"I mean it, Logan. I won't jeopardize everything for a one-night stand."

Does she honestly think once I sink inside her that one night is going to be enough?

I kick off my shoes.

"Lenna..." Stepping closer to her, my face softens at her concern for me. She halts me with her hand, which lands on my chest, heat pooling underneath her touch. My hand reaches for my belt buckle, and I undo it, throwing it to the side. Those chocolate eyes flare at the simple gesture.

"I need you to agree with me, Logan. One night only."

Huh! Why?

"One night only?" She nods her head.

"We need to get whatever sexual attraction we have for each other out of our system."

Hang on, what?

"I think we need to sleep together, and then we can go back to being friends and colleagues."

Wait. Huh? My mind and dick are very confused.

"You think that once we fuck, that's going to be it? That we won't want each other again?"

She nods her head in agreement. "It's what's best for the company."

Silence falls between us as my mind tries to catch up and compute what's happening. *Maybe she's right.* Maybe we do need to fuck and get whatever tension that's between us out of our system. Maybe it's the taste of the forbidden fruit that's making this desire between us so much more intense than it needs to be.

"Okay."

"Okay?"

Is she shocked that I've agreed?

"You've made some valid points."

"I have?"

"Yes." My eyes dip down to her breasts. "But… one night doesn't mean one fuck, okay?" Her eyes widen at my comment. "One night is literally for the next…" I stare at my watch, "… eight hours." I give her a smirk. "I think we can fuck each other out of our systems enough times in eight hours. What do you think?"

She silently nods her head in agreement.

"Good, 'cause now I want to finish what we started in the hallway." Reaching my hand out, pulling her flush against me, her gorgeous tits bounce off my hard chest. Her cheeks instantly flush. Moving forward, I place a tender kiss on the crook of her neck, and she whimpers with need.

My fingers dig into her hips as I pick her up, and she lets out a surprised squeal. Then I launch her onto the hotel bed and watch in delight as she bounces a few times. She sits up on her elbows and gives me a seductive look.

I slowly peel off my suit shirt as a smile fills her face. Then I unzip my suit pants and let them fall to the floor. I watch as her chocolate eyes zoom in on the rather large tenting in my underwear.

I toe off my socks and kick them to the side.

Her chest is moving rapidly as her eyes stay focused on me. Hooking my thumbs into the elastic of my boxers, I slowly roll them down and kick them to the side.

The tiniest of gasps leaves her pouty mouth, which makes my dick twitch with anticipation. Striding to where she's lying on the bed, I stop at the edge.

"Spread your legs for me, sweetheart."

She does exactly as she's told.

Slowly placing one knee onto the bed, I then crawl up to her. I notice Lenna's hand is over her face.

There will be no hiding from me.

"Leens?" She peeks through her fingers to look at me. "Are you okay?"

Her cheeks are pink with embarrassment. "You don't have to, you know..." She waves her hands in the direction of her pussy.

Sitting back on my haunches, I think, *Excuse me, what?*

"Do you not like your pussy being eaten, sweetheart?"

Lenna shakes her head. "Um..." She hesitates. "I don't know. Men seem to not want to go down on me."

Are they insane?

"Do you trust me?" Looking into her cocoa-colored eyes, I wait for her answer.

"Yes," her reply is a hesitant whisper.

"Then lay back..." I press my shaking hand against her taut stomach, "... and let me show you how much I want you."

Biting her bottom lip, she does as she's told. Lenna lies back against the hotel bed. Pushing ever so gently, I open her legs for me.

Her hands cover her face again. "Lenna..." my voice is low, "... watch me."

She hesitates for a couple of moments, and I can see she's building up the courage to do as I've asked. Slowly, her hand falls from her flushed face and rests beside her.

My fingers begin to peel back the lace fabric of her G-string, moving them ever so slowly down her creamy thighs until they're flung to the floor to join the rest of our clothing. Her knees instantly go to close, so she's not so exposed to me, but I stop them, pushing them aside again. Leaning forward, I place light kisses up and down her thighs that make her giggle and squirm.

Lenna's fingers dig into the white duvet cover as I reach closer and closer to her sweet spot. Taking one look up at her as I nestle myself right between her thighs, her smooth pussy is ready for me.

One... two... three licks have her arching her back and the tiniest of moans falling from her shocked lips. I'll allow her movement for a couple of moments until she's used to me.

Four... five... six licks have her twisting against me, her fingers moving from the bed to my hair, her nails digging into my scalp.

Seven... eight... nine has her pressing herself against my mouth, trying to create friction around her aching clit.

Oh, no, you don't, Lenna, I'm going to make you work for it.

I pull out all the stops with my tongue, using every trick in the book I have to make her thrash about underneath me.

"Logan... oh my God, Logan..." she screams as she almost pulls strands of my hair clean out of my scalp.

Then I give it to her, right where she needs it.

Wants it.

Feels it.

I suck and tease her clit until she's almost screaming down the room. Then I add a finger, and that's all she needed because it pushes her so far over the edge that she's coming so hard I think the rooms around us might be calling security thinking I'm killing this woman she's screaming so wildly.

"Fuck. *Fuck.* FUCK!"

Lenna pants as she slowly comes down from her orgasm with tiny aftershocks making her quake as she comes back around.

"That... fuck, Logan." Those molten brown eyes look down at me with awe. "Holy shit." She gives me an appreciative smile, and I feel like a goddamn superhero right in this moment.

"I told you we have eight hours together, and I haven't finished with you yet."

Lenna raises a brow as she sits up on her elbows, her eyes falling from my face to my cock. Then before I know it, her legs are wrapped around my waist, and she's pulling me to her.

"Show me more," she coos, her breasts heaving with desire, and they mesmerize me. That has to be the only reason why I forget the next step. *Sheathing up.* Her pretty little pussy is calling me, and the moment I sink deep inside of her, I know it's wrong, but I don't care. I know I have fucked up, but she feels too fucking good to stop now.

I know my dick has taken over my mind because never have I ever fucked without a condom.

12

LENNA

"Bend over," Logan commands. Honestly, this is the best sex of my entire life, so I do as I am told. I didn't think you could have so many orgasms in one night, or morning, or hours. I have no idea what the time is because I've lost track.

Logan enters me from behind while I'm bent over the desk in the hotel room, looking out the window over the Vegas strip below. My fingers grip the wooden desk as he fucks me wildly. My legs feel like jelly, I ache in places I shouldn't ache, and honestly, I don't know how I could possibly come anymore, but I can feel it building, that tiny flutter deep inside of me as his dick hits the place that gets me off. Some magic place deep inside of me that someone as skillful as Logan Stone can only reach because my belly quivers, my legs shake, my tits bounce as he shows me exactly what good dick feels like.

I get it now.

I get what Emma was saying about good dick.

It just sucks that this dick is attached to my boss, who has major non-fraternization and commitment issues with his employees. I guess I should be thankful that he doesn't fuck around with people in the office because that would kill me to watch.

Strong fingers dig into my hips, so much so I know I'm going to have bruises all over my body from the glorious way he has manhandled me all night.

Oh my God, there it is, that amazing sensation where you feel your orgasm building and building, and you know it's going to be incredible when you climb over that edge. Over and over, he hits me in just the right spot until he practically throws me over the cliff and into the sea, and now I'm swimming below in the glorious waters of my orgasm.

"I can't get enough of you," Logan whispers in my ear as he lays feather-light kisses against my shoulder. We stay joined for a couple more moments, enjoying the feeling of being one.

"I... um..." I am not sure what to say as I feel his dick softening inside of me but continue with, "... I should get cleaned up."

This is awkward. The man you want more than anything is pulling himself out of you, and you know that the time you have together like this, joined as one, is now coming to an end.

My body feels empty, and my hand moves to between my legs, so as not to make a mess on the carpet. Standing rather awkwardly from the desk with one hand, I turn and see Logan staring at me with a strange look on his face.

"What?"

Is there something he doesn't like about me? Is my cellulite showing? Are my tits too saggy?

"I don't know if I should say it."

Okay, now my brain is truly freaking out.

"You've just spent hours inside of me, I think you can be honest with me." Tension runs through my tone as I answer him.

"Seeing myself dripping down your leg..." he bites his lip as if he's trying to halt the words from coming out of his mouth,

"... knowing I'm still inside of you even when I'm physically not. Fuck, Lenna..." those ocean-blue eyes swirl with desire, "... it's like I just fucking branded you as mine."

My eyes widen at his caveman-like words. How the hell are you supposed to respond to that?

"I... fuck..." he runs his hand through his light brown hair, "... I'm a damn pervert, aren't I?"

"What! No," I reply because I think it's hot too.

Logan shakes his head as if he is trying to erase his wayward thoughts. "You coming?" he asks, indicating in the direction of the bathroom.

He wants me to come with him?

"Um, sure." I waddle toward the bathroom, trying not to make a mess on my way. He turns on the shower and tests the temperature, then we both step into the cubicle. The cool water feels amazing against my flushed skin.

"Let me." Logan grabs a facecloth and lathers it up with soap and slowly starts cleaning me. His hands run along my curves, over my hips, across my stomach, around my breasts, then his hand slips between my legs, the rough toweling a surprising feeling against my tender lips. Ever so slowly, he cleans himself off of me.

"I'm sorry about what I said earlier." His lips brush against my ear. "I don't know what came over me."

Turning around in his arms, the water hits my back as I look up at him. "I liked it." Wrapping my arms around his neck, I continue, "I like that side of you, Logan. The one that stops hiding behind this perfect-boss image."

"You think I'm hiding?" His question is laced with curiosity.

"Yes." My hand runs along the strong plains of his shoulders. "You show the world this perfect image, which I get, but I think that image is starting to blend into your personal life, too... the CEO who can't differentiate between work and personal life."

"I don't have a personal life," he adds.

"I know, and why is that?" I push him.

He frowns a little confused by my line of questioning. "I'm building an empire, Lenna. I thought of all people, you understood that fact?" His body tenses. It seems I'm pushing him too far out of his comfort zone with my questions, but I can't seem to stop myself.

"You can't build an empire by yourself, Logan." Those blue eyes narrow at me as he reaches behind and turns the faucet off before stepping out into the bathroom to grab a towel. I follow after him.

"Don't you get lonely in that ivory tower of yours?" The air conditioner causes goosebumps to form on my skin as I enter the bedroom. Logan begins to dry himself off, then grabs his clothing off the floor of my hotel suite.

"Just because I fucked you, doesn't mean I'm looking for more."

His words stop me in my tracks. He said them with such venom, it catches me off guard how he can turn so quickly.

"Do you seriously think I'm asking for more?" Pulling the white fluffy hotel towel tighter around me, I feel utterly foolish.

"Everyone woman wants more. They can't just fuck a guy and say 'that was great sex.' No! They always see the fairytale ending... the white knight, the happily ever after, the ring on their finger."

Hang on a minute.

What the actual fuck?

"You think that I'm dreaming of wedding bells and a happily ever after because I let you fuck me."

Logan stares at me blankly for a start then says, "You're no different to any other woman."

I'm shocked.

Stunned.

Almost overwhelmed.

I thought after five years, he might know me better than that.

"And you're no different to every other guy out there. Thinking that their dick is the best thing in the entire world and that a woman couldn't possibly want another. Well, let me tell you right now, Logan Stone..." I get right up into his face, "... your dick wasn't that great."

We stare each other down, both of our chests are heaving with tension. Then before I know it, I'm being pushed against the hotel wall, my towel has been ripped off of me, and Logan is entering me again. His lips are brutal while my hands claw at his back.

"You're mine, Lenna," he grunts into my ear. "There may be others," he says as he thrusts deeper inside of me. "But I know it will be me you're thinking about when they fuck you."

Fuck me!

I should be screaming.

Pushing him off me.

He's being a dick.

But, fuck me, it's all about his dick right now. His words make me want to punch him they're so cocky, but he's probably right because no one has fucked me like he has before.

His teeth sink into my shoulder as he comes inside of me again, and I'm not far behind him as he pushes me harder against the wall.

Holy shit, that was hot!

Now I get why people say hate sex is the best.

Logan pulls out of me, and tucks himself away into his suit pants while I'm a pile of jelly against the wall. He bends down, picks up my towel, and pushes it into my chest.

Then he turns on his heel and walks out the fucking door.

Fuck you, Logan Stone.

13

LOGAN

I can't fucking concentrate at work because every time I see Lenna, all I can think about is what we did in Vegas, and it's driving me insane. Even worse, she doesn't seem affected by it at all. She's acting as if what happened in Vegas didn't damn well happen, and it's fucking with me. I need to get away from her and clear my head.

"Hey..." Speak of the devil, Lenna pops her head into my office. "Do you have a sec?"

"Sure." Ushering her in, she takes a seat. "I was wondering if it's okay for me to head up to The Hamptons this weekend for work." Her request catches me off guard, so I reply, "Work? What work?"

"Ewan wanted me to send up some paperwork for his new guys who are starting, and I thought..." she looks a little nervous, "... that I might pop up there with it and check it out. Have a long weekend."

"With Ewan?"

Is she seeing our contractor?

How long has this been going on?

She knows the rules about our non-fraternization policy.

Lenna stills and looks a little taken aback by my comment.

"When you say 'with Ewan,' you mean working with him, don't you?" Her tone indicates a statement, not a question.

"I'm not sure," I reply honestly.

"You're not sure?" There's anger building in her tone, but that doesn't stop me.

"He's a good-looking guy."

Her jaw falls open, and she pushes back in her chair, the legs scraping against the tiled floor.

"If I want to fuck Ewan Gregor this weekend, that's none of your business," she hisses at me.

"Like hell, it isn't." Slamming my hands on the desk, my anger's getting the better of me as I stand. "I can't believe I have to remind my own HR Director about our company rules."

Lenna looks around to make sure we are alone before she speaks, "How dare you," she says slowly. "How dare you insinuate that I'm going to The Hamptons to screw the contractor."

"I mean, you screwed me easily. How do I know if it's a pattern or not?"

Lenna's hands turn into fists. I think if she could punch me right now, she would without questions.

I'm being a dick.

I'm being the biggest bastard in the history of bastards.

The problem is I can't help myself, and I know that isn't a good enough reason.

"You know what..." she states with steely determination. "Fuck you, Logan Stone." I know I have pushed her too far, I can tell by the bitter smile followed the heavy sigh. "Sleeping with you in Vegas was quite simply, the biggest mistake of my life." *Okay, that stung.* "If you're going to throw what happened between us in my face every single time we get into an argument, then fire me now." Hang on a minute, that's not what I meant. "Because in all honesty, I don't think I want to work with someone like you anymore." Turning on her heels, she walks out of my office, slamming my office door behind her.

Well, fuck.

Falling back into my chair, I know I have fucked up big time.

I've let my fucking ego get in the way of business.

"WHAT!" Anderson screams down the phone.

"Well, hello to you, too."

He groans at my comment. "You interrupted something. You've got five minutes."

"I need your advice."

"Really?" This gets his attention because he knows I would never ask for advice, and especially not from him.

"You're alone, aren't you?"

"If you mean is Noah here, then yes, I'm alone."

Of course, I've interrupted him with some girl.

"Can you please make yourself alone then?" I ask as I navigate my way through the Manhattan traffic. He huffs out something, then I hear the creak of a door, and his voice starts to echo when he speaks.

"I'm alone," he drawls.

"Okay, I fucked up with Lenna."

Silence fills the phone line.

"Are you going to say anything?"

"Sorry, just taking a moment to appreciate that Logan Stone is a human and not a cyborg, so continue."

"Lenna and I hooked up in Vegas." Anderson hums his reply. "I can't stop thinking about it or her. I got fucking jealous when she said she wanted to go to The Hamptons resort to drop off some paperwork to Ewan, and I accused her of going up there to fuck him."

"You did what?" he yells down the phone.

"Yeah, once I got on a roll, I kept putting my foot in it over and over, and now she's angry."

"I don't blame her."

"She's so angry that I think she could sleep with Ewan just to spite me."

"Are you fucking serious?" Anderson chuckles.

"Yes. Deadly. So much so, I'm on my way to The Hamptons now to make sure it doesn't happen."

"I'm sorry, what the fuck did you just say?"

"I'm on my way to The Hamptons." Now, I am not feeling as confident with my decision by the tone of Anderson's voice.

"And what the hell do you think you're going to do when you get there?" he asks.

"Stop her... from sleeping with him." Now that I'm saying this out loud, it seems totally crazy.

"Why do you care if she does?"

'She's mine,' I want to say, but I don't.

"Because it's against company policy."

"Really? That's the kind of bullshit answer you want to give me?"

"Fine! Okay, you want the truth, it's because I don't want her to sleep with him."

"There you go! Finally, some honesty." He chuckles. "And may I ask why you don't want her to?"

Because she's mine.

Mine.

Not his.

Not anyone else's.

My shoulders slump as the realization hits me—she's not mine either.

"Does it matter why." Feeling deflated, I sigh heavily.

"Not to me, it doesn't. But to you..."

"Fine." Preferring not to answer what he wants me to say out aloud, my fingers grip the steering wheel in frustration.

"Have fun in The Hamptons, and say hi to Lenna for me." He chuckles as he hangs up on me.

14

LENNA

"You didn't need to come all the way up here," Ewan, the gorgeous big lumberjack-looking builder greets me, then kisses both of my cheeks. Looking over him appreciatively, I think, *You know what, Logan Stone, I could sleep with someone like Ewan easily.* He's gorgeous. Strong. Has an accent. Is kind. Doesn't seem to have any baggage and seems like a catch.

"I needed to get out of the city for a little while." Shrugging as the sounds of the waves crashing behind, I need this, especially with how I left things with Logan yesterday. I still can't believe he threw Vegas back in my face like that. I never thought us hooking up was a mistake until that very moment. I honestly have never ever wanted to punch someone more than I did Logan at that moment in time.

"Ey, that's why I love living out of the city. Instead of sirens and traffic noise, there's the sound of the waves crashing or the birds singing. Plus, there's no traffic. Well, except for summer, but you know." He rolls his eyes while chuckling.

"I'm looking forward to chilling out on the beach, reading a good book, and reenergizing myself."

"Ey, this is the place to do it. Nothing beats sand between the toes to soothe your worries."

Sounds perfect to me.

"I've set up one of the bedrooms for you if you want to follow me."

The Stone Group purchased this gorgeous resort a couple of years ago. It was owned by a wealthy heiress who hosted the who's who of New York society. If these walls could talk, I bet they have seen so much.

We walk through the nearly completed hotel, up the grand staircase and down the corridor to the rooms. Ewan opens one of the doors for me to enter, so I walk in, and it's stunning. A large bay window covers the entire wall, and it looks directly out over the ocean with nothing but bright blue to the horizon in front of me.

"Nice, isn't it?"

"Wow!" Standing in front of the window, I can see directly all the way down to the golden sand beach, which appears deserted.

"You're going to have to head into town for food, but there are some nice places open at this time of year."

"Thanks." My eyes gaze adoringly over the beach before me with its pristine sand sparkling back, tempting and inviting me.

"Well, I'll leave you to it. You have the security codes and my number if you need anything, and I do mean anything, okay? Anytime, day or night," he tells me then gives me the biggest of smiles. *Is he flirting with me?*

"Thanks, Ewan." I wave him goodbye. Maybe after the bottle of wine I have in my car, I might need him. *Stop it, Lenna.*

Once Ewan has left, I grab the bottle of wine, head on out to the beach, and as far as the eye can see, there isn't a soul. This is exactly what I need. Taking a seat on a nice spot on the sand dunes, I twist open the bottle of wine and take a sip directly from the bottle. Yes, now this is the life. For ages, I stare off to the horizon thinking about everything and nothing all at the same time. The tiny buzz from the wine makes me feel a little better. Happier.

What the hell am I going to do about Logan? Nothing.

He is emotionally broken.

There are so many red flags with that man you could start a marching band with them.

"Are you okay?"

I'm so lost in my thoughts, I don't notice the handsome stranger walking past me. He's dressed in jeans, a chunky cable-knit sweater, and no shoes with glossy dark hair blowing in the breeze and the most gorgeous blue eyes. There are the first signs of a five o'clock shadow forming on his square jaw.

"Yes. Why?" I wonder why he's asked, perhaps I'm sitting on an angry nest of fire ants or something.

"A beautiful woman drinking from a wine bottle on the beach. Alone. Usually means something's happened." He gives me a blinding smile.

"Do you have some kind of white-knight complex? Do you think you have to save women who are drinking alone on the beach from a bottle of wine?"

He chuckles. "Do you need saving?" That killer smirk does all sorts of things to my insides.

"Not sure yet. I guess I'll know when I reach the bottom of the bottle."

The stranger chuckles again. "You live around here?" he asks.

Should I be worried? I'm not getting creeper vibes from him, but maybe I should have my guard up. Hot guys can be serial killers too.

"Yep." I point directly behind me at the incomplete resort.

"No, you're *not*," he says sternly.

"Um... yeah, I am."

Who the hell does he think he is questioning me like this?

"I know the owners. Plus, the resort isn't open yet."

Quirking my brow up at him, I say, "Really? *You* know the owners?" Not believing the bullshit that's coming from his mouth.

"Yes, Logan and Noah Stone." That's easy, everyone knows them, and it's common knowledge that they are building the resort.

"Really?" I am not convinced by his bravado, so I continue, "Prove it."

Folding my arms across my chest, in a daring move, I'm not in the mood for another hot, cocky man talking shit to me. He pulls his phone from his pocket and dials, putting the phone on speaker.

"Davenport, what do you want?" Logan's voice rasps out.

Well, shit! He does know them.

"There is a beautiful brunette sitting on the beach drinking wine directly from a bottle, and she says she's staying at *your* resort." He gives me a quick look. "Just wanted to check if it's true or if I should call the cops?"

Hang on a minute.

Then I hear Logan burst out laughing.

"Lenna. Can you hear me?"

The guy's eyes widen.

"Yes," I mumble unhappily.

"I'd like to introduce you to Rhys Davenport." *Right, that name rings a bell.* "The Stone Group's biggest competitor." Rhys chuckles. "Davenport, I'd like you to meet Lenna Lund, my HR Director."

"Well, I'm glad we could sort this all out." Rhys smirks. "See ya round, Stone." Rhys hangs up on Logan before he can even say another word, then he smiles down at me.

"You thought I was a squatter, didn't you?"

He holds his hands up and smiles. "Well, yeah, but in my defense, I thought you were a very beautiful one."

Okay, now this man has my attention.

"You can't butter me up now after nearly calling the cops on me."

Rhys laughs. "I wouldn't have called the cops on you, but I might have made a citizen's arrest."

I chuckle. "Wow! That doesn't sound creepy at all."

"I was hoping for more suave than creepy." Rhys shrugs.

"You might need to rethink your strategy."

"Well, it's been a while since I've been single, so I guess I've lost my mojo."

"I doubt someone like you will be single for long," I say while looking over the man who looks like he's just stepped out of a Nautica advertisement.

"You'd be surprised."

"Sounds like there's a story there," I reply while looking up at him.

"You'd be right," he adds a little sadly.

"I've got wine." Shaking the half-empty bottle in his direction, he takes it from me and plonks himself down on the sand beside me.

"How much time do you have?" he asks, then takes a swig from the bottle.

"I've got nothing but time at the moment."

Taking the bottle back from Rhys, I have a swig myself.

AFTER RHYS TOLD me the horrific story of his wife running off with his best friend and how he's in a bitter dispute with her over his assets, we moved from the beach, which had turned cool, to his beachfront home, which was toasty and warm from his log fire.

We continued talking in front of the fire with a glass of wine in our hands. I told him about what happened with Justin, about my hook up with Logan—omitting his name and replacing it with someone from IT, which seemed more legitimate. Well, I thought it was until Rhys laughed and said he was surprised any of the guys in IT knew how to pick up a woman. He gave me some guy logic, which was basically the IT guy is extremely jealous, doesn't know how to deal with his feelings, and was lashing out because he doesn't know how to say, 'please don't sleep with someone else because I like you, but because I'm a stubborn prick, I can't commit.' It made heaps of sense when he said it, or maybe it was the huge amounts of wine we had consumed that made it feel like he was the Dali Lama speaking to me with his profound words.

"I better get back," I say even though the fire is very cozy.

"You're more than welcome to crash here. And I promise that is not a euphemism for 'stay so I can sleep with you.'"

Thanks, I think.

"I mean... you're very beautiful, but—"

"You just had to turn creepy, didn't you?"

Rhys chuckles. "Fine! Come on, Cinderella, let's get you home before midnight strikes."

We trudge through the dark sand dunes with nothing but a torch to light our way. We tipsily giggle and laugh until we make it to the front door of the resort.

"Thankfully, Noah and Logan aren't here."

"Huh? Why?"

"Because they might think I'm spying on them." He waves his hand around.

Yeah, he's probably right.

"Shhh... our little secret."

We both laugh as Rhys walks over and pulls me into his arms. "Thanks so much for tonight, Lenna. I can't remember the last time I laughed so much."

I wrap my arms around his strong body—*oh man, is he built.*

"Thank you for a great night, too." We stay hugging a little longer than is probably appropriate, then we pull away, and I can feel it. There is an undercurrent that he's going to kiss me, and sure enough, he leans into me, but I step out of his embrace.

"I'm sorry." Rhys looks a little embarrassed, and I feel for him.

"No need to apologize. Honestly, another time I probably would have let you," I reply while looking into his azure eyes.

"Maybe another time, then." He gives me a smile. "You've got my number."

"Sure." And that's the truth because he's a really nice guy and maybe when things between Logan and me sort themselves out, I might give him a call.

"See you, Lenna."

"Bye, Rhys." Waving, I watch him disappear into the darkness.

"Wasn't expecting that when I walked into my hotel, my HR Director would be with my business competitor." Logan scares the absolute shit out of me as he stands there in the semi-darkness with a torch and a face like thunder.

Is he serious right now?

What the hell is he doing here?

My head hurts. I don't think I care enough to know the answers to those questions, so I push past him and make my way up the stairs without any words.

"Lenna," he calls out from behind me.

"Go away, Logan." I stomp up the stairs, not caring for what he has to say.

"No," he calls out to me. "What the hell were you doing with Davenport? Why was he here at my resort? What else did you show him?"

My blood boils instantly at Logan's accusations. "Are you fucking serious?" Turning around on him quickly, it makes him stop abruptly.

"He found me on the beach drinking. We got on well. He invited me over to his house."

Logan's eyes widen, and I watch his body tense at my words.

"Then he fucked me so good that I couldn't stop coming. I've never come so hard in my life."

Screw him.

Next thing I know, he has me up against the wall, caging me in. Logan's flaring nostrils and high chin make him look angry. Really fucking angry. At me.

"I'm going to ask once, and I want the truth, Lenna. Did. You. Fuck. Him?" His chest is heaving as if he's holding himself back while waiting for my answer.

"I had a threesome with Rhys and Ewan." I roll my eyes. "What the hell do you think?"

Logan snaps. He picks me up and throws me over his shoulder and marches down the hallway. He shoves open the bedroom door, then with his foot, he slams it shut behind us. Walking over to the bed, he throws me on it.

"What the hell, Logan."

"Get undressed, Lenna."

What in the ever-loving hell is going on?

"Fuck you, Logan."

"That's exactly what I'm going to do... to *you*."

My mind is swirling from way too much wine and from being upside down.

"What makes you think I want to sleep with you?"

Logan cockily raises a brow at me as he begins to undress.

"Stop!" Holding up my hand to halt him, I say, "No," and shake my head for extra emphasis. Scurrying off to the other side of the bed away from him again, I reiterate with another "No," and move as far away from him as I possibly can.

"Lenna..." His voice drops with concern.

"Don't you Lenna me." I point at him. "You don't get to come here and be all alpha male with me." I wave my hands around. "You don't get to accuse me of sleeping with all these men and think I'm just going to spread my legs for you."

"I'm sorry."

"I'm not ready to accept your apology, Logan." Folding my arms across my chest, Logan's head hangs, and his shoulders slump as he realizes he's messed up big time with me.

"I don't know what to do."

"You need to get dressed and walk out of my room. That's what you need to do."

"Lenna," he pleads.

Shaking my head. "No, Logan. What you've done to me is unacceptable."

"I came here for you."

"No, you didn't," I argue. "You came here for *you*. You came here because your ego was so big that the thought of someone else having me was too much for you. That even though you don't want me, you don't want anyone else to have me."

"It's not like that at all, Leens."

"I'm tired. I would really like to go to bed. Alone."

Logan's shoulders slump even further as he grabs his things and walks out of the door. Once the door is shut behind him, tears fall silently down my cheeks.

That utter bastard.

I hate that I want him so much.

I curl up in bed and promptly fall asleep and dream of the stupid asshole who's probably sleeping next door.

15

LENNA

There's a light knock on my door.

"Lenna." Logan's voice filters through to me, and I let out a frustrated huff before I answer, "Come in, Logan."

The door creaks open slowly, and I am not expecting the sight before me. Logan's standing there with a large bunch of flowers, two take-out coffees, and a brown paper bag filled with something. The smells filter through my room making my empty stomach growl uncontrollably.

"I'm sorry, Leens." Logan hands me the beautiful bouquet of flowers, which I rest beside me then my coffee. "The way I acted last night..." I can see it on his face how apologetic he is right now, "... that wasn't right." He silently asks if he can sit on the edge of my bed, and I let him. Logan opens the brown paper bag and pulls out two huge, flaky croissants. He knows how much I can't say no to baked goods. "Here..." He offers me the humungous croissant.

Greedily, I take it. Biting into its buttery goodness fills me with joy.

We sit in silence while we both enjoy the first couple of bites of our breakfast.

"Have I fucked things up between us?" Logan eventually asks.

"No..." After letting out a long sigh, I continue, "But you did hurt me." I need him to know he can't talk to me the way he did last night or the day before, for that matter.

"I'm sorry. I just... I don't know what's gotten into me."

"Jealousy."

Logan looks up at me, and he's ready to argue but decides not to. "Yeah, I was jealous."

Wow! I didn't think he would confess so easily.

"You know you have no right to be jealous, don't you?" I tread carefully while talking to him.

"I know." He huffs. "But..." he nervously wriggles on the edge of the bed, "... I don't think I can help it."

This is going to be a problem between us.

Sitting up straighter on the bed, I tap the space beside me. Logan moves the flowers to the side table and joins me.

"What happened between us in Vegas was fun..." Turning, I glance over at him. "Would I like to do it again?" I give him a warm smile. "Sure, but I know deep down inside it won't work." Logan's forehead crinkles into a frown. "I think the deep-seated rules you have set for yourself about mixing business and pleasure is now fundamentally ingrained in you. It's so deep-seated that if you broke them any more than we already have that..." not sure why I'm getting so emotional, "... that it will destroy you. I mean it has already started."

"Lenna..." Logan looks at me, his eyes droop.

"Pushing everything aside, I genuinely feel like we are friends, good friends. Maybe that's all we're meant to be and that Vegas... was just Vegas. We got swept up in the craziness of it all."

"I don't regret, Vegas," Logan tells me quietly. "I regret my actions after, though."

"You should, you've been a dick." My honesty makes him chuckle.

"I know," he replies while looking at me fondly. "I know I keep women at a distance. But, you..." he closes his eyes and lets his head fall back against the headboard, "... you've found a way through my defenses." Those ocean-blue eyes look at me longingly. "And I don't know how to build them back up again when it comes to you."

That hit all the feels.

"Logan..."

"I can't stop thinking about you."

No. No. No. He can't say those things to me.

"You have to, Logan."

"I know..." His hand brushes against mine, and I hate this pull we have between each other. The slightest touch, and it makes my body come alive. There's a deep throb between my legs that's becoming harder to ignore.

Our faces lean in closer to each other.

"We shouldn't."

I feel his breath across my face, and he says, "I know."

My body moves toward his. "It's a bad idea."

"Yeah, it is," he agrees, but that doesn't stop him from moving even closer.

"I..." Not sure what I'm trying to protest about because whatever it is doesn't have a chance to continue as Logan's lips meet mine. He tastes like coffee and buttery croissant as he slowly devours me, not pushing for more, but making me want it all the same. Next thing I know, I'm climbing on top of him, need now throbbing throughout my body.

"I can't stop this," I say as I grind myself against his hardness.

"Me, either." Logan's large hand wraps around my neck, pulling me closer. Devouring me.

Next thing I know, I'm pushing down his track pants and releasing him. This is escalating rather quickly, but pure need has taken over, and I'm powerless to stop it. Then I'm sinking myself onto him, both of us moaning as we join together. Running my fingers through his thick hair, he thrusts into me.

Goddamn, this was not my plan this morning. Us sleeping together again was not on the cards.

"Fuck, Leens," Logan groans as he gives me what I've been craving since Vegas, and moments later, I follow him.

"I didn't plan on that happening." Looking down at him, his hand runs along my face as he smiles at me.

"Me, either." He pulls me down into a kiss, and his eyes widen. "We forgot about protection. Again."

"I'm on the pill," I reassure him. "I took the morning after pill when I was in Vegas. The last thing I want is to get pregnant."

Logan looks relieved. "Phew, I don't even want kids, so I don't think I could handle it if there was an accident."

Note to self, *Make sure you use protection next time you sleep with Logan because you do not want to have a baby with this man.*

This is not the best conversation we could be having while he's still inside of me.

"Let's have a shower." Pushing off of him, I scurry into the bathroom, and moments later, Logan joins me in the shower.

"We need to be more careful," he tells me while resting his chin on my shoulder.

"Don't worry, it won't be happening again."

He turns me around quickly in his arms. "You want to stop?"

Has he not been listening?

"Logan..." Looking up at him, I am getting a strange sense of déjà vu. "We won't work."

"I know," he tells me, looking a little deflated.

"You want something different from what I want out of life."

"What do you want?" His question seems genuine.

"I want a partner. I want to have a family one day. I want the white picket fence, and the two-point-five kids, and a golden retriever. I never had any of that growing up." I feel completely stupid telling him all this, but maybe it's enough to scare him away for good. "Obviously, not now, but soon. I mean I'm not getting any younger."

I'm thirty-two, and yes, I have years ahead of me, but if I keep wasting my time on guys who don't want the same thing as I do, then I'm going to be forty and look back and realize I wasted my time on men who weren't right for me. I don't want to waste my chances of a happily ever after on someone who doesn't deserve it.

"I wish things were different."

"Do you seriously think we would have worked?" Chuckling awkwardly, I screw up my nose.

"I would have tried for you." My stomach flip flops in hope at his words. "But I know in the end I would have broken your heart." Then it sinks like a brick thrown into the ocean.

"Yeah, you would have."

"Are we being adults about the situation because this feels awfully mature of us."

"Guess we are." I smile.

Logan reaches out and cups my face. "I wish nothing but the best for you, Lenna." As he bends down and kisses me, ever so softly, he pulls back and declares, "I don't want to lose you."

"You have me. I'm here," I tell him.

"I promise to keep my jealousy under control. Okay?"

"Me, too."

Logan's eyes widen significantly at my confession. "You are jealous?"

"Of course, I mean..." Ugh, I can't believe I'm going to say this, but the man's been inside of me, so it doesn't really matter. "I've had a crush on you ever since you interviewed me for the job." There, it's out there in the open, and I've said it. With those words, I somehow feel lighter.

"You've had a crush on me for five years?"

Okay when he says it like that, it sounds creepy.

"Forget I said anything," I add and attempt to wrestle out of his grasp.

"Oh, no, you don't," he asserts while giving me a bemused smile. "I need to know more about this *crush*." Now he's teasing me, and somehow, I knew he would. Pulling myself out of his arms, I jump out of the shower and wrap myself in a towel. He follows behind me.

"Come on, Leens, tell me about your crush."

"Go away." My face flushes with embarrassment, but he swings me around, so I have no choice but to look at him.

"Did you think of me when you touched yourself all these years?" He doesn't need to know the answer to that. "Because I did." His voice lowers. "From the moment you stepped into our conference room, images of you have helped me relieve my stress."

Did he just confess to jerking off about me?

"Images of fucking you on the conference room table with the blinds up. People standing around, watching me eat your perfect little pussy, wishing it was their mouth devouring you." Holy hell, I like dirty-talking Logan. "Five years I've wondered what was underneath your business suits. Dreamed about tasting you. Ravaging you. Wondering what you sounded like when you came."

Is it getting hot in here?

"Now, I know, and I don't know if my hand is going to be good enough anymore."

Um... What the hell have I got myself into?

"Guess you're going to find out if your hand's up to task from now on, aren't you?"

Logan gives me a wicked smile. "Or..." he challenges me. "You could show me."

"We just decided it wasn't a good idea." Feeling very confused, I grimace and narrow my eyes.

"I know." Running his hand through his wet hair, Logan begins to pace around the room. "What I'm asking goes against everything I have ever stood for..." *Okay, that's not a great start.* "I'm fighting with everything inside of me at the moment..." *Still not sounding great.* "But my need for you outweighs everything else."

Huh. What did he say?

"Now that I know what you taste and feel like, I... I don't want to give you up."

"Logan, I'm confused."

"I know, I'm giving such mixed signals. I can't offer you anything more than a willing dick. I can't give you happily ever after. I can't give you the white picket fence. All I can give you is dirty, secretive fucks. Clandestine hookups. Cool indifference at work."

His warnings should scare me, but I already know all this.

"I won't interfere if you want to see other men. Sleep with other men. Date. I won't stand in your way if you find your Prince Charming."

"You're honestly saying you won't be upset if I sleep with someone else?"

"I'll get used to it," he says through gritted teeth.

"And what about you? Will you sleep with other people?"

Logan pauses for a moment thinking over my question. "If we are sleeping together, and you are not seeing someone else, then no, I won't be making an effort to sleep with anyone else."

"But if I'm sleeping with someone else, then you will, too?" Just want to clarify whatever this is he is offering.

"I have needs, and if you are busy with someone else, then yes, I will have mine met."

"So, this is *just sex*?" Again, I am trying to clarify what exactly I'm agreeing to.

"Yes, I like fucking you, and I'm assuming you like fucking me. We are both extremely busy people, and as you know, we are expanding the Stone Group rapidly, and that doesn't leave much time for anything else."

"What about your non-fraternization rule?" The one rule he's so strict with.

"That's why they will be secretive fucks. I'm the world's biggest hypocrite at the moment. I would like it if no one else found out about it," he says quite seriously.

Can I handle sleeping with him, and not letting my feelings get in the way?

"Can I think about it?"

Logan's eyes widen in surprise. Does he seriously think I'm going to agree to his request just like that?

"Of course." Not knowing how to deal with my answer, he adds, "I'll leave you to it."

"Logan." Halting, he turns around hope fills his face. "I'm going to need longer than getting dressed to make my decision."

"Oh."

"Tonight... I'll have an answer for you tonight."

"Sure." He bends and picks up the rest of his clothing while looking a little awkward.

"Logan..." He looks up. "I'd like to spend the day with you. It looks like it's going to be a beautiful day." Pointing to the window, which has sunlight streaming in, the water is sparkling outside.

"I'd like that."

16

LOGAN

We've spent the morning walking around the property, ironing out problems. Making notes. Working out solutions. It was nice having someone other than my brother to talk business over with.

We then headed into town for lunch and ended up at a gorgeous seafood restaurant. We spent considerable time eating, chatting, and soaking up the gorgeous view across the ocean, even if it is the off-season. I've kept my hands to myself all day, even though I have wanted nothing more than to reach out and touch Lenna, push her wind-swept hair from her face and kiss her rosy cheeks, then pull her into my arms as she enthusiastically talks about work. But I can't do any of those things. I shouldn't want to do anything about it, but I do.

My head is telling me to stick to the rules.

That things are going to get messy.

That you have gotten this far without falling for a woman.

But then there's my dick. That fucking thing has a hold over me, and every time he gets close to Lenna, he wants more. But when Lenna told me this morning in the shower about how she wants the whole happily ever after, I knew I am not the one for her.

And yet you still asked for more from her. I am a selfish motherfucker. Maybe I'm more like my father than I thought.

"Ready." Lenna walks over to me. She ran upstairs to grab a sweater for our sunset walk along the beach. Like I said, I'm a motherfucker. She hands me a beer as she swings a small bottle of wine in her hand loosely.

The air has turned cooler, and the wind has whipped up. We stroll along the sand in silence as we take in the setting sun behind us, throwing lines of pink and orange across the horizon. It's a little too romantic for friends to be walking along the beach together.

My hand itches to reach out for her, wanting to entwine our fingers together. But add in the gorgeous sunset, deserted beach, and the alcohol, and it would be considered more of a date if I do.

"This is truly beautiful." Lenna stops, placing her hand over her eyes as she stares out into the inky black ocean as the sun sets. She unscrews the cap of her bottle, I watch as her plump lips wrap around the end and my dick twitches. Her head tips back as she takes a big mouthful, then she turns and looks at me. "What?"

She really doesn't want to know what the hell is traveling through my mind right at this moment. Shaking my head trying to push away all the images of what else those lips could be wrapped around, she gives me a frown at my non-answer and turns back toward the horizon as we watch the last streaks of sunlight filter through before disappearing over the edge.

"This place is going to be a huge success, Logan." Hearing the pride in her voice sends flutter through my chest.

"It's a team effort."

"But it's your vision," she adds.

Shrugging my shoulders, I'm not my twin, and I don't accept compliments well.

She reaches out, and her cold hand touches my skin. "You should be so proud of yourself." I can hear the sincerity lacing through her words.

"All I can think about is what's next." Confessing the turmoil which is currently swirling around my brain, the never-ending search for more. To do better. To be the best.

"Do you ever sit back and enjoy everything you've created?"

Her question makes me think. H*ave I ever enjoyed a weekend at one of our resorts?* Except for that one time with Noah and Anderson where we thought we could be undercover bosses, I don't think I have. Which I guess is pretty sad when we create some of the most exclusive resorts in the world.

"Can't say that I have." Putting my hand in my pocket, I take another sip of my beer. The tiniest ray of sunlight streaks across the ocean, and the first couple of stars start to emerge from their homes and begin lighting up the night sky.

"Never?" She seemed surprised by my comment.

"I'm always looking forward. Always searching for the next site."

Lenna nods her head in understanding. "A bit like your relationships, then." Her comment catches me off guard.

"What do you mean?" Turning my back toward the ocean, I give her my full attention.

"Always looking for the next. Never satisfied with what you've got." Those chocolate eyes glare at me as she takes another large drink of her wine. *Is she talking about us?*

"Business and pleasure are two separate things."

She shrugs her shoulders, which kind of infuriates me.

"What's the point in working so hard if you can't celebrate what you've achieved." There's sadness as she says the words.

Is she sad for me? Am I missing out being so focused on my business?

"You're not your father, Logan." Her words are almost a whisper as the wind whips up around her carrying her words away out toward the ocean.

What does she mean?

Wanting to know what she's thinking inside that head of hers, I respond with, "Elaborate?"

"I think you're worried if you loosen the reigns on your business, or on your life, that it's going to spiral out of control like your father did." Those chocolate eyes stare deep within my soul, extracting my deepest and darkest fears directly from me. Her comment floors me a little because I thought that I was able to hide my fears, but she sees through all the walls I've built up around me so effectively as if they're made of glass.

Lenna shakes her head. "I shouldn't have said anything." She turns on her heel and starts to head back to the resort.

"Lenna..." Jogging after her, reaching out, I halt her with my hand. She looks up at me through dark lashes, those chocolate-colored eyes glistening with unshed tears. I cup her cheek with one of my palms.

"I shouldn't be psychoanalyzing you, Logan." She seems upset with herself for her comments, but I don't understand as they hit so close to the mark.

"You see me, Lenna." Looking up at me, she relaxes the tiniest bit. "No one's ever really seen *me*." I shouldn't be surprised that she, of all people, is the one to get me, to be the one who has pushed through all my barriers. She's been by my side for the past five years. Lenna's experienced the highs and lows of my career, and now, now she sees the real man underneath the veneer I show the world, and for the first time, I find myself lacking.

"I think you are one of the most hardworking, generous, funny, moody..." I chuckle, "... handsome men I know."

Fuck, she's perfect.

Leaning forward, I kiss her because she's rendered me

speechless. She opens willingly for me. We aren't in a hurry this time as we savior each other, softly, gently. The wind whips her hair around us. Waves crash behind us in the distance, but all I care about in this moment is Lenna and showing her that even though I may not be the right man for her forever, I am the right man for her right now. She shivers beneath my arms.

"Let's head back inside, it's getting cold."

It looks like a storm might be brewing in the distance, the way the wind and the ocean have turned more aggressive since we arrived.

Linking my hands with hers, we walk back to the resort hand in hand.

17

LENNA

Something changed between Logan and me on the beach. Something for the better, I am hoping. The tension that riddles his back and shoulders seems to have eased ever so slightly. I'm cautiously optimistic that it might be because of me. *I know I'm dreaming.* I'm also known to overthink things too. But the feeling of his hand in mine as we walked along the beach in the darkness, his large, strong hand linked with mine made me feel protected, secure, dare I say even cared for.

"What do you say to a bath?" he asks, walking up the wooden stairs into the foyer of the hotel.

"That sounds amazing." A cold shiver creeps up my spine as the wind whips around us before we enter.

"Why don't you get one started, and I'll quickly grab some take-out. Crab cakes and salad sound okay?" My stomach grumbles at the thought of food, especially after nearly knocking back a small bottle of wine at the beach.

"Sounds great."

He stops, turning me around before placing a kiss against my lips. "I won't be long." He grins, then heads to the parking lot. It felt, almost dare I say it, domesticated. I need to rein in the hearts and rainbows shit because he's told me so many times that he can't offer me anything more than a good time. Even though I know he could if he just let himself feel more than he does, instead of bottling up all those emotions that are like a heavy noose around his neck.

You want to be that girl who changes Logan Stone.

I do.

And that's why he's going to break your heart.

I let out a heavy sigh as I climb the grand staircase leading up to my bedroom.

How the hell are you going to protect your heart, Lenna? That's the million-dollar question, isn't it?

After entering my room, I walk straight to the massive bathroom, turn on the faucet to the bath and get undressed. Sinking down into the hot water feels divine. I poured in some of my body wash, and it has bubbled up. The large picture window looks out across the dark ocean and the first streaks of lightning crawl across the sky.

"It's getting crazy out there," Logan's voice startles me, making me jolt and slosh some of the water over the edge. "You look cozy in there." He comes around with a take-out bag in his hand and a grin on his face as he eyes the large stacks of foamy bubbles surrounding me.

"I don't have a bath at home, so it's an indulgence when I get to have one." I watch as he places the brown paper take-out bag on the white stone sink and pulls out two cardboard boxes.

"You think you're going to be able to see what you're eating underneath all those bubbles." He chuckles, there's a lightness to his tone.

"You could always feed me if I can't." Not meaning to sound like a weirdo or anything, Logan stills looking down at that cardboard box in his hand.

"I think I'd like that." He gives me a heated stare and

places the box back onto the side of the sink and begins to undress. I watch as his sweater, then his T-shirt hit the floor—my breath hitches when he unzips his jeans and pulls them down along with his underwear. Logan turns and stands unashamedly naked in front of me while I take him all in. His bronzed skin, his well-defined muscles, his thick, semi-hard dick that bobs in front of him. Logan Stone knows how to wear the hell out of a suit, but naked and in his glory, it is a sight to behold. He turns and empties one box into the other, discarding the empty box to the side. Then he steps into the opposite end of the bathtub with the water sloshing over the edge.

Oops, I guess I overfilled it for two.

"Guess we'll see if there are any leaks while we're here." He smiles, slowly submerging himself into the bubbles. Thick thighs rest against my legs as he tries to maneuver himself into a comfortable position around me. Once he's settled, he lays back and lets out a deep, contented sigh. Then he opens the box and plays around with the food until he's got what he needs on his fork. "Open wide, Lenna," he commands, leaning forward with a portion of crab cake on his fork.

I do as I am told and take the bite-sized piece he is offering to me. Our eyes never leave one another as I do. The tiniest twitch of his mouth gives his appreciation away.

The crab cake tastes divine, and I hum my pleasure.

Logan gives me a look through his thick lashes.

"What?"

"Moan like that again, and I'm going to throw this box and haul you into my lap and make sure that I'm the one making you moan like that."

Slowly, I chew and swallow.

Who knew Logan Stone was a dirty talker?

He leans over and feeds me slowly again and again until I'm utterly satisfied, well, maybe not that satisfied in that sense. We lay in the bath enjoying the silence, neither one of us needing to say much.

"I need a bath..." I run my hands over the vanishing bubbles, "... one just like this," I state as I sink further down into the water.

"I have one I never use," Logan adds while I look at him just over the waterline. "You're more than welcome to it."

"I thought you didn't like people invading your personal space."

"People, yes. You, I'm okay with." He gives me a grin while my heart thuds wildly in my chest.

No, he needs to stop being so cute, my heart simply can't take it.

"I don't think that would be such a good idea." Be strong, Lenna.

"Why?" Genuinely seemingly confused by my comment, how has he forgotten *his* rules so easily?

"Whatever this is..." Waving my hand between us, "... can't keep going."

Logan contemplates my words, and I'm expecting him, no, I'm hoping he will try and fight me on it, telling me that he thinks we should continue whatever this is back in the city, but he doesn't. Instead, he asks, "You want this to stop? You want the sex to stop?" Confusion mars his gorgeous face as if giving up on seeing Logan Stone naked is out of the realm of my possibilities. He'd be right, but I know the only loser in all this is going to be me.

"I think we enjoy what's left of the weekend..." be strong, "... then once we are back in the city, we continue as normal." Those blue eyes of his flare, he's not happy with my comment. "I don't think I can accept being someone's secret fuck. I know I deserve more than that." Because as much as I want to continue being with Logan, after everything I've been through with Justin, I deserve someone not keeping me in the shadows. I want to date someone who sees a future with me. Someone who wants more than clandestine fucks. Someone who wants to be seen with me out in public.

"I agree you deserve more. You deserve so much more." His voice seems somewhat sad when he says the words.

"We can worry about all this tomorrow when we go home. Tonight, let's just enjoy our little bubble one last time before we have to venture back to reality."

Logan looks at me and grins before reaching out and pulling me to him, so I'm straddling him. He maneuvers himself at my entrance and slowly enters me.

"Guess I better make it good then."

And, oh boy, does he make good on his words.

LOGAN

"Thanks for a great weekend, I think we got a lot accomplished." I am acting professional as if my tongue hasn't been tasting her all morning. "This is going to be something truly amazing."

She's truly amazing. The way she arches her back as I bring her to the brink. The way she does as she's told when I ask her to. The way she gives herself to me so freely. I don't deserve someone like her. I could only wish I was man enough for a woman like Lenna Lund, but unfortunately, these are the cards I've been dealt with.

Lenna's driving back in her car. She wouldn't hear of me asking one of my drivers to drive it back to the city for her. I wanted a couple more hours with her before having to go back to reality, but she's insistent on driving back herself. Probably eager to get away from me, thinking about what a mistake this weekend was. I know she enjoyed the sex, her screams and the scratches down my back are an indication that she did.

"Lenna." Stepping forward, I cup her face. Those doe eyes

look up at me expectantly. "I had fun this weekend, and I don't regret coming up here."

Her body sags at my confession. "I don't regret you coming up here, either." She places her hand against my chest and looks at me for more.

"I..." I want to say more, I want to say what I'm feeling deep down inside, but I don't because no matter what I may want in the end, I know I will break her heart, and I can't do that to her. Instead, I deflect by leaning in and taking her lips one last time. Savoring her taste. Taking in the feeling of her pressed against me to memory, so I never forget how perfect she feels in my arms.

"Thanks," she says rather awkwardly. Her cheeks are a little pink from our kiss. "I'll see you back in the office. Drive safe." Turning on her heel, she jumps into her car and starts it.

"Drive safe, Lenna."

As I watch her drive away with the dust kicking up around her tires, I realize I have to get back to the city, and back to my life that doesn't include Lenna Lund underneath me.

LIKE A DAMN CREEPER, my attention has been pulled by the sound of Lenna's laugh. I watch as she chats animatedly with Chloe in the office, and I wonder what they're talking about. She's wearing one of those damn pencil skirts again. Today is a bright red one with a black blouse and black heels. Her brown hair is pulled up into a high ponytail, and all I can think about is wrapping it around my hand while those bright red ruby lips service me under the table.

"Hey, dickhead." My brother surprises me, catching me off guard in a moment of weakness. Noah closes the door behind him, he has a grin on his face.

What has he done?

"What's going on?" Noah eyes me suspiciously.

"Nothing." Moving some paperwork around on my desk, I have no clue what they are, but it doesn't stop me.

"You seem pretty interested in Lenna and Chloe's conversation." His head tilts, and his green eyes bore into me as if he's trying to read my mind. *Fucker.*

"What? No, I was lost in thought thinking about something..." He's going to be annoying in less than one minute, I just know it.

"In their direction?" he questions me.

"That was simply a coincidence." See what I mean, annoying as fuck.

"How are we looking at the new Hamptons resort?"

Changing the subject to yes, work. That's what we need to be talking about.

"I checked it out on the weekend, and it's coming along well. I think we might be ready for a test in a month or so."

"I was thinking of taking Chloe up there, so we can finalize the marketing strategy for opening day."

Is he fucking serious? That's asking for trouble, and I should know.

"I'm worried about you." I see the way he looks at Chloe, the side glances when no one's watching. I know he wants her.

"Me. Why?" I hear the protest in his voice.

"You seem to be getting awfully close to Chloe." The coffee he likes to bring her on some mornings and other little things make it obvious.

Just like you used to do for Lenna.

"No, I'm not," he argues.

"You seem to be bending over backward for her. Some might say it's leaning toward favoritism." The guy rented Chloe his investment property, which is next door to his home, and if that doesn't spell trouble or temptation, then I don't know what does.

"Some might say, or are you saying?" My brother glares at me. I can see he is ready for a fight. His back's up because he knows I'm right.

"Me." Arching a brow at him. "I'm worried that feelings are involved. You have a history with her." I know I'm a hypocritic right in this moment because of the feelings I have for Lenna, but I didn't move her into the house right beside me.

"What? A kiss at a resort months ago?" He's trying to fob me off like it's no big deal.

"I heard you rescued her from her ex in Vegas."

Thanks, Anderson, for that little nugget of information.

"And where were you?" Turning the tables, he says, "You never came home after taking Lenna to her room."

Sitting up straighter in my chair, I wonder, *Does my brother know?*

"Nothing's happening," I try to reassure him, or am I trying to reassure myself?

"Didn't say there was." He gives me a knowing smirk, the fucker. "You're not Dad, you know?" Fuck him, bringing that up right now.

"I know because we stick to the rules." My body clenches at the mere mention of our father.

"Just know, I wouldn't care if something happened with Lenna."

Panic laces my body.

How the hell does he know?

What is he talking about?

"Noah..." I warn him. I don't want to talk about Lenna, especially as nothing *is* going on. My brother glares at me, urging me to come clean over what he thinks is happening. Never. He should know by now how stubborn I am.

"Is Chloe going to be a problem?" I change the subject.

"No," he replies through gritted teeth.

"But you like her?" I know I'm stating the obvious, anyone with eyes can see they like each other.

"Yes." I'm surprised he's being honest with me. "Least I'm man enough to be able to acknowledge my feelings." Noah glares at me. Is he trying to insinuate there are feelings between Lenna and myself?

"You have feelings for her?"

"Not like that!" He tries to defend his words.

"But more like friends?" I am testing him to see if I should be worried about my brother's infatuation with our Marketing Director. "Do you think taking her away to The Hamptons is a good idea?" Because let's be serious, if after a couple of wines, the moonlight, the stars, the ambiance of it all, it can easily push a friendship into something more.

"It's work," he argues.

"I know. Just, I'm concerned after what you've told me." I don't want my brother to get his heart broken. He's a romantic deep down inside, even though his exterior screams womanizer.

"I'm not a teenager with a crush. I know the difference between work and play," he tells me defensively.

"Hey, don't get pissy with me. I'm just trying to be the voice of reason here."

"So, you didn't take Lenna to The Hamptons last weekend?" Stilling at the accusation that's dripping in my brother's words.

"It was work," I seethe. "How did you find out?"

"Anderson told me."

"Fucking loudmouth."

"You hid it from me." Noah sounds a little hurt over the fact I never told him.

"Because it's nothing... just work," I reassure him. I'm going to hell for the lies dripping from my tongue right now.

"And yet, you think me taking Chloe to The Hamptons is something else?" he questions me.

Damn! He has a point, but I'm not about to tell him that.

"You and Chloe have hooked up, and you just told me you like her."

Deflect.

Deflect.

Deflect.

"So, you don't like Lenna?" he pushes.

"Of course, I like Lenna..." This subject is becoming dangerous now.

"As a colleague."

"You're so frustrating," Noah growls. "I'm taking Chloe to The Hamptons this weekend... *for work*. Nothing more."

"Okay," I agree angrily.

"Good."

And with that, my brother walks out of my office, and I feel like I've gone a couple rounds with Mike Tyson.

19

LOGAN

"**H**ey, man." EJ pops his head into my office.

"Hey." I'm surprised to see him here, he's never shown up here before. "What are you doing over here?"

"Just had lunch with Chloe. Thought I'd better make time. Things have been crazy since Vegas." I keep forgetting Chloe is EJ's sister.

"So, how are things?"

"Good. Going well. Got heaps in the pipeline. I know we have to talk about doing some things together. I am thinking maybe somewhere tropical could be nice." He's reminding me of our many chats about working together.

"I'll make a note."

"Do you have any plans tonight?" EJ asks.

"No, I'm free."

EJ's eyes light up, and a knowing grin falls across his face. "Good. Well, you and I have a double date."

Wait! What? No. No. No. No.

"Anderson, the pussy, canceled on me tonight. Not sure why... he's always up for some fun."

"Can't you handle them both by yourself?" I question. I mean, the man is a celebrity chef, women love that shit.

"Um... yes, I can. But I thought..." his eyes narrow on me, "... that you need to get out of this office and go on a freakin' date. When was the last time you went on a date?"

I have no idea, so I shrug.

He slaps his hand down hard against my desk, vibrating everything on it. "See." He smiles. "You need to get laid." *No, I don't.* "You need to enjoy good food, copious amounts of wine, and the company of a gorgeous woman to get you back into form."

"Didn't think I lost my form."

EJ rolls his eyes on a sigh. "Dude, you are the grumpiest, moodiest bastard I know, and the only thing I can think of that makes you that way is complete lack of sex."

Um, he couldn't be more wrong. The weekend of amazing sex with Lenna definitely set my mood right, but what's really messing my mood right now is the way she has effortlessly gone back to the way we were. That I don't affect her. She treats me as if I don't know what she tastes like, or that she has a cluster of freckles underneath her right breast that I like to run my finger over.

"I don't think it's a good idea."

EJ stills. Frowns. Those green eyes flicker with questions.

"Are you seeing someone?" His voice lowers.

"No," I answer, rather too quickly.

"But you have been?" he pushes.

"Does it matter?"

"It did matter, but now it doesn't?"

Why is this turning into the Spanish Inquisition?

"Let's not talk about it."

Hoping he will move on, EJ sits back and crosses his arms, silently assessing me. "You can talk to me, you know," he says with sincerity. "I'm not like Anderson, I don't gossip." He lets out a sigh.

"It doesn't matter anymore because it's not going to happen again. She's not interested, and plus..." I shuffle some papers on my desk nervously, "... I'm not the right person for her." That's as close to the truth as he's going to get.

EJ nods his head in understanding. "Then come tonight. No expectations. Enjoy the night for nothing more than getting out of the house."

"Fine! What time and where do you want me?"

He's right—Lenna and I have drawn our line in the sand between each other. She wants a happily ever after and I want? What do I want? I'm not sure, but I know it could never be the house in the suburbs, the white picket fence because I'm not my brother.

"Great. Eight, tonight at the restaurant." EJ jumps up, clapping his hands together.

"See you then."

He gives me a salute and walks out of my office.

Why do I have a sick feeling in the pit of my stomach?

"You made it." EJ claps me on the back as I enter the private room that's set up for us. Guess he's going all out. "Want a beer, bourbon, whisky?" he asks.

"A beer is fine."

EJ reaches around the private bar and grabs a bottle from the bar fridge, opens it, then pours it into a glass.

"I forgot to ask earlier..." I say as he hands me the beer. "How do you know these two women?"

EJ grins. "They're some friends who are always up for a good time." He cheers me with his glass.

"Please tell me you're not paying them?"

EJ's eyes widen over the rim of his beer glass. "I don't have to pay women to spend time with me. Look at me…" He runs his hand up and down his body—the cocky bastard. "They happen to be some model friends who are in New York for a shoot. They've finished, and now they're up for some fun."

Guess that answers my question.

"Aren't they expecting Anderson to be here instead of me?" Sipping my beer, I watch EJ shrug.

"Possibly, because he's usually my right-hand man when it comes to entertaining, but lately, he has been MIA a lot. I think he might have a side-chick-thing going on." My brows raise in surprise. Of all us, Anderson's the one who's least likely to ever settle down. I mean the man is richer than a sultan, he travels the world investing in businesses and is never usually in one spot long enough to be interested in one woman. He's the type of guy you can't hold down, he dances to the beat of his own drum.

"Doubt it."

"He's been weird since Vegas," EJ adds.

Really? Have I been that wrapped up in my own stuff to notice what's been going on with my friends?

"Maybe he's got a deal going down. You know how he gets when he's concentrating on a deal."

EJ thinks it over. "Maybe. But I swear I've heard a woman on the other end of his phone when I've called him."

"He always has a woman in his bed." Anderson's the worst of us all. Not that we're bad guys, but we do appreciate the company of beautiful women.

"You're right," EJ agrees as the door to the private dining room opens, and in walks two gorgeous women. "Ladies, you made it," EJ greets them warmly, kissing them each on their cheeks. "Let me introduce you to one of my good friends, Logan Stone."

Stepping forward, I greet them the same way, kissing each of them on their cheeks.

"He owns the best resorts in the world."

This bit of information makes the girls giggle.

Oh, no, please do not be airheads.

"This is Lindsay..." EJ points to the brunette, "... and this is Allie," he introduces the blonde who smiles at me. "Champagne, ladies?" EJ asks, and they both giggle again.

Maybe I shouldn't have come.

"CAN I COME HOME WITH YOU?" Allie, the blonde, purrs in my ear.

EJ has filled me to the brim with good food and even better bourbon. My mind's a little cloudy. I never lose control like this, but the stress of work and everything has made me indulge.

Tonight, I want to forget about everything.

Maybe I need to let loose.

Say fuck it for once.

"Yes," I agree to her question.

She leans in and kisses me. She tastes of champagne, and it feels all kinds of wrong.

"We're out of here," EJ announces with Lindsay wrapped around him like a blanket.

"So are we," Allie answers for me.

Helping me stand on unsteady legs, EJ gives me a not-too-subtle thumbs up. Allie wraps her arms around me, and we stagger our way through the back entrance of the restaurant where the VIP guests enter. My driver is waiting for me in the alley.

"Is this your car?" Allie asks.

"Yeah." My driver opens the door for me, and I say, "You coming?" Turning, I look at her. She smiles, nodding her head and slides in after me. As soon as our asses hit the leather seats, she's on me. Allie straddles me in the back of the car. Her hands are running through my hair, she's gyrating against my dick who, for some reason, should be enjoying a model rubbing herself against him, but he's not. Her lips capture mine, and I try to forget that my dick is feeling less than enthusiastic. Allie continues gyrating against me in a frenzied flurry.

It doesn't take long until we arrive at my apartment.

Grabbing her hand, I pull her through the glass doors of my apartment building, the fluorescent lights stinging my eyes as we go.

"Mr. Stone," Dion, the doorman greets me.

I nod in acknowledgment as we hurry through the main foyer until we reach the elevators. Thankfully, they're open and ready.

"Excuse me, Mr. Stone, there's—" Dion calls out but the elevator doors cutting off what he's trying to say. Then Allie's on me again, clawing at my suit, fingers entwined in my hair.

I think she's going to be wild in bed.

Maybe that's what I need, something to ease the stress, the pain of Lenna. My body stills thinking about her while Allie's lips are on mine, but she doesn't seem to notice, or if she does, she doesn't care. The elevator doors ding, and we open directly into my penthouse suite. Next thing, Allie jumps into my arms, and I push her up against the wall.

Fuck it.

As we devour each other, the sound of glass breaking stops us.

Allie looks over my shoulder.

"Um... Logan... who is she?" Allie unwraps her legs from around my waist and slides down.

Turning, my heart stops, and my entire world spins. The last person I thought I'd see in my apartment is Lenna. Her chocolate eyes are wide, her face has turned a bright shade of red when she realizes she's dropped a glass on the floor.

"Lenna?"

Why is she here?

Fuck!

Did she come here for me?

For us?

And I...

Shit! I run my hand through my hair. She's not supposed to see me with someone else. Not after everything. I...

What the hell am I doing?

Lenna quickly picks up the bits of glass she's dropped.

Rushing to her, I kneel, trying to help. "What are you doing here?"

When I look up, Lenna's gorgeous chocolate eyes are filled with hurt, they are glistening, and I know I have hurt her deeply.

"You said I could use your bath. I... I shouldn't have." She stands abruptly. "I didn't know you had a date. I..." She looks over at Allie then back to me. "I'm sorry to have interrupted."

Fuck, she's on the verge of tears as she sidesteps me, grabbing her bag off the counter.

Dammit!

"I am so sorry for interrupting," she tells Allie, who looks rather confused.

"Lenna..." I call out her name, but she ignores me, pressing the bell for the elevator, which is still on the penthouse floor. The doors open immediately, and Lenna rushes inside.

I watch on in horror as the doors close.

Lenna breaks.

Fuck.

"It seems a little late for your cleaner to be here," Allie adds. Looking over at the blonde, the one I was using to forget the woman who was here in my space, filling it with her sweet perfume.

"I don't think tonight's going to happen. I'm sorry." My shoulders sag as I scrub my face with my hand.

"Because your cleaner interrupted us?" She genuinely seems confused.

"She's not my cleaner." My voice raises. "She's the woman I was trying to forget tonight."

The blonde's eyes widen in understanding. "I can still make you forget," she purrs, slowly making her way toward me.

"Stop!" My voice is hard. "I think it's best that you leave."

Allie's thick lashes blink a couple of times slowly. "You're not serious?"

"I am. Deadly."

She throws up her arms in the air and huffs. "Fuck you! I should have gone home with EJ when I had the chance," she grumbles, hitting the button for the elevator a million times.

"I'm sure if you call him, he'll be happy to hear from you."

Allie glances over her shoulder, looking like she wants to throw something in my direction, and hard. The elevator arrives, and she walks in and leaves.

Thank goodness.

Grabbing my cell, I call Lenna, but it goes automatically to her voicemail.

I try it again.

Nothing.

And again.

Nothing.

I keep trying until her phone is switched off.

Fuck! This has turned into the worst night ever.

20

LENNA

Seeing Logan in the arms of another woman so quickly after what we shared broke me.

He's single. He has every right to screw whoever he wants. I just didn't think he was.

You turned his proposal down, Lenna. I know this, but still.

You showed up unannounced at his apartment. Again, I know this, but I was kind of hoping maybe...

Argh, I'm the biggest idiot in the world of idiots.

Logan didn't stop calling or texting me all night, of which I ignored every single one of them. I didn't want to hear what he had to say. I didn't want to know if she stayed and fucked him. Just witnessing them practically ripping each other's clothes off was enough for me to want to bleach my eyes.

Logan even tried to say sorry with coffee from our favorite Italian restaurant. I just couldn't look at him without seeing *her* hands all over him. Eventually, he gave me my space and left me alone.

So, enough of being miserable because today is Chloe's birthday. I am going to get wasted, find a cute guy, and take him home. Hopefully, that will wipe all the images of Logan Stone from my mind.

"What do you mean, he showed you his dick?" Ariana questions Chloe as we settle in her bedroom with champagne glasses in our hands.

"It was spectacular, wasn't it?" Stella giggles. "That man looks like he'd have a perfect dick."

"You know I shouldn't be hearing this." The room falls silent as they turn toward me, and I burst out laughing because, come on, I know I'm the HR Director of the company, but I'm also her friend. "Just kidding... I'm off the clock." Raising my glass in Chloe's direction, I give her a knowing wink. "It's none of my business." But if I'm really honest, I kind of want all the details because from what Chloe told us all about flashing Noah her boobs in the office while getting stuck in her new sports outfit, there's more to it than just a flash of skin, especially if he dropped his pants and flashed her too.

"It's not like that." Chloe sighs.

"Um... it kind of is." It's hard to deny that they have the hots for each other because they're always harmlessly flirting. "You guys should see them around the office. Flirting. Laughing..." I'm totally jealous because I wish things were that easy between Logan and me. "All the young girls send daggers her way as she walks past," I explain to the room.

"They what now?" Chloe seems surprised by my observation. "No, they don't, do they?" I sip my champagne and smile over the rim at her, not saying another word. "What have I ever done to them?" Concern falls across Chloe's face, but I don't want her to feel bad.

"Might be the fact that you have Noah's attention, or maybe the fact you went away with him, or perhaps the fact that he checks you out as you walk past. Every. Single. Day." It's the truth, and they all see it—you'd have to be blind not to. Chloe's such a beautiful soul, she has no idea how jealous the girls are of her.

"No, he doesn't." I see a little bit of hope shine on Chloe's face as she gently bites her lip.

I raise a brow in her direction as if to say 'really?'.

"Shit," Chloe curses.

"Hey..." Grabbing her attention, I think, *it's her birthday for goodness sake Lenna, I shouldn't be raining on her parade today.* "I'm only saying, it's not a bad thing. You might not have realized it, but some of the girls have started to emulate you by wearing those pencil skirts you love so much."

It's quite sad really because they all started wearing skirts or dresses that are short enough to be able to get away with professionally, but now, they're wearing over-the-knee pencil skirts. It's all laughable.

"Because those skirts seem to grab Noah's attention the most."

Chloe's mouth falls open, and she jerks her head back in surprise.

"That seems awfully *Single White Female* of them," Ariana adds, then takes a sip of her champagne.

"Yeah, but have you seen Chloe in one of those skirts? Her ass looks phenomenal, a gorgeous peach," Stella adds with a giggle.

"What?" Chloe stares at her in surprise.

"I'm jealous, okay? I wish I had booty instead of a pancake." She sticks her tongue out, then sips her champagne. "Anyway, back to Noah's dick... tell us more," Stella changes the subject.

"You saw Noah's dick?" Emma asks while walking into the bedroom. She hugs Chloe.

"Just another awkward situation Chloe likes to find herself in." Ariana smiles.

Chloe flips her off with a chuckle.

"Was it good?" Emma asks, getting straight to the point.

"It was amazing." Chloe's face lights up, and her cheeks turn a nice shade of pink. It's honestly the same face I probably sport when thinking about Logan's dick too.

"She's been dickmatized, hasn't she?" Ariana laughs.

Far out, that's what has happened to me. Logan has dickmatized me with his glorious dick.

"Totally. You can tell when they get one of those far-away looks, their cheeks turn pink, and they start biting their lips, remembering how amazing the D is."

I know exactly how that goes.

"I wonder if they're twinning downstairs, too?" Emma asks.

Not going to lie, the thought has crossed my mind once or twice.

"I *volunteer*," Emma yells out.

"No, I volunteer." Stella stands and bursts out laughing.

"Me, too." Ariana raises her glass of champagne in solidarity.

"I'm off the clock, so me, too." I get swept up in the craziness of the moment.

"Screw you guys," Chloe moans. "It's going to be hard—" She doesn't get to finish what she's saying before Stella starts doubling over in laughter. "Hard." She holds her belly tightly while we all burst out laughing too. The champagne is definitely going to our heads rather quickly.

"What I was trying to say is… it's going to be difficult not to picture what I saw today when I see him next. Which is going to be a problem because that's exactly what I didn't want to happen. Hence, why I've never done anything before even when I've wanted to," Chloe confesses, falling back onto her seat and letting out a hard sigh.

"The two of you have had the longest foreplay in like forever. Six months of flirting and the odd hookup—" Ariana doesn't get to finish because I'm interrupting her. "Hang on…

you've hooked up before?" I'm confused, I thought there's been only flirting between them. I didn't realize it had progressed.

"We actually ran into the twins while on holiday, months before Chloe started working with them," Stella adds.

Wait! What? Noah and Logan knew Chloe when she came in to be interviewed, and they never said anything to me? And Chloe, too?

"We met on my honeymoon," Chloe adds.

"Why didn't you tell me?" Honestly, I feel a little hurt and left out over the revelation of this bit of information.

"I never wanted to put you in a position where it would compromise your job." Chloe reaches out and takes my hand in hers, giving it a squeeze.

Am I that much of a stickler for the rules that she didn't think she could talk to me about it? But then she didn't tell me because she didn't want me to have to choose between her and my job. Damn her for being so nice.

"You silly thing." Pulling her into a hug, I'm new to all this female friend stuff. "If it isn't impacting the business, then I'm okay. Plus, we're friends. I'd talk to you first if it were serious. Unless it's something illegal." I give her a wink, and Chloe visibly relaxes.

"Fine. The honeymoon was a disaster. I kissed him, I even propositioned him, but he was a gentleman."

"Then there was a stupid misunderstanding," Emma adds.

I need to know more.

"I wasn't in the right headspace for anything, anyway," Chloe adds.

I do know the story about her fiancé and her best friend.

"Then he saved you in Vegas," Stella adds.

"You heard the story about Walker attacking me?"

It rocked me to my core when I found out, and I felt bad that I wasn't there to protect her.

"Like a knight in shining armor, he attacked Walker and saved the day," Stella romanticizes Noah's actions.

"Shame you missed it." Emma gives me the all-knowing side-eye. "But, I guess Logan was doing his own knightly duties."

Emma stumps me, and now I'm like a deer caught in the headlights at her comment. She just smiles, but I can feel my face burning up with embarrassment.

"Nothing happened." I wave my hand in the air dramatically.

Why do I feel like I'm on fire? The bedroom feels awfully small all of a sudden.

"Continue, Chloe," I say, hoping to change the subject before anyone notices.

"Nothing else has happened. Boring really. I'm wondering about you, though?" Chloe's attention swings back to me, and the whole room falls silent as I look around at the sets of eyes who are waiting expectantly for my words.

Should I say something? Maybe not.

I've never had girlfriends I can talk to about guys, and generally, I feel like I'm my own little island trying to work out my feelings. Maybe it might be okay to say something.

"Fine! We hooked up in Vegas. I was drunk, extremely drunk, thanks to you." I point in the direction of Emma. I've never been so drunk in my life as I was in Vegas.

"You're welcome." Emma raises her champagne glass in my direction.

"He disappeared after. I thought..." Letting out a heavy sigh, I close my eyes for a few seconds just trying to calm my mind.

"He had changed his mind?" Chloe questions.

"Yeah." Twisting the champagne glass in my hand, I continue, "The next morning, he acted as if it never happened. I felt humiliated because I stupidly let hope in." That's why I was reluctant for anything to happen again in The Hamptons, but this time I was the one in control.

"What about The Hamptons? Did anything happen there?" Chloe asks.

Looking up at her, she can read it on my face that something did happen, but I won't talk about it.

"Screw them," Emma states. "I've organized a wonderful birthday present for you, Chloe. Who am I kidding..." she laughs, "... I've organized it for all of us. Follow me..." We all follow her out of the bedroom and downstairs. "Voila." Waving her hands through the air, she displays six gorgeous men who are standing there waiting for us. "You're welcome." She grins.

Tonight looks like it's going to be fun.

21

LOGAN

I've been watching Lenna throughout the party while hiding out in the back garden. She's been laughing and drinking with her friends. I've even had to watch her flirt with the near-naked waiters walking around the party.

Fuck, it hurts seeing her smile being given to someone other than me. It's killing me that I fucked up and ruined whatever there might have been between us.

Throwing back the rest of my drink, I think it's time we talk about what happened that night, and in the middle of a crowded party is probably the best time because she can't escape me. Taking long strides, my laser focus is on Lenna. She's in a group chatting away, and out of her peripheral vision, she sees me. Slowly, I watch as she places her drink down and excuses herself from the group. My steps quicken as I watch her walk up the stairs to the next level. I watch in dismay as she escapes through the front door and out through the front courtyard.

I run after her, but she disappears into the night streetscape.

"Lenna," I call out while standing on the busy street looking all around me trying to figure out where the hell she's disappeared too. The sound of rattling grabs my attention, so I head in that direction. Turning into the neighbor's courtyard, I find Lenna pressed against the brick wall with tears falling down her cheeks.

"Shit."

Lenna attempts to scrub her face free of her tears, so I won't notice.

"Lenna." Stepping forward, I cup her face.

"Logan, don't!" She pulls away from me. "I don't need any more humiliation."

"Why are you humiliated?" Looking at her wrapping her arms around herself as if it's providing some sort of protection, she can barely look at me, which is ripping out my heart.

"Please, Logan." She shakes her head.

"I'm sorry, Lenna, for what you saw. I don't know how many times I can say it." Stepping closer to her, I reach out for her tentatively, but then let my hand drop.

"I get it. You're sorry, I forgive you." She waves her hand between us, but her tone suggests otherwise. I'm fairly certain she is trying to get rid of me.

"Lenna..." Stepping right into her personal space, which makes her straighten up and look at me, I sigh loudly.

"You're a single man, Logan. You owe me nothing." Her words are cold, heartless, and she's recoiling away from me.

"I was trying to forget you."

Lenna's rolls her eyes at my confession. "Of course, you were."

"My dick was limp the entire time."

She lets out a huff as if she doesn't believe me, and her attitude is showing me exactly what she thinks.

"Feel him now." Reaching out, I grab her hand and place it against my hardening length. "It seems like he only responds to you."

Those chocolate eyes flare as her fingers wrap around me. Yes.

"Knowing you were in my home, naked and wanting, it kills me. I would do anything to change what happened."

Lenna's hand lets me go, and she says, "It was the wakeup call I needed, Logan." Her words sound so final. *Have I really lost her?*

"Lenna, I fucked up, okay." I run my hand through my hair. "You told me you wanted to be friends and that you didn't want me. I was trying to forget *you*." Those chocolate eyes fall back to mine. "I can't stop fucking thinking about you."

I'm laying it all out there, and her face softens a little.

"Every damn day, I have to watch you walk around the office, knowing exactly how exquisite you taste. How plump your breasts are, the way you scream my name when my tongue hits your clit. All I want to do is flip you over my fucking desk and fuck you every damn time you walk into it." There's an audible gasp from her lips at my filthy words.

"Every time you wear that red lipstick, all I can think about is how it would look wrapped around my dick." Her teeth sink into her bottom lip as my hand rests beside her head against the cool bricks. "Every. Single. Time." I say the words slowly, hoping their meaning isn't lost.

"Fuck it!" Lenna curses before her lips are on mine in a hungry kiss.

Well fuck! This is not at all where I thought this conversation was going.

"Lenna..."

"Don't say a fucking word, or God help me, I will turn around and find the first available single man at that party and fuck him instead."

"Like hell you will," I growl against her mouth as our teeth clash in the frenzy we have found ourselves worked into.

Her hand is slipping between us and is rubbing against my

cock, that's practically bursting out of my trousers. The sound of scraping metal echoes into the night as her nimble fingers unzip me. Her hand dives into my briefs and releases me. Quickly, a loud moan falls from my lips as her hand grips my length, roughly working me over. If she keeps going like that, I'm going to end up embarrassing myself.

"Turn the fuck around, Lenna."

Those chocolate eyes widen at my command before a hungry smirk falls across her face, and she does as she's told. I press her hard against the brick wall, the sound of people walking along the street filters past us.

"Keep your mouth shut. Otherwise, we will be arrested for public indecency."

Lenna nods her head in agreement but doesn't answer me.

There's a brick alcove that's shielding us from the street, but if people really wanted to see, they could without too much effort. Lifting her dress, I expose her creamy ass to the cool night air.

"Spread them," I command while nudging her legs apart with my thigh. She does as she's told. "Good girl," I praise her.

My hand dips between her creamy thighs, testing her wetness. She's ready for me, and I wonder if Lenna's an exhibitionist at heart. Grabbing my aching dick, I run the tip through her back crease, teasing her hole. Coating myself with her wetness, bit by bit, I edge myself into her entrance making sure she's ready for me.

Lenna turns her head, a frown has formed on her forehead. "Stop teasing me, and fuck me, Logan," she growls.

This makes me smile that Lenna's that worked up for cock.

I give the woman what she wants and thrust up inside, pushing her against the cool bricks. We both grunt at the joining as she pushes back against me, matching my thrusts. Her mews start to become louder, and as much as I enjoy fucking her, I don't want us to be arrested, so I wrap my hand around her mouth.

"Hush it, Lenna, or you will get us into trouble."

She grunts into my hand as I continue punishing her.

I'm so going to hell. This is against everything I stand for, that my company stands for, but I'm not sure I can stop. She feels too good wrapped around me.

An unexpected and inopportune thought pops into my head—I'm just like my father.

I have no control.

I'm fucking one of my staff members in the middle of the street when I should be inside at an employee's birthday party.

Fuck! I'm just like Dad.

That thought hits me like a ton of bricks against my chest, and now I can't breathe. My chest tightens as the feelings of self-loathing hit me. My dick begins to lose focus.

Pulling myself out of Lenna, she sags against the wall.

"Fuck!" I whisper-shout, as I push my semi-hard dick back into my trousers.

"Logan?" Lenna straightens herself and turns. Her eyes on me, her cheeks flushed as she asks, "You okay?"

"No." Running my hands through my hair, I wave my hand between us. "I can't do this."

Lenna's face sinks, and I know instantly I've hurt her. Again.

"You're right, it was a mistake." Lenna straightens her back and pushes past me, leaving me in the darkness to wallow in my own melancholy for a while.

Reluctantly, I make my way back inside the party where things have taken a turn for the worst, with sparklers and strippers dancing around Chloe. The girls look like they are having fun watching the pumped-up men strip down to next to nothing, and Lenna's included in that list. She's happily letting some sweaty stripper touch her.

It should be me.

No, it shouldn't.
You had her and let her go.
Because I am turning into my father.
That man was obsessed with Shelly so much it killed him, and I'm following right along in his fucked-up shoes. Turning on my heel, I head outside. Maybe it's best I head home and leave Lenna to it.
You're going to leave her with a sweaty stripper?
Trying to shake the images of a stripper fucking Lenna makes my stomach curdle. The sound of stomping feet echoes through the courtyard to where I'm standing.

"You're leaving so soon?" It's Noah, who looks like he's seconds away from punching something, and I wonder if obsession is heredity.

"Yeah. We said happy birthday, no point in staying." My eyes narrow on him, where I see the pain etched on his face. I know he has feelings for Chloe. We both seem fated to follow in Dad's footsteps when it comes to women. "Guessing you didn't like the half-time entertainment?" Noah ignores me. "Are you jealous?"

Pushing him, I need to know how deep he is with Chloe, so I can assess the damage. He doesn't look impressed with my line of questions, and he doesn't answer me.

My stomach sinks.

He's totally into her.

"You are... otherwise, you wouldn't be leaving the party. Fucking hell, Chloe must have a magical pair of tits if they have made you go gaga for her." Knowing this will set him off, after Anderson let slip that Chloe accidentally flashed him with her tits while getting changed, I challenge him. He thought it would be the right thing to do to flash her his dick, so she didn't feel bad. Noah didn't come to me at the time, he went to Anderson, and that jackass is the worst advice-giver ever.

And look where we are now? In this predicament, where my brother is completely pussy whipped by one of our employees.

The next thing I know, Noah has me by the scruff and has slammed me against the wall. "Don't be so fucking disrespectful," he sneers at me.

Well, fuck. This is not at all what I thought his reaction would be. Laughter falls from my lips, and my brother tilts his head while glaring at me because I'm laughing like a damn idiot.

He lets go of me and begins to pace as he runs his hand through his hair. "Don't talk, I know the spiel you're about to give me."

My brother's posture stoops as a distant, empty stare of sadness appears. My gut twists. Am I really that bad? That much of a heartless monster? "You surprised me with your reaction." I take it easy on my brother.

"You were testing me?" He raises his brows and jerks his head back. The way he looks at Chloe, I can see it, feel it. He's as fucked up over her as I am over Lenna. Maybe one of us should have a happily ever after.

"Of course, you're as bad as me when it comes to women. But when one walks into your life and knocks you on your ass, well…" Shrugging, I push my hands in my pockets.

"Someone knock you over?" I ignore him. "Lenna perhaps?" He pushes me, and I can see the determination on his face to try and crack whatever's going on in my mind.

"I know we have the whole twin thing happening, I can deny it till I'm blue in the face, and you will still know I'm lying." My shoulders sag, not wanting to go into it. "All I'm saying is… it's complicated."

"And?" Noah questions.

"When I want you to know, I'll tell you." I shake my head because there isn't anything to tell.

"Are you fucking serious? After all the shit you've given me over Chloe, and now I find out something's happening between Lenna and you, and you're telling *me* to butt out. You're a damn dick," my brother curses at me.

So he should, but he's always known I'm a closed book. I don't overshare like he does.

"Fine! Want to hear how I've fucked up?" Throwing my hands up in the air, I let out a long sigh.

"And?"

"And... nothing." Because that's all there will ever be between Lenna and me. "If you think there's something real between you and Chloe..." my penance for killing Dad is that I will never find happiness, "... just make sure you're certain before doing anything." Giving him my brotherly warning, I don't think my brother should be down here in the watery deeps of karmic restitution alongside me.

"Logan..."

"We'll chat soon. I promise," I state as my driver pulls up to the curb.

Obsession makes you do crazy things.

I couldn't sleep when I got home after Chloe's birthday party. The images of Lenna and the stripper swirled around in my mind on a loop, sending me crazier and crazier until I couldn't take it anymore and stupidly jumped in my car, and I am now sitting out of the front of Lenna's apartment with a hot take-out coffee.

It's ass o'clock, the streets are dark, and her lights are currently off.

Is she still at Chloe's? I should have checked, she could be staying over.

Fuck! I didn't think this through.

A cab pulls up at the curb, and a giggling couple falls out of the car. Looking up, my eyes narrow, and I notice it's Lenna with a man.

Fuck! No!

The man pays the cab driver, and Lenna grabs his hand and pulls him up the stairs to her front door. He pushes her against the wall as she wraps her arms around his neck and kisses him hungrily.

That should be me doing that, not some random guy.

They break apart for a moment as she unlocks her door, the man keeps his hands all over her. The door swings open, the light in the foyer turns on, and I watch as they're all over each other again, their silhouettes dance behind the glass door. My eyes glue to the spot where they're dry humping each other.

My knuckles turn white with jealousy.

I had my chance tonight, and I pushed her away.

This is all your fault.

I continue to torture myself as I watch them fall into the elevator, the doors closing as they maul each other. It takes them a long time to make it up to her floor. I sit in my car, waiting. Eventually, the light turns on, and again the dancing silhouettes torture me as they move around her apartment.

At some point, I must fall asleep because the sound of a horn wakes me up, and bright sunlight streams through the tinted windows of my car. Looking at my watch, I register it's about nine in the morning.

Looking up at Lenna's apartment, the curtains are pulled back. She must be awake, so I turn the ignition and head home.

22

LOGAN

"Morning." Lenna smiles as she enters my office as if nothing has happened between us over the weekend. Looking up at her beautiful face, all I can see is her arms wrapped around another man, and jealousy is sitting like acid in my stomach. "I have the paperwork for you to sign." She places it in front of me with another smile.

What the hell is this for?

"For what?" Annoyance creeps into my tone, I can't help it.

"For Noah and Chloe..." her words fall away. "They are about to arrive at any moment."

What is going on? I feel like I've missed something.

"What the hell are you talking about?"

"Noah and Chloe made it official on the weekend. They are dating," she replies, slowly testing my reaction with each word.

Why the hell did my brother not call me and tell me? This is huge.

"They are signing a contract letting you and the company know they are together, officially."

"Fucking hell," I mutter to myself.

Lenna lets out a heavy sigh. "Well, I think it's great."

Looking up at her as she stands there with her shoulders back, back straight, chin up, she's daring me to argue with her.

"Of course, you would. You're still in a post-coital glow," I spit the words out like venom.

"Excuse me."

"I saw you."

"You saw me what?" Those chocolate eyes narrow on me. She's more than angry, she is furious as she holds her chin high, and the tightness in her expression, you could cut it with a knife.

"You took some guy home. Was he good? Did he make you come like I do?" I know I am stepping over the line so badly at the moment, but I can't seem to stop myself. My jealousy is out of control, and it's like a freight train barreling toward the station that I can't make stop.

"He finished the job you were unable to." Her words are like a sucker-punch to the stomach, and I almost groan out as it hits me front on. "Don't you dare make me feel bad about doing something for me for once. I put every other person's feelings before my own, and where does that get me? Fucked over... time and time again." Her eyes are glistening with unshed tears.

"Seeing you in his arms..." Raking my hand through my hair, wanting to yank the ends off in frustration, but somehow, I stop myself.

"Did you follow me home?"

"I couldn't sleep. I fucked up. I—"

"You didn't want me." Her voice tightens a little as she speaks. "I'm not going to sit around waiting for you to sort your shit out when it comes to us. You're either in, or you're out?"

The sound of the office door creaking open halts our conversation as my brother and Chloe walk in, hand in hand, looking so fucking happy I want to hurl.

"Please, take a seat." I want this over and done with because heat is crawling through my veins at Lenna's demand. "I'm assuming you've called us here today to inform us that you're dating?"

"Y-Yes..." Chloe stutters.

I'm making her nervous with my asshole behavior. The room feels hot like the walls are closing in around me.

"What the hell is your problem?" My brother eyeballs me.

"Nothing." Looking over at Lenna, I continue, "It's protocol. If this..." waving my hand in the air, "... goes foul, then I need to cover your ass."

I'm being a gigantic dick, and I can't stop the train wreck. My heart is beating so hard it feels like it's almost out of my chest. *Am I having a heart attack?* It feels like it as the beating intensifies throughout my body.

"Maybe I should be asking you the same thing, brother."

Is he fucking serious!

"I'm happy you two are together, but Chloe, I need you to fill out this paperwork to cover the brothers," Lenna smartly changes the subject.

Chloe reads over the paperwork and signs it willingly.

"Happy?" Noah looks over at me.

"Yes. Very." *Now get the fuck out of my office,* I think.

"I'm assuming, Lenna, that you've signed the same paperwork."

That motherfucking little shit. I am going to kill him. Lenna's eyes widen, then she frowns and frantically looks between Noah and me.

I am going to shut this shit down right now.

"It's not necessary. Nothing is going on, nor will ever go on between us."

Lenna's face turns pink with embarrassment. I'm a black hole of bastardry, and I'm pulling everyone's happiness into my melancholic vortex, which I'm trying to save them from.

"I better go file this paperwork." Lenna stands and picks up the paperwork, ready to make a hasty retreat from my office.

"Yeah, I better get back to work, too," Chloe adds as the two of them stand and quickly leave the tension-filled office.

As soon as the office door clicks shut, my brother is into me. "What the fuck is the matter with you?" Noah looks at me, and the look in his eyes makes me know he's ashamed of me.

"What? I'm protecting what we've worked so hard for all our lives. I'm not going to let some woman ruin it all."

Noah's face is so red with anger, I'm surprised I can't see steam shooting out his ears. "Some woman?" The chair scrapes across the floor of my office as he stands, his hands slam down on my desk hard. "You know Chloe isn't just *some woman* to me."

I don't want to hear it. Crossing my arms across my chest, I lean back in my chair as Noah gets into my personal space.

"We all know you don't have a very long attention span when it comes to dating," I state, knowing it's going to push my brother's buttons. Noah's hand twitches against the desk like he wants to punch me but hesitates.

Do it.

Take it out on me.

Hate me.

I deserve it.

"What's wrong with you?" he questions through gritted teeth.

"I'm being the sane one here. You can't see the forest for the fucking pussy." I know I have pushed him too far, and the next thing I know, he has launched himself across my desk and his fist is connecting with my jaw.

"Fuck you," Noah screams as he chokes me. "Fuck you," he yells even louder.

The office door slams open, and we're being pulled apart.

"What the fuck is going on here?" Anderson yells. "You do realize you're at fucking work?" He looks disappointed at both of us. "Act like a fucking professional, will you?"

23

LENNA

"Are you okay?" Chloe asks as we leave Logan's tension-filled office.

"I'm fine," I reassure her as we head back to my office.

However, I am anything but. My hands are shaking, my stomach feels like it's tied in knots, and I've never seen Logan so angry at me before. He's giving me whiplash with his mixed signals, and I'm at breaking point. Tears threaten to fall, but I've never been one to be emotional at work, so I suck it up.

"Wanna grab a coffee?" Chloe pushes gently.

Placing the paperwork on my desk, sucking in an uneven breath, I turn around. "It's my turn to pay." Chloe gives me a friendly smile, and I almost crack at her friendly support. I've never had girlfriends that will drop anything to help me out like Chloe and her friends, and I need to learn how to accept help when they offer. Nodding my head in acceptance, she links her arm with mine, and we head out into the sunshine. She bypasses our normal coffee shop, which is at the bottom of the building, and we head up the street.

"Where are we going?" Curiosity gets the better of me as we make our way through the crowded Manhattan streets.

"I'm taking you to the park. So, we can talk freely without running into anyone from the office."

Good idea, I'm not sure I am going to be able to hold it all in. Eventually, we reach Central Park, and Chloe orders from the café. I stand back, and she returns quickly, then we both sip our coffee in silence for a few moments savoring the caffeinated hit while walking slowly enjoying the day.

"I'm so happy you and Noah finally got together," I tell her. I really am happy that they took the leap together, Noah deserves to be happy.

"It's early days." Chloe smiles. "Logan doesn't seem too happy about it, though." She segues into what she really wants to probe me about. *Logan.*

"Logan's a complicated guy." Taking another sip of my drink, I am not entirely sure why I'm still defending him. "He thinks he's protecting his brother."

I am not sure if Chloe's aware of their past with their father.

"Do you think Noah needs protection from me?" Chloe asks with her eyebrows drawn together.

"No, of course, not. Logan can't let go of what happened with his father." Chloe nods her head in understanding. "You also can't live with a wall constantly wrapped around you."

"So, how are things between you and Logan?"

If only Logan was more like Noah, things could be so different.

"You heard him, there's nothing going on between us." Hearing Logan's words sliced through me, hard, and the pain they cause is ever-present. "Never will." My throat tightens talking about it, but I hold it together.

Why am I so emotional at the moment?

"I'm sick of pining after a man who will *never* change. A

man who doesn't want to change." Chloe looks at me with understanding as she nods her head. "I think I'm going to start looking for a new job." It's past time that I move on, I want a change, I need to rid myself of this one-sided crush I have on Logan Stone.

"Really?" Chloe's mouth falls open in disbelief.

"I can't work beside him anymore." Tears begin too well, and I try really hard not to let them fall over my lashes. "Not after everything that's happened between us." My stomach churns uncomfortably thinking about everything that's happened and the consequences of those actions. "Honestly, my heart can't take it anymore." As the first tear falls down my cheek, Chloe gives me a small smile.

"I get it..." she links her arm with mine, "... men suck." I semi-smile. "I'm going to miss you if you go, you know that." I see the sincerity in her eyes. "You're leaving me to fend for myself against all those young, vapid girls who at any second will, if given a chance, blow my boyfriend in his office."

I spit out my coffee and start laughing—this is exactly what I needed to turn my mood around.

"Stop it! You know it's true. Seriously, can't you stay? Please? Pretty, please?" Chloe pleads with me.

I want to, I really do. Maybe if Logan moved to Timbuktu, that could make things easier, but I'm pretty sure that isn't going to happen.

"I would if I could."

"Urgh... seriously, I hate Logan right now. How can two men look identical, yet be so polar opposite?" Chloe shakes her head as we continue walking through Central Park, soaking in the sunshine before heading back to the office. "You know Noah's going to be pissed when he finds out you're leaving."

"I might not be able to get another job."

Chloe waves away my concern by saying, "Please, any

company would be bonkers not to hire you. You're going to have a ton of job offers as soon as they find out you're in the market."

Maybe she's right, I have worked for the Stone brothers for so long and know the job inside and out, I'm a little worried about not being good enough anywhere else.

"Can I ask one thing, though?" Chloe turns and looks at me seriously.

"Anything?"

"Please don't hire some supermodel to take over your position, I have enough competition with those girls as it is, I don't need more."

Her request makes me laugh. "Noah's only ever had eyes for you. No one in this world would make his head turn away from you. Ever." My comment seems to reassure her.

If only Logan was the same.

Not long after getting back to the office, my cell lights up with our group chat. *What the hell is going on?*

Chloe: Urgent girls' night this Saturday. My place.

Ariana: Everything okay?

Emma: What's going on?

Stella: I'll be there.

Lenna: You ok?

What on earth has happened since our walk in the park?

Chloe: I'm all good. Great actually.

Emma: You got Noah's D.

Stella: OMG you and Noah.

Chloe: Yes. Noah and I are together.

Ariana: Finally.

Stella: Yay.

Emma: Was it good? I mean you would hope so after all that build-up.

Lenna: Noah is totally gone for her.

Ariana: Thought so.
Chloe: Guys focus. Saturday night I'll tell you all. Now get back to work you lazy bitches.

Guess we will find out on Saturday night then.

24

LENNA

Wow. Girls' night did not turn out the way I'd expected.

Emma and Anderson are married, and they go to some secret sex club.

Why can't a handsome billionaire marry me and whisk me off to a sex club? Why can't I have a handsome man to come home to?

Instead, here I am wrapped around a toilet bowl, throwing up this morning. Not sure what the hell I ate last night. We were working late at the office, getting ready for the opening of The Hamptons resort in a couple of weeks. We ordered in Chinese from our favorite place like we always do when we work late, and I've never had food poisoning from it. So, why now? When we are so fricking busy.

Maybe I can push through it.

Getting up off my bathroom floor and standing straight, the nausea hits me again. Shit. I lunge for the toilet bowl, and once I've finally emptied whatever contents were left in my stomach, I crawl back into bed and grab my cell.

"Hey," Chloe answers.

"Hey, I don't think I'm going to make it in today. Last night's Chinese has me hugging the bowl."

"Oh, babe." I hear Chloe's concern through the cell phone. "You're not sick, are you?"

"No, Noah and I are fine." Chloe covers her phone as a muffled conversation between her and Noah happens, then she comes back. "Noah says to take the day off, and we will see you tomorrow."

"Thanks, I can work from home as long as I'm close to the bathroom."

"I'll pop round after work to check in if you want?" Chloe adds.

"No... no... I'll be fine. I'll have an early night, and everything will be right in the morning." Well, hopefully, I will be as my stomach's still rolling.

"Grab some crackers and nibble them throughout the day," Chloe advises me. *Good idea.* "Got to run, feel better, and see you tomorrow." Then she's gone.

I must have passed out at some point during the day, which totally is unheard of for me, and my stomach growls as an insane hunger hits me. Jumping out of bed, I head over to my kitchen and grab some crackers and juice before sitting down in front of the television. *Can I seriously play hooky today?*

My brain's a scattered mess as I tried to read through employment contracts earlier. I'm sure that by taking one day off in your entire working life, everything isn't going to fall down around you now, will it?

I must fall asleep again because the buzz of my intercom wakes me.

Who the hell could be here?

Checking the clock on the wall, it's just after five in the afternoon.

How on earth did I sleep for another couple of hours?

Making my way over to the camera, I'm shocked to see

Logan standing there. *What the hell?* He presses the buzzer again, looking impatient and with a scowl on his face.

Do I want to let him in?

Do I even want to see him?

Looking down at my pajamas with the holes in my T-shirt, my brown hair a mess and looking as if I've stuck my finger into an electrical socket.

Who cares if he sees you like this? You're trying to forget about him.

This is true. So true. Screw him.

Pressing the buzzer, I let him in. My stomach flutters as I wait for him to walk through my front door. *Why is he's checking in on me?* I really wish my brain would tell my body to stop reacting to him. I want to move on.

He pushes my front door open and steps into my apartment, looking like a damn model selling luxury yachts on the Mediterranean. Dressed in a navy custom suit with a light blue business shirt, a tiny triangle slip of tanned skin is showing at the top of his suit because he's sans tie, he's looking effortlessly stylish. He hesitates at the front door while taking me in looking like shit.

"You don't look so good."

Gee, thanks, Captain Obvious.

"You've lost a lot of color." A concerned frown is etched on his face.

Why the hell does he care?

"What do you want, Logan?" Turning on my heel and heading back into my living room, I slump onto my sofa, crossing my arms defensively across my chest.

He follows after me, placing a brown paper bag on the coffee table. Logan shucks off his suit jacket and places it on the armchair. Then he unhooks his cufflinks and rolls up his sleeves, exposing the tanned corded muscles of his forearms.

Is he literally trying to kill me with his strip show?

My hormones seem to have kicked into overdrive, and an insane sensation of wanting to jump him and rip off his clothes has taken over me. *Where the hell did that come from?* Every molecule, every nerve ending is on high alert.

I don't like this feeling.

Why is it happening around him?

Is it hot in here all of a sudden?

"What are you doing here?" I ask him again with irritation lacing my tone.

"I wanted to check on you." Taking a seat on the armchair, he leans forward, reaching for the brown paper bag. I watch in fascination as his blue business shirt strains against his muscles. Biting down on my lip, I suppress the urge to moan at the sight.

"I brought you some saltines." He pulls the packet from the bag. "And some seltzer." Placing them on the coffee table, I so want to hate him right now, I really do because he's the biggest jerk in the history of jerks, but then he does stuff like this, and...

Stay strong, Lenna.

Logan sits back after showing me his haul and crosses his arms. My eyes narrow as his biceps push against the light blue of his shirt. *Why is that turning me on?* I need to get laid because this is becoming ridiculous. I feel like I have the hormones of a fifteen-year-old boy.

"Thanks." Mumbling my gratitude, he catches me ogling him, which makes him smirk. *Fucker.*

"How are you feeling?"

"Really tired. Exhausted, actually," I confess, this extreme exhaustion has really caught me off guard.

"You've been working too hard," he tells me. The little crease between his brows is back again as his blue eyes look over me.

"As has everyone else."

"Maybe you've caught a bug or something."

"If I've caught something, then it's been from the office. I haven't had a chance to go anywhere else."

Logan nods his head. "No dates?" His question catches me a little off guard.

"No," I answer quite defensively. "And if I have, it would be none of your damn business." Folding my arms in front of me angrily again, I huff.

"You're right. It's not my business," he mumbles.

"I bet you've been on dates since..." I trail off.

"Are you asking me or assuming?" He arches a brow at me.

"I don't care what you do in your spare time." Ignoring the pain that's settled in my chest, I put my hand on my chest as if it might help ease the agony I'm feeling.

"I've had dinners with women but haven't slept with anyone since you."

The memory of him with that woman in his apartment flashes through my mind.

"Only because I accidentally showed up." My voice is barely a whisper.

"You might be right," he answers honestly.

"What are we doing here?" Moving my hand between us, I ask, "Why are we dredging up the past when it has no bearing on our future."

"Because I can't get you out of my mind, Lenna."

No. Don't say those things to me.

My stomach does a loop de loop of emotions.

"I need to apologize for the things I said in my office after Chloe's birthday."

Nope, he needs to stop.

I don't want to hear it.

"I think you should leave." I stand quickly, the words out before I've even processed what I have said.

"Lenna." He stands, meeting me eye to eye. "I need to make this right between us."

Shaking my head, I wrap my arms around myself in an attempt to get some comfort from the pain that's lacing my chest.

"Sleeping together was the single biggest mistake I have ever made." My admission stuns him. I have hit him hard, and I can tell by the wideness of his eyes. "Five years I've had feelings for you, and I have kept them from afar. I thought that I might be the one woman who could change you. Break down those walls you have built up around you." Sadly, I chuckle to myself.

"But instead, I'm like the many others who have come before me and been sucked into the soul-destroying black hole that is Logan Stone."

Whatever's going on between us isn't healthy.

I thought I could change him.

That the years of friendship might have helped the barrier he has between happiness and guilt, but it doesn't. He's more than happy wallowing in his perceived guilt of not being able to help his father when he needed it. He likes staying in the darkness, he doesn't want to be found and brought into the light. He doesn't want to be loved even though his blue eyes glisten with emotions.

"Let me go."

"I don't know if I can." His confession is barely a whisper.

Thud... thud... thud... goes my heart in my chest.

I simply cannot do this.

Turning on my heel, I take a step to leave the room, but his hand reaches out to stop me. Logan's fingers light a fire on my skin, sending sparks to every part of my body.

No, I can't fall for this again.

Slowly his hand wraps around my arm as he turns me to him. "You're on my mind twenty-four-seven, Lenna. From the moment I wake until the minute I go to sleep."

Why is he telling me things? It means nothing anymore.

"I've tried to forget you." Those blue eyes of his sparkle with his confession. "But I can't."

Thud... thud... thud... goes my heart in my chest.

"I don't want to."

"What do you want from me, Logan?"

"I want..." biting his bottom lip, he finally says, "... you. I want us."

My eyes slowly blink in surprise.

Is he serious?

Did I hear him right?

"I can't be as open as Chloe and Noah are, but maybe we could try just the two of us. Maybe I could take you on a date? Maybe we could do things together."

"Just on the down-low?"

"It won't always be like that," he tries to reassure me. He's caught me at a vulnerable time, and my defenses are low. "I'm asking for a lot, I know," he says while stepping toward me. "I've been demanding. I'm being selfish. I've been a mind fuck," he tells me. "And through it all, all I can think about is having you in my arms again, and trying to be the man you deserve."

Damn him, my resolve crumbles right before my eyes.

"You're worth the risk, Lenna." As he reaches out and caresses my cheek, the first tear falls down my cheek at his words, and his thumb wipes it away. *Why am I being emotional?*

"Am I worth the risk for you?" he asks, his vulnerability laces right through his words. It takes me a moment to collect myself because right now, he's saying all the things I've wanted him to say.

"I'm scared, Logan." I give him an honest answer.

"I'm sorry I've made you feel that way." Pulling me to him, he wraps his arms around me, holding me tightly as his warmth seeps right through to my bones, then he kisses the top of my head. "I didn't mean to push you away, Lenna."

Leaning back as I look up into his handsome face, he's letting his walls down for me.

"I don't know what's going to happen in the future between us." A small crease forms between his brows. "I'm not sure if I can promise you a family and the white picket fence, but what I can promise you is I will try and be the man that you deserve in this moment."

Am I asking too much from Logan? The very core of him has been so set in stone that the tiniest of cracks have allowed him to let me in, but is that enough? I can't expect him to change overnight into an open guy like his brother, can I?

"I want to be the man you depend on, Lenna."

Goddammit! I'm done for.

Leaning forward, I place a tender kiss on his lips.

"I want to try." Those blue eyes rise skyward. "But..." his eyebrow raises, "... I think you need to see someone." Confusion settles across his handsome face at my words.

"See someone?" he repeats.

"I think you need to see a therapist."

"No." His objection comes out loud and clear, and that's when my stomach sinks.

"I want to give whatever's happening between us a chance." Placing my hand on his hard chest, I continue, "I just worry that if you don't deal with the issues you have with your father, then you will never find happiness, no matter how hard you try."

He steps away out of my reach, turning his back to me as he scrubs his face a couple of times. "I don't think anyone can help me?" He spins around and faces me. "I don't think I'm salvageable."

My heart breaks as I rush toward him, wrapping him in my arms. "I think you're worth the chance, Logan." Those blue eyes stare down at me, waiting for my next words. "I want to try so much, but my feelings for you might not be enough."

Logan's face falls again. "You think it might help?" His question is quiet, so much it's almost a whisper.

"It has to be better than what you're going through now."

Logan nods his head. "If I go..." he pulls me to him, "... you will give me a chance?"

Nodding my head, a smile falls across my face. I am going to take the chance he's offering me. "Yes."

Logan's face lights up with the most gorgeous smile. "Are you really going to be with me, even if it's on the low-down?"

"Yes, if you see someone. You need to work through your pain. Maybe then, you might take a chance on us not being hidden away." He cups my face and gently kisses me. "I'll wait till you're ready."

"I want to try so badly to be the man you deserve, Lenna."

"I know." I kiss him softly. "You will be."

He sucks in a deep breath as if my words are giving him the courage to face his demons. "Does that mean I have to wait until I have my first appointment with the therapist to fuck you?" His dirty grin lights up his handsome face.

There's no way in hell I can wait, not with the way my hormones are right now. "Hell, no." My answer makes him chuckle.

"Good. Because your nipples have been staring at me all night, and it's been really fucking hard to focus."

Just the mere mention has them throbbing.

Logan scoops me up into his arms and charges toward my bedroom.

The only word I can think of is yes.

25

LENNA

"Lenna, can you come here, please?" Logan calls out from his office.

The last of the remaining workers have just left for the day, even Chloe and Noah left saying something about having dinner with her brother to let him know that they are dating. Noah looked stressed, and of course, Logan teased him about it.

"What can I do for you?" Stepping inside his office, Logan looks handsome today in a light gray suit with a black business shirt. He's starting to slowly undo his black tie as I watch him—the man is pure suit porn.

"There are so many things you can do for me, Miss Lund." Raising a brow at me, he pulls his tie through his collar and then wraps it around his hands, giving it a couple of tight snaps, the sound echoing through his office.

What's gotten into him tonight?

Since we sort of got together, he's never once initiated something at work. *Is he after some role play?*

"Where would you like me to begin, Mr. Stone?" Locking

the office door behind me, Logan stands and rounds his desk then lazily sits against the edge.

"On your knees would be a start," his deep timber voice commands.

Instantly, my sex clenches and begins to throb. I'm insatiable at the moment with my hormones going crazy all of a sudden. Thankfully today, I'm in a wrap dress, otherwise falling to my knees in my usual skirt would be a mission.

I move toward Logan, swaying my hips seductively until I reach him. His arms are crossed, his face is serious. Slowly, I lower myself to my knees before him.

"Like this?" I give him my most innocent face.

"Yes, it's a start," he says, caressing my face with his warm hand. "Unbuckle me," he tells me his next command.

I do as I'm told, reaching out unbuckling his belt, pulling it slowly through the loops.

Logan takes it from me and slaps it across his palm with a sly grin. I like it. My fingers fiddle with the button and then the zipper of his trousers. He's hard against his boxer briefs, but I wait for him to direct me.

"Take me out, Miss Lund. You have made me very hard."

Biting my lower lip, my fingers peel back the black boxer briefs as if it were Christmas paper, the perfect present waiting for me beneath its wrapping. As soon as he's free from his binding, he springs back against his stomach.

Licking my lips, my legs shake with arousal.

"See what you have done to me." His voice is even, deep, and his tone has the tiniest sliver of restraint. "Prancing around the office in your tight skirts all day. Bending over my desk, giving me a glimpse down your blouse. You've wanted this, haven't you?"

"Yes." I'm practically panting. Logan's dirty talking is doing it for me so badly.

"So, you *are* teasing me on purpose, then?" He raises an inquisitive brow in my direction.

"Yes, sir."

"You've been waiting for my resolve to snap, so you can please me, haven't you?"

Good God, yes!

"I bet if my fingers disappeared underneath the hem of your dress, you would be wet, won't you, Miss Lund?"

"Yes," I pant out in agreement while his dick twitches with each dirty comment.

"Show me then."

It takes me a couple of moments to register what he's asking of me.

"Place your fingers inside that wet pussy of yours and show me."

Dammit, Logan, if I touch myself now, I'll probably come.

Lifting the hem of my dress, my fingers dip beneath the cotton of my panties and slide inside of me. I'm soaked.

"That's it," he hums while taking me in. Logan's hand moves to his dick as he begins to slide it against his velvety skin, and my fingers move in time with his hand.

"Show me your tits, Miss Lund." Those blue eyes flare with desire as I pull down the top of my wrap dress and expose my breasts to him. "So, fucking delicious," he growls as he reaches out and plucks a sensitive nipple between his fingers, while his other hand steadily strokes himself. "You like that?" He looks directly at me.

"Yes." Groaning as he does it again, my hand moves between my wet lips while he continues to pluck my nipples, alternating between the two of them, which is bringing me closer and closer to the edge.

"Do not come, Miss Lund," he growls loudly.

Wait! What? No.

He twists hard on my nipple, which gains my attention. "You will wait until I say so. Do you hear me?"

Shakily, I nod my head, my brain's in a foggy bliss.

"Show me how much you want my cock, Miss Lund."

Slowly, I pull my fingers from myself and present them to him. I'm slightly embarrassed because no other man has ever commanded to see how wet I am before Logan. Obviously, I've been missing out.

"Good girl." He grins at me. "Now, wrap your fingers around me." I do as I'm told, my wetness coating his velvety skin. "So good."

As my hand glides easily, Logan's head falls back, and his eyes close while he enjoys the sensation of my hand against his skin. Leaning forward, my mouth finally engulfs him.

"Fuck," he curses, which makes my thighs tremble.

Letting my mouth slide further and further down him, I can taste my arousal painted over his velvety skin.

"Yes," he says as his fingers grip the edge of the desk while my mouth brings him to the brink, and that thought alone makes me feel empowered, that I can bring someone like Logan Stone to the brink.

"Stop!" His hand reaches out and pulls me off his dick. "I..." His chest is heaving when he says, "When I come, I want to be inside of you." Those blue eyes flare at me hungrily.

"Stand up," he commands, and I do as I'm told. "Now bend over my desk."

On shaky legs, we swap sides, and I bend over his large wooden desk. Looking down, I see the scattered sheets of paper all over his desk. My inner neat freak wants to tidy it before I mess it all up.

"Stop thinking about the mess, Lenna," Logan tells me. God only knows how he knows my inner thoughts as I feel his heat against my body. "I want to remember the image of you coming every single time I sit at my desk and work through this godforsaken paperwork." His hand slaps against my ass, hurrying me up, so I press myself against the desk and spread my legs for him. "Perfect." I can hear the grin in his voice as his hands push up the edge of my dress and then pulls down my panties. "So beautiful," he mumbles to himself as his hands run over the fleshy globes of my ass, then his hand slides between my folds. "You ready for me?"

Nodding my head in agreement, his fingers find what they're looking for—me wet and ready for him. His fingers pump in and out of me for a couple of moments before they're replaced with the thick tip of his dick. He teases me mercifully until I'm squirming with need. Then he thrusts into me, almost pushing the desk over the floor and me right along with it.

"Yes," he roars as we connect. "So good." His fingers grip into my hips as he holds me hard against him, and from this angle, I can feel his balls hitting my clit and the sensation is overpowering. If he keeps fucking me the way he is, from this sensation alone, I'm going to come.

"So tight," he growls as he continues to fuck me. "So, fucking tight, Lenna."

My pussy clenches at his filthy words, and sweat begins to form between my breasts. My hands grip the edge of the desk, the shuffle of the papers is heard as I slide against them. The hard slap against my ass has me gasping when Logan catches me off guard. The sting feels good against his punishing thrusts.

Over and over he pushed into me until I feel the tingles all over my body, until they build to a blinding crescendo until neither one of us can take it any longer, and we both fall over the edge together.

We're both a sweaty mess, and the sound of our labored breathing fills the air.

"Fuck, Leelee, I didn't eat your pussy," Logan groans.

His comment makes me giggle. Turning my head, he's still buried deep inside of me.

"You most certainly satisfied me. I have no complaints."

Concern laces his face. "I was selfish tonight."

Shaking my head, he wasn't selfish because it was incredible, but it always is with him. He slowly slips from me. Reaching out, he grabs a few tissues and places them against me. Reluctantly, I pull myself off of his paperwork and turn over while holding the tissues between my legs.

Cleaning myself up, I grab my panties off the floor and step back into them. My dress falls around me, my head is a little light from the position I was in, and it takes me a moment to gain my bearings again. I watch as he tucks himself back into his underwear and zips his trousers.

Looking up at Logan, I give him a tentative smile and notice his flushed cheeks.

He takes a couple of steps toward me and cups my face. "I'm so thankful you're in my life." As he leans forward and captures my lips, I wrap my arms around him, pulling his body closer to me.

"What made you change your mind about fucking me in your office?" I arch an inquisitive brow in his direction.

"My dick couldn't take looking at you in this dress anymore," he tells me honestly.

"Note to self... your dick likes wrap dresses."

"He most certainly does." He smiles down at me. "I made an appointment with the therapist." His words come out in such a rush, I am not sure I hear them properly.

"You did?" I'm actually surprised, I thought he would fight me a lot more on this than he has.

"Yeah, no guarantees, though. He might not be able to fix me."

Does he think I want to fix him?

"Logan..." Looking up into the blue pools of his eyes, I tell him, "There's nothing wrong with you. You know that, right?" He shrugs his shoulders, and I'm regretful that I might have made him feel like there's something wrong with him.

"I just think you haven't dealt with some things from your past, that's all."

He nods his head, but I can see the conversation is making him uncomfortable.

"I'm doing it for you, Lenna."

"I want you to do it for yourself, Logan." I stare into his handsome face, looking at the torment swirling in his gorgeous eyes.

"You've worn me out, woman. Let's go grab something to eat and head home." Logan changes the subject swiftly.

26

LOGAN

I promised Lenna I would do this, that I would try. And if going to a damn therapist makes her orgasm the way she's done every single night since then, I'm never stopping.

It's been a week since Lenna and I decided to give things a go. It hasn't been smooth sailing as she's had a weird stomach virus for the past week, but that hasn't stopped her from practically ripping the clothes off of my body when she's seen me. I don't even get a foot into her apartment, and she's on me.

Not that I'm complaining, at all, because I'm wound up so tight from seeing her in the office all day. The way she bends over picking something up off her desk, or the way her lips move as she talks about work, and all I'm imagining is the feeling of them wrapped around my cock. It's bad. So bad that I want to lock my office and fuck her right there and then.

Screw all the rules.

Just thinking about her gets my dick hard, and that's not okay as I'm walking into my therapist's office. But then again, that thought alone has him deflating rather quickly.

Therapist.

I honestly can't believe I'm here.

There's nothing wrong with me. I couldn't have built a multi-million-dollar business if there was something wrong with me mentally. Walking toward an unassuming brownstone, there's a brass plaque on the side, the only indication that the home is something more than what it presents on the outside. Pressing the buzzer at the entrance, a video screen lights up.

"Logan Stone. I have a two o'clock with Dr. Aspen."

A buzzing noise indicates the door is now open.

Pushing against the black wooden door, I step into a home. This is not at all what I thought was going to happen. Turning to the left, one of the living rooms downstairs has been turned into the reception area.

A young woman greets me from behind a large wooden desk.

"Mr. Stone. Welcome." She smiles at me. "I need you to fill out your details on these forms, and then Dr. Aspen will be ready for you."

Taking the clipboard from her, I fill in all my health details. Once I'm done, I hand it back to her.

"Thank you, now follow me."

We walk down a long wooden floor corridor filled with modern paintings against neutral walls.

"He's the last door on the left." She points to the chestnut-colored wooden door.

Nodding my understanding reluctantly, I step toward it, my heart thundering in my chest. *I can do this.* Knocking lightly against the wood, I hear a deep voice echo from inside, "Come in."

Pushing the door open, I'm greeted by bright sunshine streaming in through large glass windows. The room is small, cozy, intimate even, but light-filled. A man is sitting in a green leather armchair, and he looks at me over his large black-rimmed glasses. To be honest, he doesn't look much older than me.

"Mr. Stone, it's nice to meet you." Standing, he's holding out his hand for me. Taking it, he gives me a strong handshake before indicating toward the large green leather sofa set up in the middle of the room. "Please sit." I do as I'm told. "How can I help you today?" He smiles, he's calm, placing his ankle against his knee and relaxing into his armchair with a notepad beside him.

"Um, I..." I have no idea where to start.

"The first session is always the toughest. You're not quite sure where to begin. It can be a little out of people's comfort zones." *He can say that again.* "So, let's just start with what prompted you to come today?"

Nervously, I twist my fingers against each other. "Someone close to me suggested I should get some help."

Dr. Aspen nods his head, picking up his notepad.

What is he going to write on there about me? I haven't said anything yet.

"Was this someone family?" he questions me. Lenna is classed as family, so I guess.

"Sort of... um... she..." The doctor continues to scribble notes, which astonishes me. "I've known her for a long time."

"Is she a friend or someone more?" he pushes.

"She's become someone more."

He nods his head in understanding. "Why do you think she wanted you to come and see me today?" He holds his pen high, waiting for me to give him the answers he's seeking, so he can scribble more stuff down on his notebook.

Fuck it! Maybe the sooner I tell him what he wants, the sooner I can get the hell out of here.

"She thinks I'm suffering guilt over my father's suicide."

Dr. Aspen pauses, his dark eyes assessing me, then he scribbles down some more notes.

"Why do you think she thinks you feel guilty over your father's suicide?" his calm voice asks.

"Because it was my fault." The words come out in a rush, and when they do, my heart starts to beat wildly in my chest, my throat constricts just thinking about him.

"Why was it your fault?" he continues to push as if what I'm saying is no big deal.

"Of course, it was." A trickle of sweat forms on my back, and I feel it run down.

"And *why* do you think it was your fault?"

Oh God! My throat becomes dry, my stomach somersaults while I twist my hands over and over again in my lap.

But Dr. Aspen just waits patiently for me to answer his simple question.

"Because he was a self-centered prick, and I was sick of hearing about how he fucked up his life. I was sick of being his emotional punching bag. I had... I had enough, and I told him so in a phone call the night he did it." The words come out in a rush thinking about that night, my face feels hot as if it's on fire.

Dr. Aspen rises from his armchair and opens a small mini-fridge beside his desk, pulling out a bottle of water and handing it to me. Gladly, I take it, opening the lid, and I take a large gulp of the cool water, hoping it will put out the fire that's raging inside of me.

"I can see that it was hard for you to tell me." Dr. Aspen gives me a small smile.

"Thank you." I pick at the lid of the bottle nervously.

"This is a great start..." he continues. "You know I'm going to ask why your father thought he'd fucked up his life, but I want to give you a moment to collect yourself before continuing." Dr. Aspen sits back and relaxes against his green leather armchair as if he has all the time in the world while a prickle of uneasiness rushes down my spine.

"I don't know if I can," I tell him honestly.

Dr. Aspen nods his head in understanding. "That's fine, Logan." He gives me a reassuring smile. "Why don't you tell me about the woman in your life who has asked you to attend today."

Damn, I am not sure the change of subject to Lenna is any better. Taking another uneasy sip of the water for strength, in all honesty, I feel like whisky or a bourbon right about now would go down better.

"She works with me." Dr. Aspen writes that little nugget down on his notebook. "She's been with my company since its inception... about five years." More scribble. "I've always been attracted to her, but..." Dr. Aspen looks up at my pause, "... we have a strict non-fraternization rule at work." The doctor nods his head and scribbles more words.

"Why such strict rules? Have you had problems in the past?"

Of course, that's the natural question he should ask, but it always comes back to my dad.

Do I have deep-seated Daddy issues? Oh, fuck, I do. Shit!

"I didn't want to turn out like my father, but it seems maybe I have."

A small frown falls across Dr. Aspen's face. "Why do you think you will turn out like your father?"

"Because I'm sleeping with one of my staff."

Dr. Aspen stills and looks up at me with his dark eyes. "And that goes against your rules?" He arches a brow at me.

"Yes, it's strictly forbidden."

He nods his head and scribbles down some more notes.

"What are you writing?" I question him. I don't like the feeling that he's dissecting me and putting it all on paper right before me.

"Just some notes to help me remember what we have spoken about for our next appointment," he tells me.

"And you think there's something wrong with me, don't you?"

Dr. Aspen places his notepad down and steeples his fingers together, those dark eyes narrow on me.

"It's too early to say, but I believe you have some deep-seated issues to work through. It seems like you have not processed your father's death at all well."

"That was a decade ago," I argue.

"And yet, you still can't talk about him."

Now it's my turn to narrow my eyes on the good doctor because I don't like the direction this is heading. "What do you want to know? You want to know that while my mother was dying of cancer, Dad was too busy fucking his secretary? That the woman who was supposed to be the love of his life was dying, and he was more interested in getting his dick wet?" Rage courses through my body thinking about what my father did to my mother while she tried to fight that insidious disease.

"I can see it still affects you deeply," Dr. Aspen advises.

No shit, doc.

"Only a few months after we laid my mother to rest, he married that whore."

Dr. Aspen flinches ever so slightly at my use of the word 'whore.'

"I understand how quickly your father moving on during such a devastating time may have had some long-lasting effects on you." He scribbles again in his book, then he sits in silence for a couple of moments as if contemplating his next words. "Is that the reason why you have the strict non-fraternization rules at your work?"

"Yes." I let out a long sigh, and he nods again.

"You think falling for someone at work makes you more like your father than you want to be?" he questions me.

"Of course," I reply with a shrug.

"Even though the two scenarios are completely different?"

There's a long pause while we wait for that question to sink in.

"What do you mean?"

"For one, you are *not* married," Dr. Aspen adds.

So? Other people work at our corporation, who are married, and if we don't have rules, they could fuck up too. I can't have our workplace destroying a marriage, especially when we deal in luxurious locations.

"Two... you're not your father."

Huh! I let his words sink in.

"Do you think falling for one of your staff members has brought up issues surrounding your father?"

Well, yes, because Lenna seems to think so.

"Lenna isn't just some random staff member, though. She's family. She's been with us from the start, and she's helped us grow our business."

"So, she's someone very special to you?"

Nodding my head, of course, she is.

"Does she know about your past?"

"Yes."

"And she's the main reason why you are here today?"

"Yes."

Dr. Aspen gives me a wide smile. "How long have you been together?"

My fingers start picking at the water bottle label again. "Officially, one week, but we have been, you know... been together for months." My heart is thundering in my chest so fast it's making me feel physically ill.

"And what do your friends and family think about the two of you being together?" Dr. Aspen asks.

"They don't know."

He stills his pen above the paper where he's writing his notes. "They don't know?" he questions.

I nod my head in agreement.

"You're hiding her?"

"No. I... I..." Oh damn, he's stumped me with this question.

"Are you ashamed of the relationship?" he probes.

"It's *not* a relationship."

Dr. Aspen's eyes narrow on me. "Then what is it?"

I open my mouth to explain that we are exploring each other, but either way I say it, it makes me sound like even more of a dick. He pushes me to continue, but I shrug my shoulders and don't say a thing.

"Why do you think she's okay with being with you in the shadows?"

"She's not," I add quickly.

"But she must be if she's willing to be with you..." he looks down at his notes, "... for a week under these conditions."

"She doesn't deserve to be in the shadows, but I just..."

Dr. Aspen nods his head. "You don't want to give her up?"

Letting out a long, defeated sigh, I shake my head. "No, but she makes me feel like I can be a better man."

"A better man than your father?" the doctor pushes.

"Yes."

"I think we've covered many topics today. Thank you, Logan, for being so open with me today."

Wait, so that's it? I'm cured?

"I think we should catch up again next week. How does that sound?"

"So, there is something wrong with me?"

"There's nothing wrong with you." Dr. Aspen places his notepad beside him. "But, I do believe you have some misplaced guilt about your father that may be hindering your future."

Oh. Just that, nothing big then?

"I want you to think about what you want your future to look like. Really dig down deep and think about every little detail, and next time we catch up, we will go through it together." He stands and opens the door to his office, then ushers me out.

My mind is a blur. I'm trying hard to push it back into Pandora's box, all the feelings about my father that Dr. Aspen has brought out.

27

LENNA

My phone rings, and it's Logan. He's just had his first session with the therapist.

"Hey, how did it go?"

"Good." His voice is monotone, and he doesn't sound that happy. "I'm not coming back to the office."

Was this a bad idea?

"Everything okay?" I cautiously ask him.

"I just need some time alone." His voice is curt, and it hurts me a little that he doesn't want to discuss it with me.

"Do you want me to bring some take-out over tonight?" We've spent every night together since he came over, so I know he will want to see me tonight.

"Not tonight."

My stomach sinks.

Have I broken Logan Stone?

"Okay."

He lets out a long sigh. "My head feels fucked up, Leens, and I just..." I can just imagine him running his fingers through his hair in frustration, "... I just need to work through some shit on my own."

"Okay. Ariana's asked me to catch up for dinner, so I'll let her know that I'm available then."

"Have fun," he says, but the tone of his voice is quite sad.

"Call me if you need anything," I let him know, but the phone line is dead. He's hung up on me.

My stomach swirls with unease.

"HEY, YOU," Ariana greets me at our favorite Italian place. She's looking gorgeous as always dressed in a bright red off-the-shoulder blouse, a black skirt teamed with red heels, and her brown hair is pulled up into a high ponytail. "You, okay?" she asks as we take our seats.

The smell of garlic hits me as a waiter walks past, which makes my stomach lunge. Oh no, that's not good. I thought I got this tummy bug under control.

"Lenna," Ariana calls my name. "You've gone pale." Her dark brows push together in a frown.

"The smell of garlic just made my stomach turn. I'm still not one hundred percent over whatever this bug is I caught the other week." Picking up the menu, I try to figure out what my stomach can tolerate.

"How long have you been feeling sick?" Ariana asks.

"On and off for a couple of weeks. I think I picked something up from somewhere, and it's really shaken me. I'm still trying to get over it." Peering at her from over the large menu, a waiter stops at our table to place a breadbasket down for us.

"Can I get you anything to drink, ladies," he asks with a thick Italian accent and looking between the two of us.

"I'll take a glass of champagne," Ariana says.

"I'll have a seltzer, please, to start with."

Ariana's eyes narrow in on me.

"What?"

She shakes her head and returns to her menu. We take a couple of minutes to work out what we want and order our food when the waiter comes back with our drinks.

"So, Chloe said the dinner between Noah and EJ ended up being a success."

"Thankfully, I mean that man is so protective over his sister, but when you see Chloe and Noah together, it's hard not to smile. They genuinely look happy," Ariana muses while sipping her champagne.

"You should see them at work." I pretend to put my finger down my throat, which makes us both laugh.

"Speaking of work, how are things going with Logan?" Ariana raises a well-manicured brow at me. A blush creeps over my skin, remembering his hands on me.

Ariana chuckles. "I see things have progressed, then."

Letting out a frustrated sigh, I say, "Things are..." running my finger over the lip of my glass, "... complicated."

"How so?" she questions.

"No one knows." Looking directly at her, I continue, "I can't say anything to Chloe because she will tell Noah."

Ariana nods in agreement. It's how she found out about Emma and Anderson was because Noah told her about it.

"And Stella... you know, she's a romantic at heart, and will be planning our wedding within two minutes of finding out."

"So true," Ariana agrees.

"And if I tell Emma, she's just going to tell me I'm being a fool." My stomach sinks.

"You know she means well. She's just very black and white," Ariana tells me.

"I know." Ripping off a bit of bread, I pop it in my mouth. I'm ravenous.

"And that's why you've come to me." She smirks. "You know your secrets are safe with me." She gives me a knowing wink.

"I know. He wants to give things a go."

Ariana's drink hangs in mid-air. "I'm surprised," she says, putting her glass onto the table. "Especially because of his *strict* rules."

"I understand why he's like that, but it's not for me to say." She nods her head. "We're still hiding what's happening between us."

"And, are you okay with that?" she pushes.

"For the moment, I am." Ripping off another piece of bread, I eat it quickly. "But not for the long term." Ariana nods again. "I've asked him to see a therapist." Ariana's eyes widen, so I quickly say, "To work through his issues… for me, for us."

"And is he?"

"Yeah, he is. He had his first session today, and…" I let out a heavy sigh.

"You're here having dinner with me instead of being at home having dirty, filthy sex." Ariana takes a sip of her champagne, then she grins widely.

"What happens if I've pushed him too far? Made him relive something so traumatic that I might have broken him?"

Ariana reaches out and places her hand over mine as tears well in my eyes. "You're simply looking out for him, Leens. It may take him a little while to process some of the bad things that have bubbled to the surface. He might need to work through it on his own. Just be your beautiful, supportive self during this time for him, and he'll come around eventually." *Maybe she's right.* "If it's as deep as you're suggesting, he might need a long time to work through it all. Be patient with him."

"Thanks." Giving her a smile, she squeezes my hand.

The waiter arrives with our meals and places them in front of us. I'm ravenous and begin to dig in.

"Did you miss lunch?" Ariana gawks at me as I shovel forks full of salad into my mouth.

"No. I just.... maybe I have a parasite or something because I can't seem to fill this hunger inside of me. Can't you see how much weight I've put on." Rubbing my belly, Ariana frowns at me.

"Don't get mad about what I'm going to ask," Ariana starts with caution. "But have you thought you might be pregnant?"

My fork falls and crashes against the ceramic bowl.

"Pregnant?" I laugh awkwardly.

As if I could be pregnant.

"Do you and Logan use protection?" Ariana pushes.

"Um, well... I'm on the pill."

"Lenna," she whisper-yells at me. "Are you serious? You and Logan don't use protection?"

"We're both monogamous with each other." I'm trying to validate the really wrong reasons for why we've been so careless.

"So..." her voice rises. "Still means you can get knocked up," she hisses through clenched teeth.

"You're being silly. There's no way in this world I could be pregnant, and especially not with Logan Stone's baby." Pushing the thoughts from my mind—thoughts I most definitely do not want to even ponder at this moment in time.

"When was your last period?" Ariana taps her well-manicured nails against the table.

"Um... I don't know. Mine are all over the place. I have no idea when they are supposed to come."

"Lenna," she hisses again through clenched teeth.

If we were at home, she'd probably have thrown something at me by now because she looks so damn angry. My mind tries to quickly calculate when was the last time I had my period. Things have been so busy at work with The Hamptons resort that my mind has lost track of the days.

Shit, I don't remember.

"I can see by the confusion on your face that you can't remember."

"I..."

Ariana shakes her head with a disappointed look on her face.

"The smell of garlic as we walked in turned your stomach." *Not everyone likes the smell of garlic, although I usually do.* "You have been sick for weeks now." *Like I said, I caught a bug.* "Has it been mostly mornings." *Ha, her theory is wrong. I've been feeling sick all day, actually.*

"No, it can hit me at any time."

Ariana pulls out her cell and types furiously away on it.

"Ha." She turns the cell around and shows me her internet search. "Morning sickness can strike at any time of the day." Looking over the words, my head becomes fuzzier the more I think about it. "Also, symptoms are... increase in appetite, tiredness, and even increased libido." She grins at me. "You also chose not to drink alcohol."

"Only because I didn't feel like it." Crossing my arms against my chest defensively, I don't like where this is heading.

"Or was it your body subconsciously knowing that drinking alcohol isn't right?"

I roll my eyes, this is ludicrous.

"There is no way in hell I'm pregnant," I state, stuffing more salad into my mouth.

"Prove it," Ariana pushes.

"Prove it?" My voice rises.

"Yeah. After dinner, let's grab a pregnancy test and see. It'll take a couple of minutes, and then you will know for sure."

The lettuce feels like a hard ball slipping down my throat at the thought of a pregnancy test.

There's no way.

No way at all.
Life wouldn't be so cruel.
My heart begins to beat wildly in my chest.
This can't be happening.

LENNA

"I need a drink," I state as my hands shake while taking the pregnancy test out of the brown paper bag. When I purchased the kit, it felt like everyone was looking and judging me at the local CVS.

"Hush. Just go and pee, and then we can put you out of your misery." On unsteady legs, I head to my bathroom. Pulling the little stick out of its packaging, I follow the instructions and pee on the damn stick. My stomach is somersaulting at the thought that this test could be positive.

Placing the cap back on, I wait for the minutes to tick by sealing my fate either way.

"Leens, you okay?" Ariana calls from the hallway.

Opening the bathroom door, tears well in my eyes. "Oh, Leelee." Ariana wraps her arms around me. "Is it good news or bad news?" she asks, looking into my eyes.

"I don't know." Bringing my shaking hand up between us, I hold the stick. "I'm too scared to look."

"Oh, Leelee." Ariana gazes at me softly. "Want me to read it?"

Nodding my head, I pass her the little stick which holds my fate, and she takes the ticking time bomb from me.

"Whatever the result is, just know I am here for you. Whatever you need, I've got you," Ariana reassures me.

I know I am lucky to have her in my life because I know she means it. She turns the white stick and looks at the little screen, and I can't read her face at all. She would be excellent at poker. Her head looks up at me as she turns the stick around. "Congratulations, Lenna, you're knocked up."

Fuck!

"No, no, no." Grabbing the stick from her hand, the little digital screen reads 'Pregnant.'

"It's going to be okay," Ariana tries to reassure me.

"What the hell am I going to do?" Feeling like the life I thought I would be living has now been completely derailed.

"Firstly, we need to get you into a doctor to double-check that everything is okay."

"Shit, I've been drinking and eating soft cheese, and…" Panic laces my body as my hand instinctively moves to my stomach. "I already suck at motherhood."

"Oh, Leelee." Ariana wraps her arms around me again and holds me tightly as my perfectly constructed life falls down all around me. "Are you going to tell Logan?"

Logan. Oh shit, oh shit, he's going to think I've done this on purpose.

Slowly, I shake my head.

"Lenna…" I hear the disapproving tone in her voice.

"Not yet. Not until I know everything's okay with the baby. Why worry him about something that might not happen."

Yeah, this could be a false positive. Those things happen, don't they?

My cell rings, so I disentangle myself from Ariana and rush over to it.

Logan flashes on the screen.

No. There's no way in the world I can speak to him at this moment.

"Lenna," Ariana warns me.

"Ariana, leave it." Ignoring his call, I say, "Give me a little time to process this. Okay?"

She smiles before leaning forward and kissing me on the cheek. "I'll leave you to it. You have much to think about," she tells me as she disappears into the night.

Much to think about.

Like what?

Are you keeping the baby? Of course, why would I not keep it?

Because Logan won't want it. Maybe he will eventually.

My internal monologue laughs at me. It knows that this is going to be the end of Logan and me. This is his greatest fear come true.

He should have used protection.

We both should have been careful.

A hell of a lot more careful.

Never in my life did I think this could happen. Never thought I could ever be this stupid. Guess when it's a good dick, you really do forget the consequences. My cell lights up, and a message comes in from Logan.

Logan: Sorry about today. Just needed some time to think. Hope you had a great night with Ariana. I miss you.

Damn him. The tears begin to fall. *Is this my hormones playing up already?*

Logan: When you get in, can we talk?

He suspects something for sure, and I know he's going to fire me for sure as panic creeps through my veins.

Me: Sure, sounds great. Night.

Turning my cell phone off, the last thing I need tonight is Logan Stone.

29

LOGAN

Lenna: Sure, sounds great. Night.

What kind of message is that?

My mind launches into conspiracy mode, a million and one things rushing through my mind. Did I interrupt something? Was she having a good time with Ariana and didn't want to talk to me? Is she over me already?

Last night's sleep was not a good one as I tossed and turned, thinking about Lenna's last text message. I've made myself go crazy with scenarios. I watch the clock on my office wall slowly tick the minutes away, waiting for Lenna to arrive. One person after another, the empty offices fill with staff, the silence being pushed away with the noise of morning chatter.

Tick, Tick, Tick.

The clock continues counting down and still no Lenna. *Where the hell is she?* Looking down at my cell to make sure I haven't missed a call from her, I try and bury myself in my work, but nothing's holding my attention. Looking up again, I notice it's nine thirty by the time Lenna makes it into the office.

Where the hell has she been?

"Miss Lund, my office, please," my command echoes through the office.

The girls all stop, their heads raising at my voice. I've never commanded Lenna so loudly and with such conviction. She throws her handbag on her desk, lets out a heavy sigh, turns, and heads toward my office.

She looks tired.

Exhausted.

As if she didn't get enough sleep last night.

Is that why she's late, she and Ariana partied on into the early hours together. Did she entertain any men? I'm sure they would have been all over her if they went out. Ariana is single. Did she push Lenna toward another guy, someone who would be better suited to her? Maybe she showed her there are better options out there instead of me.

Lenna closes the door behind her and takes a seat. She doesn't look happy to see me at all. *What the hell has happened?*

"Hey." Sitting at my desk, looking across the mess of paperwork, she's sitting there with her arms folded across her chest.

"Morning." Her one word is clipped.

"I'm sorry about last night, Lenna."

"Okay." She shrugs her response.

Have I done something that I don't know about?

"I needed to work through some things the therapist asked me to do."

Lenna nods her head, but she can't seem to look at me.

I think I've fucked up somehow.

"He wanted me to think about my future and what I see in it?" Those chocolate eyes finally fall on me. "I thought about things. About how I want my life to be." I'm nervous as I twist my fingers together, I need to just say it. Rip the Band-Aid off. "I see a future with you in it." There, it's out in the open. I was hoping Lenna would leap across the desk and into my arms and then possibly fuck me, but instead, she looks a little pale.

"I thought you didn't want the white picket fence or the two-point-five kids."

Um, how did we jump to that? I was thinking about maybe signing some paperwork like Chloe and Noah did. Maybe going public regarding us dating, then maybe a little further down the track, she might think about moving in with me.

"Is that the future you're now seeing?"

"Um, well..." I rub my neck nervously.

"That's what I want, Logan." Anger laces Lenna's tone.

"I'm not sure," I answer her honestly. "I haven't looked that far into the future."

"Do you ever want kids, Logan?" *Where is this coming from?* "Or are you just going to string me along until I'm too old to want them?"

Wait. What is going on?

Lenna's chair scrapes on the floor as she gets up abruptly.

"Lenna?" Wondering what has her so worked up, I crease my brows.

"You have a hotel to launch this weekend, I think we should be concentrating on that instead."

Well, yes, but I was kind of hoping that during that hotel opening, I might be able to be with her in public.

"But what about us?"

"I think that's something we should worry about after the hotel is launched, don't you?"

No, not really. I wince at her angry tone.

"Do you not want this?" Waving my hand between us, I become a little agitated myself.

"I don't know."

Her answer is like a harpoon to the heart. She doesn't know if she wants to be with me. What the hell happened last night?

"Did you meet someone else?"

"No."

Did she meet up with that guy from Chloe's birthday? I

never asked her about that, but maybe now isn't the right time either.

"We have so much to accomplish this week. I think let's focus on launching another amazing Stone Group property."

Why is she so cold toward me?

Is she that stressed about the hotel?

I know I am, but having her by my side makes it all seem somehow more manageable.

"So, you don't want to catch up this week?"

"Did you forget you're spending the rest of the week at The Hamptons? You're leaving this afternoon with Chloe and Noah."

Yes, I did forget, but I also thought Lenna would be there with us.

"Are you not coming?" I'm not sure what's happened, but something seems off about her.

"I'll be up Friday," is all she gives me.

Walking around my desk, I move to her. Reaching out, I touch her face, and she flinches ever so slightly. "We okay?"

She nods her head, moving away from me. "We're good, I've just got loads on my plate." As she moves closer to the door, she turns back and says, "Have a safe trip." And then she's out of my office.

And I don't think we're okay.

At all.

LENNA

"Thanks so much for coming with me." I am gripping Ariana's hand so tightly, I'm sure I am cutting off the circulation.

"Of course, I'm so excited, we get to see your baby today." She gives me a reassuring smile.

"It hasn't sunk in yet that this is happening. What if I'm not pregnant? What if something's wrong?"

"Lenna, don't worry." She pats my hand. "Everything's going to be fine."

"Miss Lund," the doctor calls me into her office.

Nervously, I sit and answer her questions.

"Let's give you a checkup." The doctor indicates to the bed, and I lay down. "If you could lift your shirt up, it's going to be a little cold." She squirts the gel onto my stomach, then she says, "We will see if we can see anything this way first, and if not, then we will have to go internally."

What on earth does that mean? She moves the wand over my stomach until a sound echoes on the screen. My eyes look up at Ariana, wondering if she heard that too. She looks at me, and I can see her eyes begin to well up.

"See this..." The doctor points to a jellybean that looks like a tiny human. "That is your baby."

It takes me a couple of moments for that information to sink in—I'm having a baby.

Ariana squeezes my hand.

"Judging by the size, you look to be almost ten weeks."

Oh no.

Ariana looks at me. "You okay?"

Nodding my head, that was the weekend in The Hamptons.

"Is everything okay?" I ask the doctor.

"The baby has a strong heartbeat. Listen..." She turns up the sound, and the tiny thud, thud, thud filters through the room. That's my baby's heartbeat. My eyes begin to fill with tears looking at the grainy black and white pictures in front of me.

Logan and my baby. That thought hits me hard and makes my stomach turn.

He's never going to want this baby.

He doesn't want the white picket fence.

He doesn't want a family.

"I can print out the picture for you if you like," the doctor adds. "I'll give you both a moment." The doctor hands me the black and white image, and I run my finger over the little jellybean.

"This is so magical, Lenna." Ariana sounds in awe, just looking at the picture.

"It is, it really is."

I promise you, bean, that it's going to be you and me against the world. I'm going to make up for the love your father can't give you, I promise.

"When are you going to tell Logan?" Ariana asks as we enter my apartment.

"After the opening. I don't want to ruin his weekend."

Ariana frowns at me. "Why do you think it will ruin his weekend?"

Giving her an are-you-fucking-serious look, she winces, but reiterates her feelings again just like she did in the doctor's office, "You have to tell him."

"I know." Rolling my eyes, I go grab a water from the kitchen.

"But do you?" she pushes. "I know this may not be what he wants, but you have to give him the chance to make that choice. You can't take that right away from him," Ariana raises her voice.

"I'm confused, okay. It's a lot to process," I tell her.

"But you don't have to do it alone," she argues.

"I have to get used to doing it on my own... because I know exactly what he's going to say when he finds out. And it will be two words... you're fired."

"He won't do that. He can't do that. Noah won't let him do that," Ariana adds.

"Yeah, well, we all know that Chloe snagged the Stone brother who has a heart."

"Lenna," Ariana raises her voice. "Don't assume you know how he's going to react."

This is turning into a fight, and I'm not in the mood for it.

"I asked Logan before he left if he saw a family in his future, and he said no."

Ariana sighs, I can tell she's losing patience with me.

"Probably, because in his mind, it's all hypothetical."

"It doesn't matter." Waving my hand around in the air, I sigh. "Look, I'm tired. Thanks for coming with me today, but I might have an early night."

Ariana's frown softens as she walks over and hugs me tight.

"I know this new future seems scary, and you may think keeping something like this from Logan is the right thing to do. But it's going to backfire, Lenna. He may never forgive you if you don't tell him."

Pushing out of her judgmental embrace, a dark cloud forms around me. "Your comments on the situation are noted, Ari. But, regardless, I am going to do what's best for my baby, not what's best for Logan Stone."

I see the immediate disappointment in her eyes as she turns and leaves my apartment.

My cell buzzes wildly beside me, and I pick it up without looking.

"Leens…" Hearing Logan's voice down the line wakes me up. "I haven't been able to get in touch with you all day. You okay?"

"Yeah, just busy. How's everything going?"

"Really good. It would be better if you were here, though."

Tears well in my eyes at his words where an alternative future flashes in front of me. One where Logan's holding our baby and is looking down at it with love and adoration, and he's standing in front of a white picket fence out the front of our brand new home. My bubble quickly bursts with the realization that the image will never come true.

"I'll be up in a couple of days."

"Are we okay, Lenna?" Hesitation filters through his words.

"Fine," I say through gritted teeth.

"You don't sound fine."

"Just a lot going on at the moment," I tell him truthfully.

"Things will settle down again once the opening is over," he tries to reassure me.

"Yeah," I agree unenthusiastically.

"Lenna, have I done something? I feel like I've done something, and I don't know what it is." The vulnerability in his voice almost breaks me into telling him.

"It's not you, it's me."

"That sounds like a breakup answer to me."

"Maybe it is." The words are out before I even process what I'm saying.

"Oh," he states before silence falls between us.

"I don't think we're going to work, Logan." More silence. "I didn't want to say anything until after your weekend."

"Did I do something wrong?" he asks.

"No, you didn't," I am trying to reassure him. "We want different things in life."

"I told you I'm working on myself... to be a better man for you."

Shaking my head, the tears rush down my cheeks. "I don't think it's our time."

"Are you saying it's not our time yet, or ever?" he questions me.

"I don't know."

"Has someone said something to you?" He's so confused by my three-sixty degree turnaround, and I can't blame him. The poor guy probably has whiplash, but this is no longer about me and my wants anymore. I have something precious I need to be thinking about.

"No," I reply while shaking my head even though he can't see it. "Your therapist's homework about working out what you want in your life got me thinking about mine."

"Oh." Silence falls between us again. "And I'm assuming by the way this phone call is going, you don't see me in *that* future." My heart is breaking, listening to him question my feelings for him.

"No." The word feels like acid on my tongue, but it's for the best. He will only break my heart if I let him in now.

"Right..." He clears his throat. "Guess that's it, then." His tone turns tough like steel. "I wish nothing but the best for you, Lenna," he adds, which breaks me even more. "Because of you,

I've started the path to be a better man, and I thank you for that. I'll always love you, Lenna." And with that bombshell dropped, he hangs up.

What have I done?

Collapsing into a heap on my bed, I cry a river of tears.

31

LOGAN

"**F**uck," I roar into the room, throwing my cell against the hotel wall. "Fuck." Pulling my hair, I realize she doesn't want me. Kicking the chair, but the desk moves away from me, and the wood hits the wall with a thud. Next thing I know, there's banging on my door.

"Logan," my brother calls through the door.

"Leave me alone," I yell back.

"What the hell has happened in there."

"Nothing." I pace the room like a caged fucking tiger, my anger has reached a pivotal point where I may just combust.

"Let me in." Noah pounds on the door again. "I'm not leaving until you show me you're okay."

The annoying fuck! I know he won't leave until he's checked on me, so I stomp over to the door and open it.

"Happy? See, I'm fine."

Noah's green eyes narrow. He then pushes past me into my bedroom, where he surveys the semi-destruction of my room. Slamming the door shut, I head on over to the minibar and pour myself a bourbon and throw it back in one gulp.

"What's going on?" his voice softens.

"It doesn't matter." Shaking my head, I pour myself another glass of bourbon before throwing it back.

"Pour me one, too." Noah points to the bottle. "If you're wanting to drink away whatever's going on with you, then you're not doing it alone." I pour my brother a drink and hand it to him.

We clink our glasses and throw back the shot together.

"You going to tell me what's going on?"

The warmth of the bourbon has taken the edge off of my darkness.

"Things haven't gone well with Lenna." My brother stays silent, waiting for me to elaborate. "I can't stay away from her." Letting my head fall back against the bed, we both end up sitting on the floor.

"What happened?"

"Does it really matter now?" Running my fingers over the woolen carpet on the floor, the pile feels like sandpaper.

"It does when you want to drink yourself into a stupor and throw things around your room."

Letting out a heavy sigh. "I wanted to try. I even started seeing a therapist."

"You did?" He seems surprised by my admission.

"Just the once, not sure if I'll go back again. He's the reason everything seems to have blown up in my face."

"How so?" Noah asks.

"He asked me to write down what I want my future to look like."

"And what do you want?" he pushes.

"What do you want?" I turn the question back on him.

"I see Chloe and me together. A house in the suburbs. A dog. Kids, like loads of kids. I see our business thriving as we continue to grow together. I see happiness and love."

Urgh, of course, my brother sees all that. He's a typical

romantic. Lenna would be better off with someone like my brother than me.

"And you?" He turns the question back on me.

"I told Lenna I saw her in my future." Noah's eyes widen at my honesty. "And it looks like now she doesn't see me in her life anymore."

Noah's forehead crinkles in confusion. "I feel like I'm missing something."

"Welcome to the club." With frustration, I scrub my hand over my face. "We had a couple of weeks of being happy together. Then she told me tonight that she's been thinking about her future, and she doesn't see me in it."

"I don't believe that," Noah adds. "Lenna's had a crush on you since day one. You two are perfect for each other. Out of all the women you have dated, Lenna was always the one I thought you would end up with."

"So did I for a moment." Not sure how I have managed to fuck it all up, though.

"You talked to the therapist about Dad?" Noah asks quietly, knowing how much that topic is a no-go zone around me.

"Sort of."

"And what did he say?"

"Nothing much, he listened. Maybe this is my karma for not helping Dad. You know... losing the woman I love."

Silence falls heavy between us.

"You think karma is kicking your ass because you didn't help Dad?" Noah turns to look at me, but I can't look at him, so I just nod. "Logan...." His voice is hard and stern. "Logan, look at me."

Reluctantly, I turn to look at him.

"Have you been blaming yourself all these years for Dad's death?" Noah asks.

He has no idea that it's my fault. All my fault. The sting of tears begins to fester in my tear ducts.

"Logan," his voice calm, yet hard. "Dad's death is *not* your fault."

"I pushed him over the edge." My confession's barely a whisper. "I was more interested in getting my dick sucked by a fucking cheerleader than listening to him go on and on about losing Shelley." Noah runs his hands through his hair, and I can tell he is annoyed with me. "It's my fault. You lost your dad because of me." The first drip of salty water slides down my cheek, and I swipe it away angrily with the back of my hand.

"What the fuck, man. No!" Noah grabs hold of my shoulders and wraps his arms around me. "Dad had problems, lots of them. Anyone could have said anything to him that night, and it was always going to end up the same way," my brother tells me angrily. "And how fucking dare he make you feel responsible for his death after all these years," Noah tells me.

"I fucking hate him. I hate that he's robbed you of happiness all these years. That his death molded you into who you are today. Fuck! I'm sorry I let you down, bro."

What does he mean, he let me down. No way in the world has he let me down. Noah's been the best through everything, dealing with my demons and still being there for me regardless.

"You deserve happiness, Logan." His grips me tighter in a brotherly embrace. "You deserve someone to love you the way Lenna does."

"You think she loves me?" I question him.

"Yeah, I do." Pulling away from me, he continues, "I think she's scared, but I also think maybe it's not the right time."

"You're thinking, right woman, wrong time?"

He nods his head in agreement.

"We've had a semi-breakthrough, you and I. Something you've seemed to have bottled up all these years." He gives me a stern look. "You need to keep seeing the therapist, work through the residual trauma of Dad's death and how it has affected you. Then I think you might be ready for Lenna. Be ready to fight for what you want."

How and when did my brother become so wise?

"You happy with Chloe?" I ask.

We haven't really had much one-on-one brother time over the years.

The guilt.

The walls I built between us.

"Yeah, she's the one, man." He grins. "I love her."

Slapping him on the back, I say, "I'm happy for you, you deserve it."

"And, so do you, Logan," he adds.

Maybe, just maybe, I might start believing him.

LENNA

"I can't believe Camryn, our event planner, managed to sign Dirty Texas and Sons of Brooklyn to play at the opening of the resort," Chloe screams wildly as she sings away to one their songs.

"Best grand opening ever," Stella screams along with everyone else at the party.

It's been an amazing the grand opening of The Hamptons resort. Memberships for the year have sold out already, and Chloe's idea of making the resort 'members-only' was a stroke of brilliance. Seeing Logan and how happy he looks makes me feel like I've made the biggest mistake in the world, pushing him away. We haven't really spoken at all. There hasn't been time, but I'm chicken feeling like I might cave in easily if I talk to him.

I've spent the day watching Logan walk around the resort and chat with everyone. I've watched him flirt with the beautiful women in bikinis as they notice him walk by. Each woman who touches him is like a dagger directly to my chest. It will always be like this if I stay. Maybe distance is what we need. I mean, I have accomplished so much since starting at the Stone Group five years ago, so now maybe it's time for a change.

But what the hell will I do?

"Hey, you." Emma wraps her arm around me, pulling me close. "You must be so fucking proud, this resort rocks." She's more than a little tipsy.

"Yeah, it's great."

She stills and looks at me, those jade green eyes narrow. "What's going on with my Lenna bug?" She starts pulling me away from the crowd.

"I think I need a change."

Her champagne glass stills in mid-air before falling back to her side. "You want to leave... all this." She waves her hand around at the luxurious surroundings. "Or, do you want to leave a certain someone."

"A little of both."

She nods her head in understanding. "Sometimes, what you thought you wanted in your life maybe isn't what you really wanted." *Cryptic.*

"Is that you and Anderson?" I question her.

"Yeah, I never thought I wanted to get married, but being married to him doesn't seem so bad now." She shrugs.

"Is that because you still get to sleep with other people?"

Turning her head, she lets out a sigh. "Somehow, that side of our relationship has changed."

My brows raise in surprise that the anti-monogamous woman is now monogamous.

"Wow, never thought I'd see the day Anderson would settle down. But if any woman could tame him, it most definitely would be you."

"Why, thank you." Emma giggles, then takes a sip of her champagne. "He most certainly is *not* tame." She gives me an elbow to the side, and this makes me laugh.

"I'm happy for you."

Emma gives me a large smile. "Why don't you come work for me?" Her question catches me off guard. "My business is growing, and I have to employ more staff. If you need a change, I'd love you to come work with me."

Is she serious?

"But only if you're serious about leaving." She takes a sip of her champagne as if she hasn't just offered me the world.

"And you would hire me... just like that?"

"Of course... I mean, hello, look around, you're part of all this. I think working with me might be a walk in the park for you. Plus, I'm sure you could use the eye candy with all the male models that pop in every now and again."

Her words make me chuckle. Maybe she's right. Maybe now is the time to change the course of my life because it's certainly not turning out the way I thought it was going to.

"Can I think about it, or do you need an answer straight away."

She shakes her head. "The job is yours, anytime you want it." She gives me a grin. "Now, I need to go find that yummy husband of mine and fuck his brains out." As she saunters off into the crowd, she gives me a small wave.

I think putting distance between Logan and me is for the best.

Oh, I need to pee—stupid pregnancy bladder.

Finally, the sun is setting, the extreme heat of the day has exhausted me. I think I might take myself for a walk along the beach to cool off a bit and watch the sun slowly move toward the horizon. I find myself a nice little seat nestled in the long grass and lay back to look up at the pink dusted sky and let the excitement of the day finally set in.

Closing my eyes for a couple of moments, I listen to the

waves crash against the beach. The sound of the music pumping from the DJ and the voices of people having fun, filters through the air.

Huh, wait.

Sitting up all of a sudden.

Where the hell am I?

Looking around at the darkness, I must have fallen asleep, so I pull out my phone to look at the time. My Instagram has gone crazy with notifications—Noah and Chloe have gone public with their romance, and I couldn't be happier for them.

"What's going on with you and Lenna?"

Hearing my name in the darkness has my attention.

Is that Anderson? Is he with Logan?

Crouching further into the grass, even though it's dark, I don't want them to see me.

"Nothing's going on with Lenna." Logan sounds angry, answering Anderson's question. I watch as their shadows stop not far away from me as they stare out into the darkened ocean.

"But I thought..."

"Well, you thought wrong, Ando."

There's silence between them for a couple of moments.

"What happened?" he questions.

"Nothing happened. We needed to get the sexual tension between us over and done with."

"So, you're saying it was just sex and nothing more?" Anderson pressures him.

"Yes, once the tension was over, we both realized we are better off as friends."

Friends? My hand instinctively clutches our baby.

"So, you never saw anything more with her?"

My body stills, waiting for Logan to answer Anderson's question.

"No."

My heart breaks open there and then. I really was naïve

when I thought that Logan Stone had changed. Thank God I now know how he really feels. Tears fall down my cheeks as my heart breaks into tiny pieces.

"Well, I'm sorry." Anderson slaps him on the back. "Least there are plenty of hot chicks here to help ease your pain." He chuckles.

"I know. Think I might take them up on their offers."

They both burst out laughing as they continue walking along the beach back toward the party.

I DIDN'T MEAN to kiss Johnny from Sons of Brooklyn, it just kind of just happened. Hormones and low self-esteem took over, and I thought fuck it. Why not? It was a stupid thing to do, but the boy knows how to kiss. I decided to leave The Hamptons early and head back into the city. I didn't want to run into Logan again, not after what I overheard him say at the beach.

My cell buzzes uncontrollably beside me, and I have a couple of missed calls from Emma.

"Finally." She sighs into the phone.

"Sorry, I was taking a nap." This seems to be a common occurrence more and more recently. Hopefully, that doesn't continue to happen for the entire pregnancy.

"Shit's hit the fan. Chloe's ex has lost his mind about her going public with Noah. He's threatened them in the media. We're having a group pow-wow at the hotel, you need to be there."

Wow! This doesn't sound good, but it also means I'm going to run into Logan.

"Do you really need me there? I might just be in the way."

"Yes," Emma yells. "Chloe needs her friends around her."

Yeah, she's right. I'm a horrible friend thinking about my

own needs when I know if the roles were reversed, Chloe would be there for me.

"I'll see you in twenty."

Walking into the hotel, the boys have moved to one room, and the girls are in the other.

"Guys, I'm fine. I had no idea Noah and I going public would cause so much drama. I was kind of hoping it would lessen it. Obviously, I was wrong!"

"It's a cute pic," Stella adds. "Very swoon-worthy."

Emma pours champagne for everyone, and I decline.

"Why are you not drinking?" Emma questions me, those green eyes narrowing. I can see her mind ticking over. "You never say no to champagne."

"I just don't want any, thanks." Not liking the attention on me, I look over at Ariana, who gives me a small smile.

"How are things with..." Chloe flicks her thumb in the direction of the other room.

"You have enough going on, try not to worry about me." My emotions are getting the better of me, and I don't want to break down.

"What's going on?" Chloe ignores my protests and moves forward, grabbing a sandwich off the platter and taking a bite.

"Nothing. It's no big deal. Don't worry about me. Really." Putting on a big smile, I let them all know I'm fine.

"We can't do much for Chloe at the moment, but maybe we can help you," Ariana adds.

What the fuck, Ari? I thought she was on my side, now she's throwing me under the bus in front of everyone.

I feel my hormones kicking in, and my emotions begin to bubble just under the surface. I *will not* cry. Looking around the room at all of my friends' expectant looks, I need to throw them off the scent. I'm not ready for them to know about how much of a fuck up I really am. Once they know my secret, especially Chloe, she's not going to want to be around me anymore. She's going to side with the man she loves, and who shares the same DNA as his brother.

"I love my job, but I can't work there anymore." Trying to hold back the tears, I shake my head. "Not with him."

"Oh, my Lenna bug." Emma sits and pulls me into arms. "No man is worth your tears... especially not one so emotionally stunted as he is. No offense, Chloe. You got the good twin," Emma tells her.

"He made it obvious this weekend whatever fleeting thing we had was done and dusted. I can't turn my feelings off like that, I'm not a robot." Ariana doesn't look happy with me. "I'm sorry, guys. Seriously, Chloe has more important things going on than my stupid crush."

"Hey, no, this is just as important," Chloe tells me.

See, I am a bad friend.

"I can't do it anymore. I thought I was stronger than this, but I'm not," I tell the group, the tears now falling fast and heavy down my cheeks.

"Does it have anything to do with you not having any champagne?"

Flinching at Emma's question, I stand quickly. "No!"

They are going to find out, and they are going to tell Logan, and fucking hell, I can't do this.

Not yet.

I haven't been able to sort things out in my mind yet.

33

LOGAN

This weekend's been a success, and I should be on top of the world, but I'm not. Seeing Lenna flirting with one of the guys from the Sons of Brooklyn, put a real damper on my evening, especially when he leaned over and kissed her. It took everything in me not to march over there and rip his tattooed fucking hands off her.

I never thought Lenna would be a groupie, but then again, maybe I don't know her like I thought I did.

Was she waiting for someone more successful, or maybe even richer than me, to come along? I never thought she was like that, but how easy she's been able to move on from me has me second-guessing her.

I could have taken up any number of offers given to me over the weekend, but I chose not to because of her. Maybe I should have just said 'fuck it' and gotten laid, so I wouldn't feel like I want to punch the walls of my apartment right now.

My cell rings, it's Anderson, so I ignore it because I'm not in the mood. It starts again. Shouldn't he be at home getting laid by his wife? I let it go to voicemail, but it rings again.

Damn! Maybe it's actually something, so I pick it up.

"Finally, you fuck," he yells down the line. "Looks like Chloe's ex isn't too damn happy about Chloe and Noah going public. He's made threats against them." *He did what?* "We are heading to the hotel because the paparazzi won't let them into their home."

"I'm on my way," I tell him as the phone line goes dead.

STEPPING BACK into the living room where the girls are seated, after we spoke to Jackson, our security contractor, who was going to look into Walker Randoff for us, the last person I thought I would be seeing is Lenna.

Looking over to where she's standing, I can see she's been crying, and for a moment I want to reach out and pull her to me to comfort and help her work through the pain, but then I see the images of her with the rock star and anger replaces my compassion.

Lenna looks up at me. She looks exhausted, her normal luminous skin appears pale and gaunt. It's as if she's lost weight.

Is she just as affected by our parting as I am?

"Logan, Noah... I want to let you know that I'm giving you two weeks' notice." The room falls so silent you could hear a pin drop.

"Lenna..." Noah steps forward. "No, we don't want you to leave," he tries to reassure her.

What the hell just happened?

I am standing here frozen to the spot.

Did I just hear Lenna correctly—she's quitting?

"Say something, dickhead." Anderson elbows me, and my mind's blank.

"You're a fantastic employee, we don't want you to go," Anderson says.

I watch as Lenna's face turns bright red with embarrassment.

Why is she embarrassed? She's just quit her job in front of everyone.

"Urgh... men," she huffs out, frustrated. "I have to go." She grabs her bag. "I can't be here anymore." Her eyes glare at me.

What the fuck have I done?

All of the girls rally around Lenna, trying to reassure her that she shouldn't leave, while they all throw icy glares in my direction.

Why am I the bad guy?

Then she's gone.

"You're a damn dick." Emma points to me.

Seriously, what the hell have I done?

"You should have begged her to stay. She was waiting for you to man up."

"If she wants to move on, then that's her choice," I tell Emma. Lenna's made it crystal clear she doesn't want me.

"Seriously, did you get dropped on the head as a child?" Emma yells.

"This has nothing to do with you," I tell her. I understand she's sticking up for her friend, but she really needs to butt the hell out of *our* business.

"Like hell, it does. I'm her friend."

I scoff. I'm not going to listen to whatever bullshit story Lenna has told the girls about me, to fit whatever narrative she's has going on to justify her fucking around on me.

"You're a selfish bastard."

Wait a fucking minute, I've fucking done nothing wrong here.

"Anderson, control your wife."

Anderson turns to me, and he looks furious.

"Don't involve him. Are you not man enough to take on a woman?" Emma places a hand on Anderson's chest. What the hell has Lenna been saying to the girls? It looks like she's painted me out to be the fucking monster in this situation.

Well, fuck this.

"I don't have time for this bullshit. I never thought you were one for the dramatics," I say while looking over at Emma. I always had her pegged as the one who was more open-minded about things, especially since she's married to Anderson.

"Back the fuck off," Anderson booms putting himself between Emma and me. "You *will* show my wife some respect."

"Your fake wife."

He's so fucking pussy whipped it's not funny. Anderson's hand comes out at lightning speed and grabs me by the front of my shirt. *What the hell?*

"Whoa, hold on." Noah jumps in, wrestling Anderson away from me.

"Emma's a part of my life, a permanent part of my life. You better get used to it."

"I don't get how you can stay with a gold digger like her." The words tumble out before I have a moment to process what I've just said.

"What the fuck, Logan?" Noah turns on me.

EJ restrains Anderson from knocking me out because even I know I've gone too far.

"I'm not a fucking gold digger," Emma screams at me. "I have my own shit."

"Ems..." Chloe tugs on her arm, "... just leave it."

"You're siding with that dick after the way he's treated Lenna. Your friend. You do remember that?"

This is turning into a shitshow of epic proportions.

"I'm not siding with anyone. I don't think hurling insults at each other is working either," Chloe tells her friend.

Emma pulls her arm away from her.

"I'm out." She reaches out, grabbing her bag.

"Me, too," Anderson agrees with her, leaving the suite with a black cloud hanging over it.

"What the hell is wrong with you?" Noah asks me.

"Leave me the fuck alone." Pulling myself out of his grip, he won't understand. He's found his one. My head is swimming with so many thoughts, feelings, and regrets as I storm off into the other room.

Lenna just quit.

Just like that.

Five years thrown away all because I broke the fucking rules and fell for her. Running my hands through my hair, I groan out loud.

"You okay?" EJ hesitantly asks as he follows me.

"What the hell just happened?" Noah's yelling as he follows after me.

"I don't know. They're the ones coming at me." I throw my hands up in the air.

"Because you were being a damn dick," Noah tells me.

Well, fuck him, so I flip him off.

"I think everyone's a little touchy at the moment, and everyone is trying to protect everyone," EJ adds. "I've also known Emma for a really long time. She's no gold digger, man," he tells me.

I know she's not, I'm just lashing out.

"Fine, I was wrong. I owe her an apology." Letting out a heavy sigh, I rub my chin.

"You also insulted a man's wife," EJ adds. "I know they have some weird, fake marriage thing going on, but the way he stood up for her tonight that didn't seem fake."

EJ's right, I went too far. I was angry over everything, a switch flipped in me, and I lost it.

"Fine, I'll apologize to everyone. Happy?" Throwing my hands up in the air, I seem not to be able to do anything right at the moment.

EJ and Noah look at each other, and the concern written on their faces is telling me something.

"You okay about the whole Lenna thing?" Noah asks.

Shooting him a death stare, hoping he will change the subject, I know he won't let this go so easily.

"Mixing business and pleasure is hard. That's why I don't do it," EJ adds.

"You haven't even once with Stella?" Noah asks the obvious question.

"No way. She's a good girl. I mean look at her, she has wholesome written all over her. She's marriage material, not banging material," EJ muses.

"You started off so strong, then fucked it all up in the end," I tell him.

"But then there are people like Chloe and me, whose workplace romance works," Noah adds cockily.

"I don't want to hear about it," EJ grumbles.

"You're the exception," I tell him.

"What are you going to do about Lenna?" Noah asks again. See, I knew he wouldn't let it go!

"Nothing." It's obvious she wants nothing more to do with me, so there's no point in pursuing it anymore.

"Are you just going to let her quit?" Noah raises his voice.

"She can't work with me anymore. What more can I do? I fucked up. I've fucked it all up," I answer while running my hands through my hair.

"Lenna's a valuable employee. Honestly, *I* don't want to lose her. There has to be another way. We have two weeks to change her mind." Noah tries a different approach on me. The problem is he's right, losing her would be a huge issue for the company.

"Fine!" I let out a defeated sigh.

A PERSONAL APOLOGY IS REQUIRED, and I need to give it to Anderson and Emma right now. I took my frustrations out on them, and they were totally misdirected. I have sent them both a peace offering of alcohol, lots of expensive wines, and a note that contains an apology. They must be angry still as I haven't heard back from them.

Picking up my cell, I need to suck it up and call them personally because they deserve that. Pressing the button on my cell, I hit Anderson's name.

"Yes," he answers gruffly.

"I'm sorry."

"Good. So you should be." He sighs. "You're going to have to apologize to Emma. But I warn you now, she's going to be tougher than me to convince."

"Is she there."

"You're on speaker." *Asshole*. I can hear the grin in Anderson's voice.

"Hey, Emma..."

"Stone," she replies curtly. "I appreciate the gift."

Well, that's a start, I guess.

"I'm truly sorry for the things I said to you, Emma. On that day, I..." rubbing the back of my neck, I continue, "... I was a little taken aback by everything that happened."

There's silence for a couple of beats.

"Do you really think I'm a gold digger, Logan?" Her voice is a little softer this time, maybe even sounding vulnerable.

"No. I definitely don't. Honestly, I think you might be good for my friend."

"Let's not go crazy," Anderson adds, which has us all chuckling.

"I took my frustration with Lenna out on you guys, and I shouldn't have done that," I tell them being quite open and honest with them.

"What happened, Logan?" Emma asks. "Lenna's tight-lipped over your relationship."

I'm surprised, I assumed the girls knew what had happened between us, they seem to share everything else.

"I don't know. I asked her to give me a chance, she agreed. Something has happened to change her mind because she broke it off after I asked her to go public with our relationship."

The line is silent again for a few seconds.

"You wanted to go public?" Emma reiterates.

"Yes, I've started seeing a therapist who's helping me to work through some stuff—"

"Wait! What?" Anderson interrupts. "You went to a therapist?"

"Yeah. Lenna suggested that I have residual issues over my father's death and that I need to work through them. She was right. He's made me think about things differently. I need to keep going to therapy, but life has gotten in the way of that lately. But I will be going back."

"I'm proud of you," Anderson tells me, which makes me sit up a little straighter.

"I wanted to do it for me, but even more so for her. I wanted to make myself better for her."

"I'm so confused, Logan," Emma adds. "I had no idea this is how you felt."

Shrugging my shoulders, I reply, "I can't make someone want me."

"I accept your apology, Logan," Emma tells me.

"Thank you."

"Have you given up on her?" Emma asks.

"I think I have to. Maybe time will heal, but she's not going to give me that time. I'm not usually a quitter, but you have to know when to take a step back, and I am more than aware now is the time."

"You know she's coming to work for me," Emma confesses,

but I did already know because Noah mentioned it. "I'll look after her."

"Thanks. She's going to be a great asset to your business."

"She will be, but you can be upset she's leaving, Logan," Emma tells me.

"It's her choice."

"Well, leave it with me. I'm going to get to the bottom of what's going on, and if I think you should know, I'll tell you."

That's very kind of her, and really I don't deserve her loyalty after what happened, but I appreciate it.

We end the call on a happier note.

34

LENNA

Two weeks go by so quickly. Logan's been out of his office for most of that time. Every single day either Noah or Chloe have begged me to stay, but now that I'm here, I think the time is right. I promoted my assistant, Francis, and she's going to be the most amazing replacement.

"I can't believe today is your last day." Chloe hugs me tightly then gives me a sad pout.

"It's gone quickly," I reply while I shuffle some papers around my bare desk.

"Well, there's cake in the break room." Chloe winks at me.

I could do with cake, I mean I'm eating for two now so why not indulge, so I head to the break room, and we all enjoy the time.

Coming back from demolishing a couple of slices and a cup of tea, I notice Noah's in Logan's office. That's good because it will be safer with him there to give them both their thank you present for my time here in their company. I managed to find a nice bottle of The Macallan 18-Year-Old Whisky, which I knew the boys would like. Mustering up the courage, I make my way toward Logan's office where the door is slightly ajar, and I can hear them arguing.

"You think what happened between Lenna and me was love? Hardly. It was a couple of convenient fucks," Logan hisses at Noah.

Oh. The shock of hearing Logan's real thoughts about me causes me to loosen my fingers around the neck of the bottle of whisky, and before I realize what's happening, I'm turning on my heel and getting the hell out of there. I'm gone before the bottle has time to smash all over the tiled floor.

I've got to get out of here.

I can't be here anymore.

I head toward the fire escape, trying to catch my breath.

"Lenna," Logan follows after me. He pauses, his chest heaving from running down the corridor after me as I turn around.

"You don't have to explain anything."

"I think I do."

Shaking my head, I really don't want to hear his bullshit excuses, explaining away his reasons for getting caught and voicing his true feelings toward me.

"I don't care anymore, Logan." Tears are falling down my cheeks as I look up at his hurt face.

"I don't understand how things have gone so bad between us, Lenna." The look on his face is imploring me to explain to him how fucked up we've become, but I can't, not after hearing that.

"You were right about having the rules of non-fraternization. We should never have stepped over that line."

"You think we were a mistake?"

"I think we should have stayed friends."

Logan shakes his head. "I disagree. We were good, you and I, when we gave in and finally gave it a go. It was the happiest I have ever been with anyone in my life." He needs to stop saying those things to me, I simply don't want to hear it. I can't hear it. I need to protect myself, protect my heart.

"I can't risk my heart." There I've said it out loud.

"Oh." He shoves his hands into his pockets. "I understand now. Why am I not surprised you would weigh up all the pros and cons of our relationship exactly like you do in business." He shakes his head as if he's just cracked some unseen code. "You've found me risk-averse and decided it was better to cut your losses now rather than later. Smart."

His words make my stomach sink.

"I wish you luck with your new adventure, Lenna."

He's actually letting me go.

"Emma has gained one of the best employees the Stone Group has ever had, and you will be a tough act to follow around here. You *will* be sorely missed." Once he's finished speaking, he turns on his heels and leaves me in the stairwell where I collapse in a miserable heap on the concrete.

This is what I wanted.

This is what I thought I needed.

But seeing Logan walk away so defeated, I'm not sure that I've made the right decision.

"To new beginnings." Emma raises her glass of champagne in the air, and we all do the same.

Ariana gives me a dirty look as I hold a champagne glass in my hand too. A pregnant woman can hold a glass of champagne, it doesn't mean I'm going to drink what's in there.

"Welcome to chaos." Emma grins.

"I hate you," Chloe pouts. "I'm going to miss my daily lunch with my Leens."

"I'm pretty sure Noah will be happy to have you all to himself," I give her a grin.

"So true." She smiles, taking a sip of champagne.

"I still can't believe he let you go." Emma looks at me over the rim of her champagne glass, her eyes questioning.

"He didn't have a choice." Twisting the full glass between my fingers, I avoid drinking it.

"But he wanted you to stay?" Emma pushes.

"Only because I'm good at my job."

"You sure that's the *only* reason?"

Where the hell is this coming from.

"I doubt that's the only reason," Stella interjects.

"This isn't a fairytale. There's no happily ever after."

Why are my friends turning against me?

"But, there could be," Ariana suggests, and I shoot her a warning glare.

"Guys, what's with the Spanish inquisition?" Chloe asks while looking at our friends. "We're here to celebrate Lenna's new beginnings, not worry about her disastrous love life." She chuckles.

The girls all agree, and they stop asking questions about Logan. I don't like lying to my friends, but until I work out how to get my life back on track, I will wait to tell them my news, but I do know it has to be sooner rather than later.

35

LOGAN

"Mr. Stone, it's good to see you again, it's been a while." Dr. Aspen gives me the look of 'you missed a couple of sessions, why is that?'

"Sorry. Things have been complicated. You're probably going to need a bigger notepad."

Dr. Aspen's eyes widen a little at my candor. "Well, then, I guess you better start at the beginning..."

So, I do. I tell him how I left his office feeling confused and exhausted about my past. That it took me a while to work through my feelings, and that I realized more than anything, I wanted Lenna in my life. I told him how things were great for a couple of weeks, perfect in fact until I asked her about going public with our relationship.

Dr. Aspen furiously writes down so many notes I am sure his hand must be cramping.

I then explained that Lenna wasn't interested in the future I saw. I told him how she got upset that I couldn't give her the white picket fence and the two-point-five kids.

Of course, Dr. Aspen asked me why.

I told him that I hadn't thought that far ahead, that publicly outing us as a couple was a huge step for me. I wasn't against the future Lenna foresaw for us, but I just wasn't ready to admit it yet.

The doctor asked me what she said when I told her.

I replied with I didn't get a chance to because she broke up with me and then quit her employment with our company.

"She just quit! Didn't give you a reason?" Dr. Aspen asks.

"Her reason was simply that she couldn't work with me anymore," I reply, shrugging my shoulders in defeat.

"Why do you think she *couldn't* work with you anymore?"

Frowning, I contemplate our conversations over the weeks.

"Her feelings changed, I guess."

Dr. Aspen's eyes narrow on me. "If her feelings changed for you, why would she have to quit? She wouldn't have feelings, so working with you shouldn't affect her at all?"

His question gives me pause to think.

"Are you saying working with me might affect her?"

"Usually, if you don't have feelings for someone, it's easy to move on and not let them affect you. Don't you think?"

Is what the doctor saying correct?

"Everything's a mess, and I don't know how we got to this place. I feel like I'm missing a giant piece of the puzzle."

"Do you have feelings for her, or do you just want to know what happened between the two of you?" Dr. Aspen asks.

"Can't it be both?" I question.

"You may never know what triggered Lenna to pull away. Would you be okay with that?"

His question pauses me for a moment.

Does it matter why Lenna got scared if she truly does see a future with me? What's a couple months of sadness when we could have a lifetime of happiness.

The doctor grins as he watches me process what's running through my mind.

"I would give Lenna some time. You know the saying, absence makes the heart grow fonder."

"But what happens if she meets someone else?" My gut twists with so much jealousy it physically hurts.

"There is a risk that could happen. But she could also be concentrating on her new life. You said she's starting in a new position with a friend?" I nod my head. "Just like you are growing and transitioning into a new version of yourself, perhaps she is too. Maybe seeing you getting yourself together has promoted her to reevaluate her life."

Maybe the doc's right. Lenna has been working for us for years. Perhaps we didn't challenge her enough? Or praise her enough? Maybe she wasn't truly happy with us?

"Lenna might be on a different path for the moment, but it doesn't mean you both can't come together again. Maybe, if it does happen, you both might be ready for the future." Dr. Aspen raises his brow at me.

He's right, I need to focus on putting the demons of my past behind me. I must begin to concentrate on a better work-life balance. Maybe then, I might be the man who is deserved of Lenna Lund.

Maybe therapy isn't such a bad thing after all.

"You seem different." Noah throws the basketball at me.

"I feel different," I answer, grinning at my brother as I throw the ball back to him.

"Did you get laid?" He pauses, holding the ball against his chest.

"Who got laid?" Anderson joins our conversation.

"No one," I reply while shaking my head

"Logan seems happy. I'm worried," my brother adds as he pegs the ball back at me.

"Happy?" Anderson tilts his head.

"You guys are fucking dicks." I pass the ball over to Anderson.

"What's going on?" Noah continues to question me. "Have you patched things up with Lenna?"

"No, not yet."

Noah and Anderson still, then give me their full attention.

"You've seen her?" Anderson asks.

"No, but I had another great session with my therapist, who helped me to look at things differently." Anderson and Noah look at each other skeptically. "I'm serious."

"And your therapist is a man?" Anderson asks.

"Yes." With a frown, I ask, "What does that have to do with anything?"

"I thought the therapist might have been giving you something, you know... extra on the side." Anderson grins.

"Fuck you." Grabbing the basketball from his clutches, I start bouncing it in front of me. "This is why I don't talk to you two."

"Logan," my brother moans. "Sorry, we're just busting your chops... if this is helping you deal with everything, then I'm all for it."

"Me, too," Anderson adds.

"Don't get your hopes up." I look at them both. "I think it will be a long time before I join your pussy-whipped brotherhood."

"Well, I'm thoroughly enjoying being pussy-whipped." Noah grins. My brother is a lost cause, I know this, so I turn my attention to Anderson.

"I'm the one whipping the pussy, not the other way around." Anderson grins.

Noah and I groan at his words.

36

LENNA

It's been a couple of weeks since I started working with Emma, and it's crazy, hectic, and new. Emma is a total boss bitch the way she handles everything from diva-like designers to snobby fashion writers.

It still feels weird not walking into my old office, grabbing my coffee from my regular barista, Kate, and having lunch with Chloe, then seeing Logan's grumpy face.

Letting out a heavy sigh, I thought leaving the Stone Group would have helped these feelings I have for Logan subside, but they're still there bubbling away beneath the surface like magma, just waiting to erupt to the surface at any moment.

My emotions have been all over the place with the pregnancy, and it's been a very confusing time, especially watching my stomach grow. The guilt that follows from the joy of watching my body change is eating away at me. It doesn't help when I receive Ariana's daily messages asking if I've spoken to Logan yet, which adds to my stress levels.

I want to wait for the dust to settle so I can figure out the next step. But Ariana's right, I'm taking away Logan's rights and depriving him of enjoying his baby growing inside me. She told me I should give him a choice, not take it away from him. She's right, and I know I've fucked everything up so badly.

"You okay?" Emma surprises me as I am having a teary moment thinking about Logan.

"Um... yeah." Trying to wipe my tears away quickly, Emma frowns at me. She closes my office door and then proceeds to sit down before me.

"Is the work too much?" she asks, and I shake my head. "Is it Logan?" she presses.

Sucking in a deep breath, I know I have to tell her. I mean, she's about to find out when I have to take maternity leave anyway.

"Kind of." Rubbing my hands together nervously, I prepare to tell her what I have been keeping hidden from everyone.

"Did something happen?" Concern falls across her gorgeous face, and I love that she cares for me so much.

"I did something." My voice hitches with panic, and her jade-green eyes widen at my confession. "I think I've fucked up."

"Leelee." Emma reaches out and takes my hand. "Whatever's happened, it's going to be okay."

The tears fall freely now, as I shake my head. "Everyone is going to hate me." She squeezes my hand tighter. "I've never had girlfriends before. I've never had people care about me like you all do. And I've gone and messed it all up."

Emma rises from her chair and sits on the edge of my desk. "Whatever it is, we *will* get through it together. There is nothing you can say that could make me not be your friend anymore." Tilting her head, she looks down at me. "Even if you fucked my husband. I'd be angry, of course, but then I'd give you a high-five because let's be serious, it's rare to find a dick that big and everyone should be able to experience that at least once in their lifetime."

Wait! What? Looking up at her, she's grinning, and I know

she's joking, but then she continues, "I won't mind if I catch you checking out his crotch next time he comes in." She gives me a wink.

Shaking my head from the thoughts of Anderson and his huge dick, which is something I shouldn't be thinking about at all, but now it's there at the forefront of my mind.

"I think it's worse than that, Ems." My voice is barely a whisper.

"Do I need to hide a body? Because I can. I mean, I will for you," she adds.

Damn her and her niceness.

Just rip the Band-Aid off, Lenna.

"I'm pregnant."

Emma stills, her jade-green eyes flare with so many questions.

"How far along are you?" Her words are slow and precise.

"Over three months."

Her eyes widen again with my words. "Well, fuck." She stands. "It's Logan's, isn't it?" I nod my head as tears well again. "Fuck!" She paces. "Oh my God, Lenna." She stops and stares at me. "Wait..." her eyes focus in on me, "... Logan doesn't know, does he?"

Shaking my head, I hiccup on my emotions.

"Oh, Leens." Emma rushes over and pulls me up into her embrace and holds me tightly as I come undone, tears running down my chin and onto her blouse.

"I'm... so... sorry... I... didn't... tell... you," I choke out, sniffling into her shoulder.

"Have you seriously been going through this alone?" Pulling away from me, she starts questioning me.

"Ariana knows, but that's it."

"Ariana knows!" Emma raises her voice.

"She's the one who told me she thought I was pregnant and actually made me do a test."

"Oh my God, I bet she's been harassing you every day to tell Logan." I nod my head in agreement. "Why didn't you come to me?"

"Because you're married to Anderson."

She turns her head at my answer. "Fake married." She waves her hands in the air. "Girl code still reigns supreme with me. Maybe not Chloe, though, she will definitely tell Noah everything."

"I know."

"Oh, Leelee..." Her face softens. "Is this why you pushed him away?" Nodding my head again, the enormity of it all hitting me square in the chest. "You know you have to tell him."

"He's going to hate me, though." My stomach is somersaulting at the prospect of the argument that we are going to have, or the fact that he will shut me out altogether from his life.

"He's going to be angry at first..." she shrugs, "... but he needs to know. You can't keep this from him, it's not fair."

"I know. I... I've messed it all up."

Emma reaches out and rubs my arm. "A little," she replies honestly. "Logan thinks he's done something wrong. That he did something to push you away."

"I heard him the night of The Hamptons openly talking to Anderson about me. That he wasn't interested."

Emma frowns. "That's why you kissed the hot rock star."

Nodding my head, I answer, "Not my finest hour."

"I wouldn't say that." Emma gently elbows me with a smile. "The rock star was cute."

"I wanted to hurt him like he did me. I know, utterly childish, right?"

"Pregnancy hormones... apparently, they make you do crazy shit." Emma grins. "Can turn you into a completely different person, I hear."

"That's what it feels like at the moment." I let out a long

sigh. "My last day at the Stone Group, I heard Logan telling Noah that I was nothing more than a fling."

"Oh, Lenna." She wraps her arm around me again.

"I am stupid for wanting something with someone who doesn't want me."

"Logan has feelings for you, we can all see it," she tries to reassure me.

"There's a big difference between sexual tension and something... *more*," I reply while trying not to feel too sorry for myself.

"I know it might be scary to put your heart out there, but it's not just your heart any longer, it's you and your baby's." Her eyes fall to my stomach before coming back to mine. "You have to give Logan a choice, Lenna. You can't take that away from him. It's cruel." Emma's serious, and I know she's right. It's the same sentiment that Ariana keeps telling me too.

"What do I do?"

"Let Anderson and I mediate." Her face lights up as a scheme brews in her mind. "We will invite Logan over for dinner. Hopefully, when he sees you, he will be happy. Then, you lay it all out for him, and you both live happily ever after." She grins.

"I somehow don't think that's how the night is going to go."

Emma shoos my concern away. "Don't be a Negative Nelly. I've got you. Plus, Anderson is a giant, and he can pin him to the floor and hold him there until he listens." She shrugs. "Actually, now that I think about it, that might be hot. Very homo-erotic, don't you think?" She smiles, lost in her thought.

"And if it doesn't work."

Emma snaps back from her fantasy land. "Then you will be the best co-parents that baby could ever have. And it's going to be surrounded by so much love from its favorite Aunty Emma that it's not going to even notice that Mommy and Daddy aren't together."

Could it really be that simple?

LOGAN

I had a very weird phone call from Emma last week, insisting I come to dinner at Anderson's place. Anderson's never invited me to his home for dinner. Is this the kind of shit that happens when you get married?

Anyway, my curiosity has gotten the better of me, and here I am with a bottle of Jim and a bouquet of flowers for Emma, and I am heading up to his penthouse suite. The chrome elevator doors open, and I step straight into his home, and the aroma that's coming from the kitchen smells delicious.

Turning the corner, I see Anderson walking toward me with a smile on his face.

"Glad you could make it." He slaps me on the back as I hand him the bottle of Jim Beam. "Thanks."

"And these are for your lovely wife." Shaking the flowers at him, I try to peer over his large shoulder and notice briefly that Emma is talking to someone in the kitchen.

Oh, for fuck's sake, is this a blind date?

Dammit! I didn't think Anderson would play me like that.

"Dude, if this is a blind date, I am turning around and getting the hell out of here," I hiss under my breath.

"I can assure you it's not." He gives me the most serious of stares.

Oh. Has something happened?

There's tension in his shoulders all of a sudden.

"Come on, let's get this over with."

Why does he sound so off?

Turning around, I follow my giant friend further into his apartment. Once he steps toward his wife, I soon realize who the other person is. *Lenna.*

She's beautiful.

As she slowly turns around in slow motion, her hair appears glossy and sleek pulled up into a high ponytail. She has color back in her cheeks again, and she's not looking pale and gaunt like she had done weeks ago. She almost—dare I say it—looks glowing.

Maybe she is better off without me.

She's dressed in a gorgeous dark green wrap dress which hugs her curves in all the right places, even her breasts look fuller since the last time I saw her. I wonder what she's doing here?

Looking between Emma and Anderson, I wonder if this is this some kind of intervention?

"Well, this is awkward as fuck," Anderson breaks the tension.

Lenna gives me a small smile.

"What's going on?"

Emma looks over at Lenna, motioning for her to talk to me. It seems as if Lenna's lost the ability to speak.

"Logan, you're going to need a drink for this," Emma tells me as she busies herself in the kitchen with Lenna.

"What is going on?" I ask my best friend.

"Take a seat. It's going to be a long night." Anderson motions to his sofa, while unease prickles my skin.

"Here..." Emma hands me a large glass of bourbon and

hands one to Anderson as well. She takes a seat on the sofa opposite me with Lenna, who still can't bring herself to look at me.

"Babe, I think you're going to have to break the ice." Anderson nods to his wife.

I'm still not sure what the hell I'm doing here?

Emma gives Lenna one last look and lets out a sigh. "Recently, some information was brought to my attention." Emma side-eyes Lenna again, who fidgets nervously beside her. "And it involves you."

Me? Turning my attention to Lenna, I'm utterly confused, and if I am honest, a little worried.

"You can do it," Emma whispers to Lenna, who finally looks over at me.

I notice her eyes welling up as she tries and wrangles with herself with whatever it is she's about to say. My heart is beating furiously inside my chest. I think I'm going to have a heart attack waiting for her to spit out the words.

Emma reaches over and clasps her hand with Lenna's as if to give her some sort of hidden strength.

"I'm pregnant," Lenna whispers.

The world around me shifts on its axis.

Lenna is pregnant.

What?

No.

Fuck! No. I've completely missed my chance with her now.

"Congratulations." The words spill out, but my brain has disappeared into some kind of vortex that resembles a black hole. Is this why they wanted me here to tell me in person, so I wouldn't hear it through the grapevine somewhere else?

I've missed my chance with her.

This is what she wanted.

She's getting her happily ever after, and it's not with me.

"Um... yeah..." standing on shaky legs, "... I think... um...

yeah. Have a great night, guys." Turning on my heel, I've taken a couple of steps away from the group when I hear Lenna speak again.

"It's yours, Logan."

Hang on, what?

Turning around quickly, Lenna's standing, and her face is a mixture of emotion.

"Mine?" Pointing to myself in disbelief, she nods her head once. I'm not good with the whole woman's reproductive system, but it's been a while since Lenna and I slept together. "Are you sure?"

Lenna takes a step back as if my question had physically hit her.

"Logan, what the hell?" Emma stands and places a protective arm around Lenna.

"I'm not the bad guy here," my tone elevates ever so slightly. "It's been a long time since Lenna and I have been together—"

"I'm almost four months, Logan," Lenna's words are like a slap to the face when she interrupts me, and I recoil at this new information.

She's almost four months pregnant.

My eyes fall to her belly, and I can see the tiniest of swell against her tight-fitting dress. *Four months?* As I mentally do the calculation that would bring us to around the weekend in The Hamptons.

Has she known all this time?

Did she not want me to know?

Was she ever going to tell me?

"When did you find out?" my question is curt as hurt filters through my veins that she's been hiding this from me. Something this huge. Something that I should have been a part of. Lenna can't look at me. "You've known… all this time," I ask, raising my voice. "And you kept this from me." I thump my chest angrily.

"Logan... I—"

"I don't want to fucking hear it." Raking my fingers through my hair, I almost pull it out by the roots.

"Logan." Anderson gets up and puts himself between Lenna and me.

Does he think I'm going to do something? Is he fucking serious right now?

"You made me think I did something wrong, Lenna. I poured my heart out to you. I've started therapy. I was willing to do anything to be the man you could love." Lenna gasps at my declaration. "Are you ashamed that someone like me knocked you up? Is that why you've kept it from me?" Thumping my fist against my chest again, I know I am becoming too agitated over this, but I can't help it.

"Oh, Logan... no." Tears are falling down Lenna's face in a constant stream.

"I'm sorry, I... I can't be here anymore." Turning on my heel, I rush to the elevator and press the brass button a million fucking times. Why the fuck is the elevator never here when you need it?

Lenna's whimpering echoes through the apartment, but I can't be compassionate or caring right now. How could she *not* include me?

"Logan." Anderson large hand lands on my shoulder, but I shrug it off.

"Don't," I give him a one-word warning as the doors open, and I step into the metal box.

Pulling my cell out, I call the one person I can count on as the door closes.

"Can I come over? It's urgent."

38

LENNA

"It's going to be okay," Emma tries to soothe me.

"You saw his face." I look between Emma and Anderson. "He hates me. Like... *really* hates me."

"Give him time, I think he's in shock," Anderson tells me as he shoves his hands into his pockets.

"I've fucked everything up. Not telling him as soon as I found out makes me a selfish fucking bitch, and the problem is I knew that all along."

"Leens..." Emma wraps her arms around me. "Don't be so hard on yourself."

"It's true, Ems. Don't sugarcoat it. Me not pulling up my big girl panties and dealing with this head-on instead of sticking my head in the damn fucking sand like a stupid ostrich, has messed up any semblance of an amicable co-parenting."

"Yes. You fucked up," Anderson answers.

Emma shoots him a death stare.

"What, babe? She has." He shrugs.

Emma throws her hands up in the air in disgust. "Okay, you made some decisions that, with hindsight, may not have been the right ones."

Okay, I know I said don't sugarcoat it, but I think I want the sugarcoating again.

"It's hard for men because we're on the outside of pregnancy. We don't know what it's like to have a parasite move inside of us..." Emma elbows him in the ribs. "Ouch."

Rolling his eyes at his wife, he continues, "We don't know what it's like to have our bodies change every day because of it, that better?" Emma smiles. "All we know is that when you're sick, we hold your hair back while you hurl into the bowl. All we know how to do is when it's two in the morning, we call out to get pickles and ice cream, or rub your feet, or cook a meal... shit, no, I mean... pay someone to cook you a meal."

This brings a smile to my face.

"All I'm saying is it must be hard for a man to watch his woman go through so much and not be a part of it. Men are fixers, we need to fix shit. So, when you're pregnant, the only thing we can do is fix it, and that means being there on the sidelines as your biggest cheerleader."

"Fuck, Anderson, that speech was hot." Emma looks over at her husband with awe and hunger.

"Thanks," I answer while looking up at him.

"I know Logan can come off as aloof, grumpy, or Mr. Playboy, but deep down inside, he's a simple man. Noah may be the flamboyant romantic of the two, but just because Logan doesn't show it the same way Noah does, doesn't mean he doesn't have a heart."

He's right, Logan would make simple gestures for me. If I was having a really busy day and didn't have time to stop for lunch, there would be a delivery of mozzarella sticks and salad from our favorite Italian restaurant. Or, if it was that time of the month and I was grumpy, a chocolate bar would magically appear on my desk. He remembered how I liked my coffee, what wine I drank, my favorite food without being prompted.

When I broke up with Justin, he was there at my door with

the type of flowers I deserved and dinner as well. When I was sick with morning sickness and didn't realize at the time what it was, he was there for me with crackers. Everyday little things a partner knows about you, he knew about me.

Two years with that jerk, Justin, and he still had to ask me if I drank red or white wine. *Red, always red.* I've been a fool.

Why the hell did I think Logan would be any different when it came to me telling him I was pregnant? He would have been beside me in this journey the entire time, and he would have instinctively known what I needed and when I needed it. Instead, I've been trying to figure it all by myself because I thought that's what I had to do. He has every right to be angry with me. I took time away from him with his baby, and that's something he can never get back.

"I heard him talking to you at The Hamptons opening." Mentioning one of the niggling things about our miscommunication, Anderson raises a brow in my direction. "Logan said he only ever saw us as friends, that there wasn't anything else there." Anderson frowns as he tries to recollect the conversation.

"You might not realize this, but we're guys." He chuckles. "And guys don't talk about their feelings. You had just called time on whatever was going on between the two of you. He was probably trying to save face in front of me. Us men have egos the size of our dicks." Anderson bursts out laughing.

Really? Could it be that simple?

"We know how big your ego is." Emma grins.

"Oh, for fuck's sake, I'm out of here. I'm leaving you two alone before you decide to rip each other's clothes off in front of me." I laugh as I gather my things together to leave.

"You're welcome to watch, Lenna." Anderson chuckles.

My cheeks heat at his statement. Damn these hormones.

Rushing to the elevator, I leave before they put that statement to the test.

39

LOGAN

"What's going on?" Noah answers the door with a concerned look on his face. His green eyes widen when he sees me. "Are you okay?"

Shaking my head, he ushers for me to come inside.

Chloe's in the kitchen, puttering around, and she looks up at me arriving. "I can give you both a moment."

"You will need to hear this, Chloe." Noah and Chloe give each other a look. "I don't know what to do." As I begin to pace the living room, almost pulling my hair out, I start, "I..."

"Logan..." My brother stops me by placing a concerned hand on my shoulder. "Whatever it is, we have your back, okay?" he tries to reassure me.

"I had dinner with Anderson and Emma tonight..." They nod their heads. "Lenna was there." Their eyes widen, but I don't give them time to register anything else before I blurt out, "She's pregnant."

Chloe gasps, and Noah shakes his head.

"Lenna is pregnant?" Chloe asks slowly, the news seems to have caught her off guard too.

Did Lenna keep this from her best friend? So, I'm not the only one who's been left in the dark.

"Are you sure?" Chloe frowns.

"Whose baby is it?" Noah asks.

Looking at my twin, his face registers my silent answer.

"It's yours?" His voice is barely a whisper.

My shoulders slump, and the fight leaves my body as I fall lifelessly against the sofa.

"Yours?" Chloe reiterates.

"Apparently." Hanging my head in my hands, I sigh heavily. "She's almost four months."

"Four months." Chloe's voice raises. "She's been hiding this for *four months*?" Anger and hurt lace her voice.

"She's kept it from me all this time." My eyes well with emotion.

Would she have had the baby and never told me? Would I have gone through my life never knowing my child? I feel utterly betrayed.

Chloe rushes over and wraps her arms around me. Her concern surprises me, and I take the comfort she's giving me.

"I'm so sorry, Logan," she says while holding me. "I had no idea. No idea at all."

Noah joins me and places a hand against my back. "We're here for you."

I spend the rest of the night getting drunk with my family, trying to forget the hurt that Lenna's deception has caused me.

As I finally begin to fall asleep, my cell buzzes beside me. Lenna's name flashes with a message. Against my better judgment, I open the text message.

Lenna: I'm so sorry, Logan.

Feels a little too late for apologies.

"Logan, I'm surprised to see you so soon," Dr. Aspen greets me. "You're looking a little worse for wear if I may say so."

"Doc, it's been a shitshow that's for sure."

He nods and ushers me into his room. "Want to tell me what's going on?" Taking his normal seat in his armchair, he reads over his notepad.

"Lenna's pregnant. About four months. It's mine. She hid it from me. I don't know what to do." Giving him the CliffsNotes version of what I've been dealing with, I look up and can see I've stumped the poor doctor.

"Okay, that's a lot to unpack." Madly scribbling down whatever he usually does on his pad, he finally looks up. "What I'm getting from you is that you're angry."

"Damn right, I'm angry, doc."

He nods his head. "Well, now you know the reason why she pushed you away." My body stills as the realization hits me. "Seems like she went into shock, and her coping mechanism was to hide away and deal with it by herself. Is that how she normally deals with stress?" the doctor asks me.

"No. I..." Trying to think back, the last time she was upset was when Justin dumped her, and she took the day off. But she bounced back relatively easily after that, I think, or maybe I'm wrong. "I don't know."

Dr. Aspen scribbles on his notepad. "Do you think she retreated because of her feelings toward you?"

She kept her pregnancy from me because she loves me.

"Perhaps she didn't know how to process everything," Dr. Aspen states.

"Lenna's a planner. Generally, when she has a goal, she sets about achieving it."

Dr. Aspen nods and continues writing. "So, do you think if Lenna is a planner that accidentally falling pregnant, in a job that has strictly forbidden relationships, that someone like that might panic, especially if she knows you as well as you have said she does..." Dr. Aspen pauses, letting that bit of information settle in.

"Do you think the reason she asked you those questions early on about your future, if you saw a family in the suburbs, that she might have been gauging your reaction to that image?"

"I'm not a mind reader, doc?"

He chuckles. "I understand that, but neither is Lenna. She may have found this surprising information out at the same time you were working out how you saw your future, and when it didn't align with her plans because, like you said, she's a planner, she might have gotten spooked and bolted?"

"Maybe, but she should have told me. She shouldn't have hidden it from me. I've missed out on her first scan, seeing our baby for the first time."

Dr. Aspen nods. "This is valid. Have you spoken to her about all this?" I shake my head, not really knowing how to answer. "And why not?"

"I'm too angry. I'm confused. I'm in shock. I feel like I've already let our baby down by not being there. I don't want to be a fuck-up like my dad was."

"And how do you feel about the prospect of being a father?"

"I'm still processing because, honestly, I didn't think it would happen for me. I always thought I'd be the cool uncle instead." Smiling to myself, I always thought Noah and Chloe would have a family together before me. Heck, maybe even Anderson. "All I know is, I want to be the best father I can be to my baby."

Dr. Aspen smiles. "Then you need to talk to Lenna. Your feelings of betrayal are valid, but at some point, in your co-parenting relationship with Lenna, you are going to have to move on. You and Lenna are now tethered to each other for life."

LENNA

Chloe: Urgent girls meeting at Emma's place this weekend.

    Stella: Everything okay?

Ariana: Last time you summoned us to a meeting we found out Emma had married Anderson.

Stella: Please tell me you didn't run off to Vegas and marry Noah?

Emma: Please tell me you did?

Chloe: Hell no. EJ would kill me.

Lenna: I'll be there.

I know this meeting is about me.

It wouldn't have been long before Logan told Noah and, of course, Chloe along with it. I'm dreading this, but I need to suck it up and deal with the consequences of my actions. I've hurt a lot of people by trying to deal with this on my own. Now I need to suck it up and be an adult.

"Thanks for coming," Emma greets me at the door. "I've got your back."

I hear the others laughing and clinking glasses as I enter Emma's apartment. Stepping further in, I see Chloe glance up, and she doesn't look happy with me at all. Ariana gives me a questioning look, and Stella has a smile on her face, totally oblivious to the bombshell I'm about to drop.

"Hey, guys." I wave awkwardly at my friends as I take a seat on the sofa beside Stella.

Emma gives me a glass of water and sits beside me.

"So why the hell are we here?" Stella questions Chloe.

"Maybe Lenna would like to start?" Chloe throws the grenade right in my lap.

"I've been a bad friend, guys." I let out a stuttering sigh. "I'm not used to having such a great group of girlfriends around me, and I thought I could do it all on my own. I was wrong." Looking over at Chloe, then Ariana, I blurt out, "I'm pregnant."

"I knew it," Stella squeals. "I called it ages ago."

My eyes widen in shock. She what?

"You refused champagne when we were at that hotel meeting about Walker." She grins.

The rest of the girls stay quiet.

Stella looks around and notices no one else is as excited by the news as she is. "You all knew."

"I just found out," Chloe adds. "Just like Logan did."

"Wait! What?" Stella's head turns to me. "It's Logan's baby? Holy shit!"

"I'm sorry, Chloe, for not telling you, but you and Noah are a package deal at the moment."

"I get it, but still, you should have told Logan. That poor guy is torn up about it."

Tears well in my eyes thinking about Logan. "I'm sorry." Crumbling into a teary mess, I hate being so damn emotional all the time. "I'm sorry," I say again.

Chloe kneels in front of me. "You do *not* have to apologize."

Looking down at her. "I've messed up big time. I can't change the past, but I sure as hell am going to change the future," I tell her.

"Does Logan know that?" Chloe asks.

"We have our first scan together next week. I've texted him, but he's been distant."

"Give him time, Leelee," Emma says beside me.

I know I have to respect Logan's feelings and give him time, so he can hopefully one day forgive me.

"Now that the boring stuff is out of the way, can we get excited that Lenna is having a baby? Because that means... baby shower, clothes shopping, nursery decorating." Stella grins.

Oh my, I hadn't even given myself time to think about all that.

"Stella's right." Chloe smiles. "We're all about to become aunties." She whoops loudly and throws her arm in the air on each whoop.

How did I get so lucky to have these girls in my life?

As our conversations descend into guesses about whether or not I'm having a boy or a girl, excitement swirls in my stomach for the first time.

NERVES FLUTTER through my body as I wait outside the doctor's office for Logan. This is the first time seeing him since delivering the life-changing news a couple of weeks ago. I guess it's a step in the right direction that he's here with me today.

Of course, he will be here. He's a good guy.

Urgh, shaking my head at myself at my insane stupidity, I watch in slow motion as he turns the corner with his cell in hand. He hasn't spotted me yet, so I can take my time drinking him in. He's dressed in a white business shirt, the sleeves are rolled up casually exposing his tanned, corded arms while his titanium watch glistens under the fluorescent lights overhead. Navy trousers with tan shoes and his suit jacket are resting casually over his arm. It's as if he's come directly off a luxury yacht from some exotic island. His light brown hair is looking a little disheveled as if he's been raking his hand through it.

Is he nervous too?

He's started growing some stubble. Usually, Logan is clean-shaven, but there it is and it suits him.

Biting my lower lip, I unashamedly drink him in. Then when he gets a little closer, he looks up from his cell, and his blue eyes strike me to the core as they sparkle with warmth.

Is he happy to see me?

Hope blooms inside my chest before it crashes down in a fiery ball of flames. His jaw tenses, his sparkle dims, and his hand tightens around his cell.

So, I plaster on a smile to greet him. "Thanks for coming."

"Of course, I wouldn't miss it for anything." Logan opens the door for me as we make our way into the waiting room. We check in and wait for the doctor to call my name. Looking around the room, I see it's filled with happy, smiling couples. A man rubs his partner's large stomach as she tries to sit in a comfortable position.

Is that going to be me? *It will be, but instead, you will be alone.* That thought curdles in my stomach.

"How's work?" I attempt to fill the awkward silence between us while we wait.

"Good," he replies as he fiddles on his cell while ignoring me.

"Pretty cool that Emma and Chloe are off to Bali next month. What a brilliant idea to shoot the designer's collection at your resort."

"Yes, indeed." He taps furiously away on his cell, but before I can push him further, the doctor is calling us into her office.

After some questions and a quick checkup, she moves me to the sonogram. I lift my top and Logan's breath hitches. It's the first time he's seen the start of my growing belly. Turning, I notice his eyes are fixated on it. The doctor does her thing with the gel and the wand, and before we know it, the images of our baby are being displayed on the screen. The bean looks more like a baby this time. Turning, I look at Logan, who seems a little shell-shocked. Then the baby's heartbeat kicks in through the speakers and echoes through the room, and it makes me smile.

"That's your baby's heartbeat. It's nice and strong," the doctor tells us.

Reaching, I take Logan's hand and entwine it with mine. Thankfully, he lets me.

"That's our baby?" I ask as tears well in our eyes.

"Yes."

Trying to hold back my emotions, which are in hyperdrive at the moment, Logan asks the doctor, "Can we tell what sex it is?"

"Not yet. Next month probably. Would you like to know?"

Logan looks at me for guidance.

"It's up to you," I answer, giving him this decision.

"I... yes, I would love to know." He turns and grins at me. "Lenna is a planner, so I know it will kill her not knowing."

He's one hundred percent right, the suspense is killing me. Plus, I want to know what clothes to buy. What color to paint the nursery. There are so many things around the sex of the baby.

"I want to know."

Logan chuckles, and the nerves from earlier seemingly vanished as we both finally relax around each other.

"I'll let you clean up." The doctor disappears from the room.

Logan hands me some tissues to wipe the gel from my stomach. I notice Logan's still staring at my stomach.

"Would you like to touch?" My question pulls him from whatever thoughts were going through his mind, and it flusters him. Not letting him back out, I grab his hand and place it against my stomach, his large tanned hand a stark contrast on my pale skin.

"I can't feel anything?" His brows crinkle.

"Not yet, you won't. It's still early... they say about twenty weeks." He nods his head. "Logan—"

"We have a lot to talk about, Lenna." He removes his hand from my stomach. "I have a meeting I have to attend after this." Hope slowly begins to fade away from my grasp. "But..." he pauses, "... tomorrow night, come to my place, and we will discuss everything."

"Okay."

Taking his hand, he helps me off the table. "It's going to be okay."

He stares down at me, and this time the sparkle is back in his blue eyes.

41

LOGAN

Seeing our baby on the monitor was crazy and almost surreal. It put everything into perspective that in five months, there's going to be a living, breathing, screaming, tiny human arriving, and its parents need to get their shit together.

I've ordered from our favorite Italian place for dinner. I bought all the baby books I could find, and I have been trying to catch up on the baby's development. I want to be the best father I can be to this baby, no matter what happens with Lenna.

The doors ping open, Lenna walks through, and she looks as gorgeous as ever. Her brunette hair is falling loosely around her shoulders. She's dressed in a black blouse, the animal print skirt falls well below her knees, and she's wearing a pair of black heels. Her makeup is natural, and she looks almost luminescent.

"Dinner smells amazing." She gives me a timid smile.

"I bought all your favorites."

Lenna's chocolate eyes sparkle with excitement. "Good, I'm starving. This baby doesn't stop eating."

Talking about the elephant in the room, I give Lenna a nervous shrug.

"Well, then, let's get some food into you. Take a seat at the dining table." I busy myself in the kitchen, pouring the contents of everything I purchased into bowls, and then arrange them neatly on the table. "Can I get you something to drink?"

"Just water is fine, thanks."

Heading back into the kitchen, I grab Lenna a bottle of water and pour myself a glass of red wine. Finally, taking a seat, we start to eat dinner. We chat about mundane stuff as we slowly make our way through the pasta dishes.

"I can't take it anymore, Logan," Lenna eventually breaks. "Being so close to you, yet so far away... I know I messed up. And I messed up in one of the cruelest ways possible, and I don't ever expect you to forgive me..." she rambles on.

Reaching out, I take her hand in mine, and she stops talking.

"I could never hate you," I tell her. "I am hurt, though." She nods her head in understanding. "I feel like we need to start again. I'd like to start over again if you want that?"

"You mean as friends?"

"Yes," I reply while running my thumb over her hand. "I think for the sake of our little one, we need to rebuild our relationship."

Lenna's hand tightens in mine. "I'd like that." She gives me a small smile. "I know nothing can make up for the bad choices I've made the past couple of months where I chose to pull away from you instead of being an adult and dealing with the situation head-on." She lets out an exhausted sigh. "A series of stupid and immature miscommunications on my part seems to have messed it up even more."

"I think we're both at fault with that. We both don't communicate well, which I think we need to work on, especially regarding how we will bring up the little one." Lenna nods in agreement. "Which is what I wanted to talk to you about." Her brows rise at my comment, and I am not sure how she will take my idea. I'm not even sure now if it's what I want, but here goes. "I want you to move in with me."

Lenna chokes on her water at my question. "You want me to do what?"

"I can buy us a more family-friendly home if you want. I know an apartment is probably not that great for kids."

"Kids? As in plural?" she questions me.

"We might make a cute one. So, you never know, we might have to create more." I give her a wide grin.

"I'm really confused, at the moment, I thought you said we would be just friends?"

"Can't friends co-parent their kids together?" Her forehead crinkles as she contemplates my idea. "I don't want to miss a moment of my baby's life, and if we aren't together, then I will. Plus, you're going to need help with the baby, and that help should be mine. I helped create our child."

"I just..." She's floored by my suggestions, I can tell.

"The books say that babies wake up all the time. I may not have the boobs to feed the baby, but I can definitely change diapers in the middle of the night." She laughs. "I'm sure I can work it out." Taking a sip of my wine, I continue, "You can decorate the baby's room however you want, and the same will go for your room, too."

She nods her head. "You've made a lot of good points." Twisting her bottle of water around in a circle in her hands, I can tell she has more to say. "Just know if I take you up on your offer, I won't cramp your style if you want to have a lady friend over. We will make ourselves scarce."

Huh? What is she talking about?

"Lady friend?"

"Yeah. Just because I'm knocked up or have just had our baby, it doesn't mean it should cramp your dating life."

Dating life?

Is she serious?

"I don't have a dating life, and I most certainly am not interested in one after the baby is born either."

"But if we are living together as friends, then I'm sure at some stage you will need... well, you know... companionship."

"Maybe the same can be said for you, too?" I pass the question back to her.

"Yeah, I'm sure a single mom with stretch marks, saggy boobs, and spit-up all over them is a 'real' catch." She uses air quotes and then rolls her eyes.

"And yet, you will still look beautiful." The words are out before I have a moment to push them back.

Lenna's face softens. "You think we can seriously live together, and it not become awkward?"

"Guess we're going to have to put our new communication skills to the test."

"Okay."

Did I hear her correctly?

"You have given perfectly valid reasons for why we should be together as a family. It will be nice for our little one to have its parents living together after he or she is born." She gives me a wide smile. "We are going to encounter bumps in the road navigating our co-parenting relationship, but I think we know each other well enough that we can do what's right for our little one. Plus, your home is way bigger than mine." She grins.

"So, we are doing this, then?"

Lenna nods.

"Well, welcome home, Lenna Lund."

Raising my wine glass in her direction, we cheer to a new chapter in our lives.

42

LENNA

"I can't believe you are moving in with him." Emma smirks as she helps me pack up my apartment.

"It makes sense."

"It's romantic." Stella grins.

"I think it's exciting," Chloe adds, popping her head into the living room from my study.

"That's because you moved in on day one of your relationship with Noah," Ariana teases, and she flips her off.

"I bet you one hundred dollars something happens by the end of the week," Emma tells the group.

Wait! What?

"Is that one hundred dollars if they sleep together, or should it be fifty for a kiss and fifty for some heavy petting," Ariana questions.

What the hell are my friends talking about?

"I bet fifty they kiss by the end of the week," Stella shouts.

"No way. They will be boning by the time this week's out," Emma adds. "I've heard pregnancy hormones make you aroused as fuck." She grins at me. Yes, my little friend located in the side table has been getting a bit of a workout recently with all my urges.

"I think Lenna will have more restraint. I say one hundred dollars for the second week that *she* jumps Logan."

I end up throwing a pillow at Chloe, which has her in fits of giggles.

"I can assure you I will *not* be sleeping with my baby daddy... *at all*."

My friends burst out laughing.

"You do realize how you got into this mess in the first place," Stella adds. "Suppressing your sexual tension." She wiggles her eyebrows at me.

No, this time, I'm going to be able to control myself. I have a lot more riding on this working with us than before.

"Logan and I are in a good place, and no matter how crazy my hormones may be, I don't want to jeopardize where we're at right now."

"What happens if he offers?" Stella asks. "You said he's been reading all the baby books. There must be a chapter on crazy sexy hormones and how to deal with them."

Is there? I haven't had a chance to read any baby books yet. *Would they seriously have a chapter on that?* No, my friends are just winding me up.

"Maybe he's not up to that chapter yet." Emma chuckles.

"He can *never* read that chapter," I warn them all. "It is what it is, guys. Logan and I are trying to have a healthy relationship with one another, and sex complicates it."

"So, you have thought about having sex with Logan once you've moved in," Chloe questions me.

"No." Which is a bald-faced lie, and my friends all know it because they burst out laughing. "Fuck you all. I'm trying to be an adult."

"Yep, definitely one hundred, she bones him by the end of

the week," Emma adds as she hastily runs out of the living room, disappearing from my wrath.

"THAT'S the last of the stuff," Logan tells me as our friends wave us goodbye after helping me move. Logan obviously spoke to an interior designer, and I don't know how he did it, but the guest room which is now my room has been freshly designed just the way I would have chosen. "You like it?" He rests his shoulder against the door jam, dressed in a white polo shirt and gray sweatpants with bare feet. His long legs are crossed over casually as he waits for me to answer.

Wicked thoughts of him and me in this bedroom swirl through my mind.

Shut it down, Lenna.

Day one isn't even over, and you're already thinking about him in your bed.

"Leens, you okay? Your cheeks look a little flushed."

Shaking myself from my thoughts, Logan strides over to me quickly and sits on the side of the bed. "Just overdid it today, I think."

His hand reaches out and tests my forehead. "You feeling sick?"

Oh God, tingles spark all over my body when his skin touches mine. I attempt to suppress a moan, but it's not easy.

"I'm fine. Just tired. Thank you for all this." Waving my hand around the gorgeous room, I smile.

"I'd do anything for you, Lenna." Those blue eyes dip ever so slightly to my lips.

No. No. No.

Danger.

Danger.

The air in the room swirls with tension, the walls feel like they have moved in a couple of feet, and the sounds of my beating heart echo in my ears. Logan's warm breath sends sparks of white-hot heat all over my body.

"Well, thanks again." Sitting up straight, I pull myself from the handsome swirling vortex that is Logan Stone. "I might have an early night." Fiddling with my hands, I hope he understands.

"Right, yes, well, I'm just across the hall if you need anything." He clears his throat and stands, then disappears.

Falling back against the softest bed known to man, I curse Logan Stone for being so damn irresistible.

43

LOGAN

Lenna's been in my home for a couple of weeks now, and I thought her being in my personal space would be hard, but it's not at all. In fact, it's perfectly normal. I find myself looking forward to coming home to catch up on her day over dinner. The friendly chats we used to have before things became complicated has returned. It's looking like our friendship is back on track, even if I'm starting to picture her naked every single time she's in the shower, or how much I want to kiss her while we watch television together every night. The berry scent of her shower gel makes me instantly hard.

I shouldn't be thinking these things. I know that. It's wrong. It's against everything we agreed upon when she moved in, but I can't seem to help my thoughts and what I want.

"Hey," she greets me with a kiss on the cheek as I wait for her outside the doctor's office. She's dressed in a pink dress that's molded to her gorgeous bump. Seeing her stomach bloom stirs something inside of me, something protective, a deep-seated desire to claim her as mine.

"You ready to find out what we're having? I'm so excited."

Her face lights up, and I know right now she's the most beautiful woman in the world.

We don't have to wait long before we are called into the doctor's office, and Lenna is lying down on the bed again, only this time her stomach is a little larger.

"You ready to find out what you're having today?" the doctor asks.

The doctor moves the wand around Lenna's stomach until she's in the right position. "See that there..." she points at the screen, but I don't see anything. "That's a penis." *Wait, what did she just say?* "Congratulations, you're having a boy."

A boy.

I'm having a boy.

Tears well in my eyes as I look down at Lenna, and see she too is as emotional as I am. Leaning down, I place a kiss on her forehead as the doctor checks all the measurements to make sure our little man is healthy.

"We're having a boy," I exclaim excitedly while helping Lenna up from the bed. "A son. Thank you." Leaning forward again, I place a chaste kiss against her lips. We both pause at my over-enthusiasm, which has spilled into very dangerous territory. "I'm sorry, I got caught up in everything."

Lenna shakes her head. "Don't be, it's exciting. We're having a little mini-you."

"Don't wish that upon us."

My comment makes us both laugh ending the awkward tension.

I CAN'T WAIT to get home after work to celebrate with Lenna that we're having a boy. As soon as I step into our apartment, I catch Lenna holding her stomach, and she's crying.

Dropping the flowers I've bought her, I rush to her side.

"Are you okay? Is the baby okay?" Panic takes over at the thought that something catastrophic might have happened.

"He kicked." A smile falls across her face. "Here..." grabbing my hand, she places it on her stomach, "... feel him." My hand is pushed against her hard stomach and the tiniest little movement occurs under my hand. My eyes widen with wonder. "I feel it."

Tears are falling down Lenna's face as we're connected in this moment. My heart begins to beat out of time in my chest as we both stay still just staring at each other.

"It's magical."

Sucking in a shaky breath, she nods her head.

Reaching out, I push a lock of her hair behind her ear. "You look so beautiful." I'm unable to control the words that want to tumble from my mouth. My thumb caresses her cheek making her shiver. *Does she feel this pull between us again?*

Her eyes fall to my lips. *Does she want to kiss me?* I thought I had overstepped in the doctor's office, but perhaps I didn't. "Tell me to stop." My thumb catches her lip as I gently touch it.

Lenna opens her mouth ever so slightly. "I don't think I can," her voice says shakily.

I'm treading on uneasy ground, but fuck it, I need her. I want her. Leaning forward, my lips press against hers as her mouth falls open for me. Her hands move from mine and rest on my hips, pulling me closer as our tongues collide. The moment that they do, it's like throwing a match into a tinder box, and we both go up in flames.

"I've missed this," I say, then our lips collide in another frenzied kiss.

"Fuck, I've missed your lips."

Lenna moans as she tries to claw at me as if she can't get close enough. "More, I need more," Lenna moans as my hand begins to roam freely over her body. Touching her curves freely, just as I have imagined for the past couple of weeks now, my dick's pressing hard against my zipper. Dammit! I don't think I've ever been so hard. I need her. I need to be inside her.

It's okay for us to have sex, isn't it?

Stilling, I reluctantly pull myself away from her perfect lips. "If I turn you around and fuck you, will that hurt the baby?"

Lenna bites her bottom lip, her cheeks are flushed from our kiss.

"As long as you don't squish him, it should be fine from what I've read."

Well, damn! She's read about having sex while pregnant. Did I skip those chapters in the baby book?

"Show me, guide me," I tell her.

Turning around in my arms, she places her hands on the kitchen counter, and her ass gives me a little wiggle. My hand reaches out and grips her pert little ass in my hands.

"Have you been thinking about this, Lenna?"

She nods her head as my fingers pull up the hem of her dress.

"Do you remember how my fingers make you come?" My hand slips beneath the elastic of her cotton panties where I find her soaked, and my thumb finds her aching clit. "Goddammit, Lenna..." I suppress a groan, "... you're fucking soaked."

"Yes," she moans at the connection. "Oh, God, I need this," she tells me. "I'm turned on All. The. Time."

This little tidbit of information stills me. "What did you say?" My breath caresses her cheek as my chest is pressed against her back.

"Being pregnant, my hormones are out of control. I need..."

My fingers sink inside of her. "What do you need, sweetheart?"

"I need... *you*. I need your fingers. Your cock. Your mouth. Sex. I need sex all the time."

"Have you been in your bedroom these past weeks desperate for my cock?"

"Yes." Her head falls back as my fingers slide between her folds.

"Lenna, why the fuck did you not tell me? I could have..."

Could have what Logan?

She shakes her head. "I couldn't."

"I promised you... whatever you need, I will provide." Her pussy constricts around my fingers as I take her higher and higher. "That includes my cock, do you hear me?"

She hums in agreement as I push her over the edge.

Fuck me, I've never been so turned on in my life. Pulling my fingers from her quaking pussy, I unzip myself and pull her panties to the side.

"Get ready for me, Lenna." She widens her legs and gets into a comfortable position. Running my aching tip between her wet folds, I slowly slide into her, making sure I'm not hurting her in any way.

"Yes," Lenna moans as she clenches around me.

Fuck. She could make me come just like that.

My fingers dig into her hips as I try and slow myself down.

"More, Logan, I need more." She pushes back against me, and I quicken my pace. She meets me thrust for thrust, taking what her body's been craving, and I give it to her. I may not be able to give her much, but I can give her a release.

Frantic need takes over as we both try to catch our orgasm until she clenches down on me, and I swear I see stars and the Holy Ghost as she pushes me over the edge.

"Fuck, Lenna," I yell out as she milks every last bit of my orgasm from me.

Our labored breathing fills the kitchen as we each try to come down from an epic orgasm. Slowly, I slide myself from her tightness and tuck myself back into my pants.

She straightens herself up then turns around. Her face is flushed, her chocolate eyes are almost molten, and her skin is practically glowing. "That was..." She is unsure of the words to use.

"Just what we needed."

She giggles, looking slightly embarrassed now that the flushes of our orgasm have subsided.

"You okay?" My hand rests comfortably against her stomach.

"I am, and so is he," she reassures me.

"I thought it was a myth about pregnant women and sex." Anderson ribbed me about it the other day.

"Not all women feel that way." She bites her lip.

"I don't care about other women." My eyes narrow on her. "I'm talking about you?"

"Yes, I've found my hormones have increased my sex drive."

"And what have you been doing about it?" Lenna looks away from me, and I know what I'm asking is embarrassing for her, but I am genuinely curious. "Lenna..." I turn her head back to face me.

"Does it matter," she pushes back.

"To me, it does. I want to know."

"Fine. My vibrator has helped... a lot."

"If you need to use it when I'm not here, then do it. But..." making sure I have her full attention, "... when I'm home, and you have needs, let me fulfill them. I told you anything to do with the baby, I want to help."

She pushes me hard in the chest. "I'm no one's pity fuck." She storms out of the kitchen, and I wonder, how the fuck did this just turn into a fight.

"Lenna." I chase after her. "What the hell did I do?" Grabbing her arm, I turn her around. "Why would you think that?"

"Did you even want to have sex with me?" She thumps her hand against her chest. "Or was I just convenient for you?"

Wrapping my hand around her neck, I pull her forehead forcefully to mine. "I cannot get you out of my mind, no matter how much I try, Lenna." Her face softens slightly. "I know things are all out of whack between us at the moment, but the thought you might seek a reprieve from someone else fucking kills me."

"Logan, I would never..."

"Seeing my baby growing inside of you has turned me into a possessive man. I'm ashamed I feel this way, but I do. I don't want another man touching what's mine."

"Logan?"

"I don't want to think about anything other than being the only man you need."

"Okay." I'm surprised she's not fighting me on it. "I only want you, Logan. No one else." Leaning forward, she presses her lips against mine.

44

LOGAN

A couple days after Lenna and I finally reconnected on a sexual level, I was on a flight to Australia with EJ, Anderson, and Noah. We'd had this trip planned for such a long time, and I couldn't not go.

After all, I couldn't say, 'Sorry guys, I can't go because I am Lenna's real-life vibrator who's on-call twenty-four-seven.' They would think I've gone insane.

Thing is, they wouldn't be wrong because, honestly, Lenna's sexual appetite has been insatiable.

Logan: Arrived. You're probably asleep. Miss you.

Sending the text off as I lie down on my hotel bed, my cell starts buzzing, and it's Lenna FaceTiming me.

"Hey." Her tired face comes into focus.

"I didn't wake you, did I, with that text?"

She shakes her head. "Couldn't sleep, got indigestion pretty bad." That shouldn't make me smile, but it does.

"Well, we just arrived. Going to have a power nap before we head out for dinner tonight."

She yawns. "Okay, well, I hope it's nice down there. I've always wanted to travel to Australia."

"With a new hotel in the planning, we might be down here a lot more. I'm sure our little one would love a trip." Making family holiday plans isn't what you do as co-parents, it's what you do as a family. Just because we may not be together doesn't mean we aren't a family.

But aren't you together?

"You're frowning." Lenna pulls me from my thoughts.

"Are you okay making plans with me as a family?"

"Yeah. Why?"

"It's a long flight to Australia." She smiles. "It gave me a lot of time to think." Lenna nods her head. "I want to make plans with you, Lenna." Silence falls between us. "Lenna?"

"Yeah, I'm here."

"Leaving you in my bed was hard. Sitting on that long-haul flight was even harder because I realized the only place I want to be is with you and the little one. Together as a family. I miss the fuck out of you, Lenna."

Sniffles echo through the cell phone. *Is she crying?*

"I miss you, too, Logan." She snorts while trying to hold in her tears.

"When I get home, I want us to try."

"Try?" she repeats my word, hiccupping through her tears.

"Yeah, try. I think you and I owe the little one that much. We owe him the chance to see his parents together and loving each other."

"You want to love me?" Her thick lashes blink rapidly as she tries hard to keep herself together.

"I already do, Lenna."

EVERYTHING FELL to shit right after that.

Chloe disappeared.

She was supposed to be on a plane heading to Bali for work

and meeting up with Noah on his way home from Australia, where he was going to propose.

Instead, her crazy ex-best friend kidnaps her because she had some *Single White Female* obsession with Chloe.

My poor brother's a mess stuck halfway across the world away from the woman he loves, and not being able to do a damn thing to help her. I understand his helplessness. If anything like that had happened to Lenna, especially while pregnant, I would have reacted the same way my brother did. I would move heaven and earth to get the woman I love back to me.

Unfortunately, things took a sinister twist when her friend took her own life before the cops were able to arrest her, and she left a wave of destruction in her wake.

My soon to be sister-in-law is struggling with PTSD from the shooting. Chloe's ex-fiancé, Walker Randoff's Superbowl career is over after taking a couple of bullets meant for Chloe.

Helping my brother through that harrowing time made me reassess everything in my life. Knowing that in an instant, everything can be taken away from you. So, I've decided I'm going to propose to Lenna today at her baby shower.

It's been a couple of months since Chloe's kidnapping, but she's been so strong, asking us all to treat her normally again. She wants to put the pain of that time behind her because she has so much to look forward to in her life, and I totally understand her sentiment.

"Where the hell is this baby shower?" Lenna moans as we head out of the city to the suburbs of Greenwich, Connecticut.

"This is *all* on *your* friends. I can tell you now that I have had no hand in planning this baby shower." Our hands are linked together as I drive.

"Ouch, that hurt." She scolds our son, who's been kicking up a storm in her stomach.

We lay on the couch at night, and I see this little foot

pressed out in her stomach. It's kind of freaky, but oh so cute, in the same breath. But I dare not say that because I did once, and Lenna practically bit my head off.

"He's excited about his party."

Thinking about the surprise I have in store for her, I grin widely.

"How much longer, I need to pee," Lenna moans beside me.

"Not much, I promise." She lets out a couple of frustrated huffs beside me.

Finally, we arrive at the large stone gates of the luxury home. Rolling down the window of my SUV, something Lenna was insistent on us purchasing as she said my sports car was not going to cut it for a family, I decided on mixing the two and bought us a Porsche Macan in matte black. It's going to fit nicely in the suburbs, that's for sure. Leaning out, I type in the passcode, and the large metal gates creak open slowly.

"Fancy." Lenna grins as we make our way past the gates and drive up the long winding road that leads to the home. "This is so pretty." She stares out of the window, looking at the lush green trees that wind along the side of the road. "These gardens are magnificent. This is seriously one long driveway."

"We're almost there," I reassure her.

We turn the corner, and the lush greenery gives away to three stories of stone, wood, and shingles.

"Oh, wow!" Lenna gasps beside me. "Wow. Oh, wow! This ... wow." Seems that's all she can say. I guess she's speechless, and that's exactly what I wanted.

A blue balloon arch is set up around the front entry as we drive up, and there's even a blue carpet for Lenna's arrival. "I'm guessing the theme for today is blue?" Lenna looks over at me with a smile.

"Like I said, the girls did it all." Taking her hand, we walk through the front door.

"Ooh, look at those stairs." She eyes the white wooden stairs as we enter. "Oh, and the floors." Lenna points to the freshly polished wooden floorboards. "Oh, and the living room. This place is a dream."

"Wait till you see outside," I say, pulling her further through the home and out toward the back, which has glass doors all along one side of the building.

She pauses, taking in the view. "It's on the water." As she admires the view over Long Island Sound, she says, "That view... it's spectacular. Imagine waking up to that every day?"

"Lenna, Logan... you made it," Stella squeals noticing us standing there.

THE BABY SHOWER was a huge success, Lenna's enjoying her day. She is sitting on a large blue throne with a blue flower crown atop her head, and she's opening the last of her baby shower gifts.

"There's just one more gift." Stepping over to where Lenna is sitting, I hand her a large white box, which is gift wrapped with a blue ribbon. I have to keep with the theme. "It's from me."

Those gorgeous chocolate eyes sparkle up at me.

"You didn't need to get me anything," she whispers. "You and little one are enough."

"Open it!" I push her to open my gift.

Slowly she undoes the blue ribbon, and with each step, my nerves intensify. She lifts off the white lid and places it beside her. Pulling out the top box, she undoes the blue ribbon and opens the smaller white box.

"It's a key?" She looks up at me, trying to work out what it could mean.

"The place may not have a white picket fence, but I thought

it might do," I answer her question while waving my hands around me at the house.

"Wait!" Lenna frowns. "You bought *this* house?" Her eyes look around, taking it all in again.

"Yep, it's all ours."

"And we bought the house next door, too. We're neighbors," Chloe adds.

"What?" Lenna smiles.

Little does she know that there's so much more to come.

"Logan?" She reaches out for me, and once I'm close enough, she pulls me in for a heated kiss. "Thank you." Her eyes well up with unshed tears. "I can't…" Words fail her this time.

"But wait, there's more." I point to the second box, the most important one. Lenna shakes her head but does as she's told. Slowly, she unwraps that little box as well. She pauses as she opens the white velvet box, and when she looks up, she sees me down on one knee before her.

"I thought about where I saw myself in five years' time, and the picture of this house came to mind. What I saw inside of it was filled with laughter, love, and the pitter-patter of tiny feet against the hardwood floors. Then I would turn and see you, the most beautiful woman in the world, with the biggest smile on her face. And when she looked at me, all I feel is that I'm the luckiest man in the world. Lenna Lund, will you allow me to love you forever and ever?"

Tears are falling down her cheeks as her shaky hands pull out the three-carat flawless cut diamond ring.

"Will you marry me?" I ask once the ring is on her finger.

"Yes, yes, yes." She jumps up from her chair and wraps her arms around me. "I love you, Logan Stone," she whispers into my ear.

45

LENNA

Three Years Later

"Congratulations." Rushing into the hospital room where Chloe is lying after she has given birth to their first babies, twin boys, Remy and Theo. "You look amazing." I give my sister-in-law a kiss on the cheek.

"Stop it! I look like shit. I just pushed two watermelons out of my hoo-ha."

It's quite the twin menagerie in the Stone family at the moment, as Logan and I popped out the cutest set of twin girls last year, Millie and Ella. They were quite the unexpected surprise, especially as we were celebrating our first night away from Jagger, then Logan knocked me up with twins.

Twins!

One was hard enough, but two? It's been quite the struggle having three kids under three, but thank goodness Logan is right there beside me being the best father and husband I could ever have dreamed of.

Looking around the hospital room, I take in the sight,

which is filled with our family and friends, I couldn't imagine my life any other way.

THE END

COMING NEXT

The Merger

Playboys of New York - Book 3

Emma Banks is a strong, single, independent woman who's busy building her fashion empire. She doesn't have time for men unless it's on her terms–quick and convenient.

Emma makes no apologies for the way she lives her life.

That was until Anderson West walked in.

All six-foot-six of him.

He was supposed to be a bit of fun to pass the time.

But then Vegas happened.

And they woke with the mother of all headaches and gold bands on their fingers.

Two people allergic to commitment have merged as one.

They thought it would be a funny story they could laugh about, until Anderson's family made her an offer she could not refuse.

ABOUT THE AUTHOR

JA Low lives in the Australian Outback. When she's not writing steamy scenes and admiring hot cowboy's, she's tending to her husband and two sons, and dreaming up the next epic romance.

Come follow her

Facebook: www.facebook.com/jalowbooks
Twitter: www.twitter.com/jalowbooks
Instagram: www.instagram.com/jalowbooks
Pinterest: www.pinterest.com/jalowbooks
Website: www.jalowbooks.com
Goodreads: https://www.goodreads.com/author/show/14918059.J_A_Low
BookBub: https://www.bookbub.com/authors/ja-low

ABOUT THE AUTHOR

Come join JA Low's Block
www.facebook.com/groups/1682783088643205/

www.jalowbooks.com
jalowbooks@gmail.com

INTERCONNECTING SERIES 1

Reading order for interconnected characters.

Dirty Texas Series

Suddenly Dirty

Suddenly Together

Suddenly Bound

Suddenly Trouble

Suddenly Broken

Paradise Club Series

Paradise

Playboys of New York

Off Limits

Strictly Forbidden

The Merger

ALSO BY JA LOW

The Dirty Texas Box Set

Five full length novels and Five Novellas included in the set.

One band. Five dirty talking rock stars and the women that bring them to their knees.

This collection includes:

Suddenly Dirty

He was everything she wasn't looking for.

She was everything he wasn't ready for.

A workplace romance with your celebrity hall pass.

Suddenly Together

She was everything he always wanted.

He was everything she could never have.

A best friend to lover's romance with the one man who's off limits.

Suddenly Bound

He was everything she could never have.

She was everything he couldn't possess.

An opposites attract romance with family loyalty tested to its limits.

Suddenly Trouble

She was everything he wasn't allowed to have.

He was everything she couldn't have.

A brother's best friend romance with a twist.

Suddenly Broken

He was everything she wasn't looking for.

She was everything he wasn't ready for.

A friend's with benefits romance that takes a wild ride.

One little taste can't hurt; can it?

If you like your rock stars dirty talking, alpha's with hearts of gold this series is for you.

ALSO BY JA LOW

The Paradise Club Series

Paradise

Standalone Spin off from the Dirty Texas Series

My name's Nate Lewis, owner of The Paradise Club.

I can bring every little dirty fantasy you have ever dreamed of to reality.

My business is your pleasure. I'm good at it.

So good it's made me a wealthy and powerful man.

I have one rule—never mix business and pleasure, and I've lived by it from day one.

Until her.

** WARNING: If you do not like your books with a lot of heat then do not read this book. **

ALSO BY JA LOW

Bratva Jewels Duet Box Set

SAPPHIRE - BOOK 1

An unconventional love is tested to its limits.

Mateo is used to being in the spotlight, he craves it in everything he does... except when it comes to his love life - that is firmly in the closet.

Tomas shuns the spotlight, the one he was born into, he wants nothing to do with it or his high-flying family who now reject him for his choices in love.

But Tomas' and Mateo's carefully constructed lives are turned inside out when they discover a beautiful, battered woman on their doorstep. The woman with the sapphire eyes has no memory of who she is or how she got there. She doesn't know about the Bratva Jewels - the Russian mafia's most desired escorts - or how her story intersects with theirs. Can Tomas and Mateo help her remember before the men who are after her find her first?

DIAMOND - BOOK 2

Round 2 with the Devil begins.

Grace thought she had left the nightmare of the Bratva Jewels behind her. Her days spent as one of the Russian Mafia's most desired escorts were some of the darkest of her life, but she was safe now. Or so she thought.

When Russian mobster Dmitri seeks revenge, he gets it, and Grace knows she must call on every ounce of inner strength she has to withstand what he has in store for her. What she didn't expect was to meet someone like Maxim...

Maxim is one of the Bratva's most skilled, and most feared, assassins. But his relationship to the Bratva is a complicated one. And when he meets Grace, suddenly everything becomes clear.

ALSO BY JA LOW

International Bad Boys Set

Book 1 - The Sexy Stranger

Lilly

This is not how I saw my life panning out. Flying halfway across the world, leaving my dream job behind me all because my fiancé couldn't keep it in his pants. Coming home to my family is the exact cure I need for my broken heart.

What I wasn't expecting to see in my living room is a hot, naked, Italian man.

Did I mention, naked. I really shouldn't be looking at his...

Luca

I've always lived by my family's rules, but where has that gotten me?

A cheating fiancée. A scandal that will be national news by morning.

I need to get away and plan my next move. A remote cottage in the middle of Scotland seems the right place.

That is until an awkwardly cute brunette stumbles into my cottage in the middle of a snowstorm where I'm standing. Naked.

She can't take her eyes off of my... I should go and put some pants on... shouldn't I?

ALSO BY JA LOW

International Bad Boys Set

Book 2 - The Arrogant Artist

Louis Marchant—artist of our generation.

More like the most arrogant artist of our generation.

The man looks like Michelago has carved him with his bare hands.

Kissable soft lips.

The perfect amount of five o'clock shadow stretched across his square jaw.

Add in that delicious French accent and oh là là.

And then there's his giant... Um, never mind, it's still connected to him.

No amount of magnificence can take away the fact that he's the most arrogant man in the history of France—no, the world.

He also happens to be my new boss.

INTERCONNECTING SERIES 2

Reading order for Interconnecting Series

Bratva Jewels Series

The Sexy Stranger

Printed in Great Britain
by Amazon

29396041R00159